C000069751

October Day

To Kathleen

October Day
– A Novel –

Frank Griffin

Introduced by *Andy Croft*

New London Editions
www.fiveleaves.co.uk

October Day

Published in 2011
by New London Editions

New London Editions
is an imprint of
Five Leaves Publications,
PO Box 8786, Nottingham NG1 9AW
www.fiveleaves.co.uk

New London Editions 5

October Day was first published by
Secker and Warburg in 1939
Published by New London Editions/Five Leaves
for the 75th anniversary of
The Battle of Cable Street
with the support of
Barry Amiel and Norman Melburn Trust

ISBN: 978 1 907869 15 0

Five Leaves acknowledges financial support
from Arts Council England

Typeset and design by
Four Sheets Design and Print, Derbyshire
Printed by Imprint Digital, Exeter

Introduction

OCTOBER Day is an extraordinary book about an extraordinary event. It is a novel about 'The Battle of Cable Street', when 100,000 Londoners took to the streets on 4 October 1936 to prevent Oswald Mosley and the British Union of Fascists marching through the Jewish East End. Published less than three years after the event, the central chapters of *October Day* are a vivid eye-witness record of a famous victory in the history of anti-Fascism.

Although 'The Battle of Cable Street' has been written about in memoirs like Phil Piratin's *Our Flag Stays Red* and Joe Jacobs's *Out of the Ghetto*, and celebrated on the stage in Arnold Wesker's *Chicken Soup with Barley*, Steven Berkoff's *East* and Simon Blumenfeld's *The Battle of Cable Street,* this book represents the only sustained attempt to use the narrative possibilities of fiction in order to record the complexity and the scale of those events. Moreover, while most of the famous British anti-Fascist novelists of the period set their work in Germany (Christopher Isherwood, Phyllis Bottome, Louis Golding), in Spain (Ralph Bates) or in Italy (Eric Ambler), *October Day* is one of the few British novels from the Popular Front period which tried to address the threat of home-grown Fascism and its supporters.

All the more extraordinary then, that *October Day* has been forgotten and out of print for over seventy years. It is not mentioned in any of the usual literary or political histories of the period, and its author is these days almost completely unknown.

Frank Griffin was born in 1911 at Alwalton, near Peterborough. He grew up in Richmond in North Yorkshire, then in Piercebridge near Darlington. Griffin's father was a farm labourer. The boy was not encouraged

5

to attend school, since he was expected to follow his father and work on the land. When he was fourteen, Frank Griffin ran away to sea. Unable to find a ship, he drifted through several jobs, working as a miner, a labourer and a lorry-driver. In 1929, after three months without work, he joined the Army, initially in the Royal Tank Corps. 'There was nothing else for me to do,' he later wrote, 'in the northern town where I lived half the normal adult population was out of work... I was sure I would like the life as soon as I became settled. The recruiting sergeant told me I should too. He told all of us that.' Griffin left the Army six years later with the rank of corporal, a first-class Certificate of Education and a burning determination to write a book that would expose the brutal conditions then endured by ordinary soldiers.

I Joined the Army (by 'Private XYZ') was published in 1937 by the new and radical publishing firm of Secker and Warburg. It was a shocking documentary account of life in the Army, a picture of systematic violence, brutal victimisation and managerial incompetence. It put the case for improved conditions, specifically higher pay, more leave, less severe punishments, better food and better accommodation. And it was an argument about the radical potential of the armed forces:

> 'Intimidation, and fear of the military machine, prevents the soldier from taking any active part in politics, and at the same time robs him of political freedom. However, the soldier, despite the handicaps, is undoubtedly interested in his position in the class society: he is loyal to his class, and to the best of his ability gives support, if only at heart to industrial struggles and those millions of unemployed who become ever more oppressed. He knows that, eventually, he too will be unemployed or having to face wage cuts and abominable working conditions.'

The book was controversial, to say the least (the Invergordon Mutiny had taken place only six years earlier). When an extract from the book appeared in the left-wing journal *Fact,* the editors were accused of sensationalism and a lack of patriotism (the issue appeared on the eve of the Coronation). One rival magazine even suggested that the book was a work of fiction, and that 'Private XYZ' was a pseudonym of *Fact* editors Raymond Postgate and GDH Cole. Meanwhile, the magazine's distributors refused to handle the issue for fear that it might be seditious and WH Smith announced that they would no longer stock the magazine because they disliked its 'tone'. The editors could not help wondering if the affair was connected to the way that 'the Coronation and the rearmament programme together are whipping up a spurt of "patriotic" sentiment' — 'is this sentiment fostered and protected by unofficial instructions which set up a censorship which legally has no existence?'

In 1934 Griffin married Kathleen Cawood. To support his family — they eventually had seven girls and two boys — Griffin worked variously as a civil-servant, an audit clerk, a garage-mechanic and a book-keeper. At some point in the late 1930s he joined the Communist Party in London. He wrote regularly for the *Daily Worker* on London County Council issues. He was also involved in establishing the NUGMW paper *The Gasworker.*

In early 1939 Secker and Warburg published Griffin's second book, *October Day*, with considerable fanfare — 'a novel of the people', 'the throbbing pulse of London', 'this remarkable book establishes [the author's] high place among proletarian writers'.

The action of the novel takes place on a single day — Sunday 4 October 1936. The story begins early in the morning with a sleepy murmur and ends as, 'in the street outside, in all the other streets in London, the night was pressing gently onto another October day.' And in between is an account of the anti-Fascist demonstration told through the shifting, and sometimes overlapping, points of view of seven main characters — an unemployed labourer, a bus-conductor, a young woman just out of prison, a policeman, two young Communists and the titled widow of a beer baron — whose lives suddenly collide on the streets:

7

'shouting and hooting and whistling and waving their raised clenched fists at the cops... bald heads, covered heads, slim or brawny shoulders... red and white fists thrust up in salute. And what a motley of colours! Blonde hair, dark hair, no hair at all; red hats, black hats, grey hats, and brown. And then the suits and dresses, all manner of suits and all manner of dresses, but a lot of them with red – a hell of a lot of them with red... You'd think they were all going into battle, the sun shining, weapons in hand and red flags flying and all... Surely they weren't all communists! There couldn't be so many as that or there'd soon be a Bloody Revolution, like the papers told you about. Then there must be Labour as well, and some of those Co-op people who were always on about dividends. But even so, a lot of them couldn't be either – Then what the devil were they? People like himself, just there to watch?.. whatever they were, they made you feel like one of themselves...'

The *Daily Worker* welcomed the appearance of a novel 'alive with the shouting and booing, the police charges and the crowd's resistance, the hot pushing and shoving, the cursing, the indignation and the triumph of that day... a living and human book, an exciting story.' 'A highly readable novel,' wrote John Mair in the *New Statesman*, 'holding the stage from which Eisenstein has been thrown... Frank Griffin, by snapshotting the reactions of a number of ordinary, unrelated people, tries to show how the demonstrations came about and to what they owed their success... we see them awaken under the twin stimuli of baton charges and casual conversations to an understanding of what it all "means".'

As the reference to Eisenstein and 'snapshotting' suggests, *October Day* was seen at the time as an example of the new 'cinematic' fiction of the late 1930s. Among the best-known exponents of this new and experimental kind of novel were Communist novelists like James Barke, Patrick Hamilton, Arthur Calder-Marshall and John Sommerfield, whose 1936 novel *May Day* was also built around a large political demonstration in London. Influenced by novelists like Dos Passos and Jules

Romains, by Expressionist filmmakers like Fritz Lang and Walter Ruttman and by documentary film-makers like John Grierson and Ralph Bond, these *romans à fleuve* represented a break with the traditional unities of character and plot in favour of a large cast of characters connected only by historical accident.

Beginning with a suicide and ending with a car-crash, *October Day* is structured by a series of chance incidents. Although none of the characters have previously met, they are linked in ways they never realise. At the beginning of the novel Joe Slessor storms out of the house after another row about money; when he stops to buy some cigarettes at the local newsagent he hears about a female suicide fished out of the Thames the previous night. Meanwhile Elsie, who was with the woman when she killed herself, is afraid that the police will want to question her; she jumps on a bus, where she meets Bert the conductor, who invites her to go to the pictures; since the cinemas are shut on a Sunday afternoon, they go for a walk and end up watching the anti-Fascist demonstration; there Elsie sees her previous employer, the Hitler-admiring Lady Stroud talking to a policeman, who is killed later that night in a road-accident — which is witnessed by Joe on his way home after the demonstration.

If the novel has a main character it is Joe. He is clearly related to Eugene O'Neill's 'Yank' ('a short hairy-legged figure whose shoulders were bowed as if with the cares of the world'), full of rage and frustration and innocent anger. His ignorance is a blank page on which the novel's arguments can we written (interestingly both the *New Statesman* and the *Daily Worker* found the CP characters too preachy). Joe thinks that politics is a racket ('They're all after the same thing — the money and the best jobs going, no matter whether they call themselves fascist or labour'). He hates trades unions ('All they want is your money. When they get that they forget about you.'). He is shocked by the police brutality ('The devils! There was no need for that! No bloody need at all!'). He is horrified to find that the pretty girl he saves from being hit by a mounted policeman is a member of the Communist Party ('just fancy *her* being a communist!'). When Joe is beaten up by some young Fascists on the way home, he is first shocked to realise that they think he is Jewish ('A Jew! But I'm not a Jew!'); he soon learns that the Fascists do not care to distinguish between a Jew and someone attending an anti-Fascist demonstration. By the end of the novel, Joe returns home, bloodied but changed:

'I've been wrong all the time! I've been a bloody fool! I ought to have joined the union years ago. Everybody ought to join a union. Don't you see?... We must all stand together. All us working folks must be organised. That's the only way we'll ever fight the bosses, that's the only way we'll ever get the rich off our backs.'

October Day is a novel about political process, about the relationship between the individual and the crowd, the private and the public. Like Chaplin in *Modern Times*, the novel's characters are swept along by historical forces they cannot see. The narrative of events that brings them together on the streets of London on this particular Sunday is driven variously by anger, idleness, hunger, loneliness, idealism, love and despair, connecting the domestic and the local to the national and the international, a street in the East End of London to Spain and Nazi Germany. They are transformed — they transform themselves — from spectators to participants, audience to actors. On their way home from the demonstration Bert and Else buy an evening paper, excited and amazed to see an account of the anti-Fascist demonstration, suddenly disappointed that they cannot see themselves in the photographs. It is a fascinating fictional study in the anthropology of the crowd, its personality and collective instincts, the strength found in unity that is greater than the sum of its parts:

'His thoughts wandered back to the march, to those scenes of spontaneous welcome; the cheers, the songs, the saluting and that triumphantly shouted slogan; the flags at the windows of the working-class flats, the next street with its Jewish shops, and the street after that, when the column had broadened with newcomers, and then on to the Town Hall, full to overflowing, and his own swift rush of disappointment when he found that he couldn't get in. He thought back further to the afternoon, to those dense, angry crowds of people, hundreds of thousands of them, seething and swaying and protesting hour after hour, and winning in the end. That was what being united meant, he thought approvingly. If you stood together you could win; you were invincible. There were so many of you that no power on earth could resist you, once you stood together.'

'The genuine East End flesh and blood,' enthused the *News Chronicle*. 'A dramatic picture,' said the *Sydney Morning Herald*, of 'what must have been the greatest demonstration of working-class hatred that England has seen in the past 50 years.'

During the Second World War Frank Griffin contributed regular articles to the magazine *Britanskiy Soyuznik* (British Ally), sponsored by the Ministry of Information and published in Moscow. He also helped John Hilton set up his Industrial Advice Bureau at the *News of the World*. After the War Griffin made a living as a freelance journalist, contributing anonymous features for Fleet Street newspapers, writing for magazines devoted to DIY, cooking and motor-racing, and writing stories for popular magazines at two guineas a story. He also published more than a dozen *noir*-ish thrillers, mostly two-shilling paperbacks pitched somewhere between James Hadley Chase and Gerald Kersh — *Death Takes a Hand, Appointment with My Lady, Danger at Midnight, Death after Dark, His Sort of Girl, So Only Mugs Work, All Set For Murder, Ladies Must Love, Killer's Progress, Strumpet's Fool, Miss Lucas Takes a Lover, A Rope for Christmas* and *She*

Deserved to Die. He also wrote a children's novel, *Black Rock Island.* His last published book appeared in 1951.

Frank Griffin died in 1984 of a heart-attack at his home in Cornwall.

I am grateful to Josephine Clarke and Ken Worpole for their comments on an early draft of this introduction, also to Lynette Cawthra at the Working Class Movement Library, Salford.

Andy Croft

Author's Note

THIS novel is based on the events of a single day, Sunday, 4 October 1936, when, with the assistance of some five thousand policemen, the British Union of Fascists attempted to hold a march from Royal Mint Street, near the Tower of London, through the densely populated working class districts of the East End. To oppose the march, a quarter of a million people assembled in the East End streets. There were severe clashes with the police, individual assaults, barricades erected in Cable Street, Stepney, eighty-four arrests and a countless number of injured. So overwhelming was opposition to the march that the police were compelled to divert the fascists from their intended route to a point on The Embankment, where they dispersed — having marched west instead of east.

Most of the scenes of violence described in this novel are based on the facts as recorded by cameramen in scores of Sunday and daily newspapers (to which any doubting reader is referred) and on the author's own observations. But every one of the characters is entirely fictitious, and bears, to the author's knowledge and belief, no physical, mental, moral, or any other resemblance to any living person. The author hopes, however, that the reader who witnessed the events of that October day, and the reader who did not, will feel in some manner that the fictitious characters were really there in the flesh, among those two hundred and fifty thousand living people who made a new chapter in London's history.

Chapter I

A slanting shaft of sunlight had pierced the bedroom curtains since early dawn. Starting high on the ceiling, an oblong patch of light on the paper-covered wall, it had crept stealthily lower to the brass-topped head of the bed. Here it had seemed to pause, playing a while on the brasswork, before its final move to the pillow. Now it suddenly shone on Joe Slesser's face, bathing his square, bristly chin, his slightly hooked nose, lined, sallow cheeks, and grey brown hair in a soft, warm glow. Slesser's heavy breathing ceased abruptly. With a sleepy murmur, he opened his eyes and sat up in the bed, squinting at the clock which ticked monotonously on the mantelpiece.

"Twenty past seven," he muttered doubtfully. "But it's broad daylight already. That clock must have stopped and started again in the night. It must be gone eight."

He listened a moment to his wife's slow, regular breathing, and then climbed cautiously out of bed. Despite his care, she woke up immediately, and saw him standing there in his shirt — a short, hairy-legged figure whose shoulders were bowed as if with the care of the world. She flung back the clothes and asked, with a touch of resentment, "What are you getting up so early for? It's Sunday."

"This clock's been stopped," Slesser said, scratching his hairy legs. "I was going to look at the kitchen clock to find out the right time."

"Clock's going," said his wife, nodding at the mantelpiece.

"Ah, I know. But it's been stopped."

"How do you know that? You haven't been lying awake all night, have you?"

"No, but it must have been. You can tell by the sun, if you look," Slesser retorted impatiently. "It isn't as light as this at twenty past seven of a morning. It's nearly dark."

She gave her unvarying, tittering laugh. Annoyed and flushing darkly, he raised his voice.

"What are *you* cackling at all of a sudden? There's nothing funny about it, is there?"

She laughed again. "You ought to know. You put the clocks back, didn't you?"

"Ah!" said Slesser. He felt a fool. Of course, summertime had ended the night before. He had altered the clocks himself and should have remembered that it would be lighter this morning and darker tonight. Cursing inwardly, he snatched his trousers from the bed end and savagely pulled them on to his hairy legs.

"You're not going to get up now, are you?" his wife asked, in a wondering tone. "It's Sunday."

"Might as well get up now," Slesser grumbled, "Sunday or not."

"Then I will," she announced, sitting up and rolling back the bedclothes until her legs and feet were uncovered. "Reach me my clothes off the chair, will you?"

"Pity you can't get them yourself," Slesser grumbled and threw her clothes on the bed. He was angry with himself because of the clock. He knew she would make fun of him when her sister Rose came to visit them that afternoon. 'Couple of old hens,' he thought, tugging at his braces. 'Drag everything up they can. Pity they've nothing else to cackle about. Wish I had a bloody job and could get out of this hole for a bit, by Christ I do!'

He glanced at his wife. She had taken off her nightgown and now sat in a vest that had once been his own. Her face was sickly pale and on it was stamped an expression of extreme worry. Something seemed to grip at his heart, stopping its beat. Then it raced away again at double speed, thud, thud, thud. He knew when she lifted her head what she was going to say, he knew what had happened — rather, what had not happened.

"There's no sign again," she said, in a voice charged with meaning, looking up at him with resentful eyes. "It's five weeks now..."

Slesser said nothing; but his lips tightened and his forehead wrinkled in a sudden frown, making him look older than his thirty-eight years.

"As if I haven't enough already," she went on in a whining tone. "What with four kids and two miscarriages in ten years — And of course you would have to be on the dole, wouldn't you?"

"You talk as if I was to blame!" Slesser cried out, in a tone made angry with fear of the coming child. "Couldn't help losing my job, could I? Bloody work got slack —"

"I'm not talking about that. I'm talking about the other. You should have taken more care, especially now. We can't afford another kid, even if we wanted one. You know that as well as I do. And God knows," she added, "the others have nothing to stand up in since you've been out of work. Nigh on two years now, it is, and don't forget it."

"Others have been out longer than I have," Slesser reminded her. "And it isn't my fault those bloody tablets didn't work. *You* said they were all right —"

"My sister's never caught with them, and she's used them for years, that I know of. They're all right for her —"

"Ah, she's barren — or he is," Slesser interrupted savagely. "Counter jumper, that's him! *You've* caught, anyway."

He couldn't help the sneer. He disliked his sister-in-law and her shop assistant husband with his fancy clothes and nancy ways and a regular job. They weren't burdened with children they couldn't afford. 'Too bloody clever!' Slesser thought, sitting down heavily on the chair and beginning to pull on his socks.

"Why you should blame me," he said aloud to his wife, "I don't know. It isn't my fault the tablets haven't worked. I didn't make them. But if I knew who did," he added rashly, "I'd wring his bloody neck, selling fakes and letting folks in for a brat they don't want and can't afford to keep. If I had my way we'd never have tried the damned things and then you wouldn't be like you are. You listen too much to that sister of yours —"

"You leave Rose out of it!" Mrs Slesser snapped, struggling to pull a tightly-fitting dress over her head. "You can't blame her for what's our trouble."

"Can't blame her for anything, according to you," Slesser retorted hotly. "Think she was an angel to hear the way you go on about her —"

"You can talk, but where would you be without her, eh? That's what I'd like to know. If it weren't for her tipping you off you wouldn't have got that last job you had on the council, nor the one before, at the garage. And even now she's trying to get you back on the council, if you did but know."

"She needn't bother," said Slesser, to whom this information was quite new. "I don't want no more jobs with the Labour Council."

"What!" gasped Mrs Slesser, getting out of bed. "You don't want a job...!"

"Not with that Labour lot," he repeated, adamant. "So you can tell her from me she needn't paint her face and go sheikhing the councillors on my account. That's flat!"

"She doesn't paint her face and sheikh the councillors, so you needn't say that. She only gets to know when there are vacancies —"

"Ah, we know, we know," Slesser said impatiently, and jumped up from the chair, snatched his jacket from the bedpost and shuffled out of the room in his stockinged feet.

He paused to listen outside the children's bedroom door; but no sound came from within. Evidently they were still asleep, packed like sardines in their double bed in the stuffy little room which looked out on the back yard. 'Poor little devils,' he thought as he made his way along the passage to the kitchen. 'It's a nice sort of life they've got. So've we all. Not fit to live, it isn't.'

The Slessers rented the ground floor flat of a house off South Park Road. They had three rooms and a cellar for fifteen shillings a week. Two of the rooms were used as bedrooms, and quite remarkably they did not house any bugs in the crumbling walls. The kitchen, also without bugs, had a tiny scullery attached and jutted out on a small backyard, at the end of which towered an eight storeyed warehouse in an advanced state of disrepair. Even in the middle of a summer day the sun never reached the kitchen; and in the early morning, while it was low in the sky, the place was as dark as a vault. In the four years they had lived there, Slesser had never accustomed himself to that damp-smelling darkness: and now, as he dug his feet into a pair of thin-soled shoes, he felt the cold, clammy air press on his flesh like a wave of death. It struck deeply to his bones, and, shivering, he left his shoes unlaced and stood up and lit the gas. That would warm the room. He knew his wife would object to the extravagance when she came through from the bedroom, and usually he left the light alone, fearing her tongue. But this morning he was sick of everything. Nothing seemed to matter now another child was on the way. 'Let her nag and cackle,' he thought defiantly, and bent down to lace his shoes, close under the hissing gas.

Mrs Slesser pattered into the kitchen in a pair of carpet slippers that had once belonged to her sister. To Slesser's surprise she said nothing about the gas; she had another thing on her mind.

"What do you mean by not taking a job on the council?" she demanded, picking up the kettle from the hearth and brandishing it near his head. "I should have thought you'd been on the dole long enough and would be glad to work for anybody, Labour or whatever they are. But no! You must have funny ideas. What have you got against the council, anyway?"

"You know what I've got against them, without *me* having to tell you again," Slesser replied. "So you needn't pretend you don't."

"What? Because the men try to get you to join a union? Well, why not? Others're in it, so why shouldn't you be, if it means a job? You're always on about how much you'd like work, but when you get a chance you turn it down — and just because you don't like being in a union."

"I won't be forced into a union, not for you nor anybody else. And what do you mean — when I get a chance of a job? There is no job, and never will be, so for Christ's sake stop cackling about something that doesn't exist!" Slesser exploded, and pulled so savagely at his shoelace that it snapped. "There! Now I've broken the bloody lace through your damned row! Why don't you get on with the break-fast and leave me alone, damn you!" he shouted, red in the face with temper. "It's nag, nag, nag and cackle, cackle, cackle all day long!"

"All right, all right. You needn't wake the whole house with your ravings," she replied tartly and, temporarily silenced by his outburst, took the kettle to the scullery tap.

Slesser mended the lace and then washed at a tap in the backyard, swilling the water carelessly over his neck until it ran in icy cold streams down his chest and back. He needed a shave, but he felt too miserable to bother this morning. 'Why shave?' he asked himself moodily. 'There's no need, no need at all. Besides, it'll save blades. And we'll have to save if there's going to be another brat, like hell we will! Three bob a week they'll give us, down at the dole, but if it was a bloody illegitimate they'd make the father pay ten bob or more to the mother. Strikes me there's something wrong somewhere... What we need is another war, then I could get out of it, away from this hell of a life. Nothing but nag, nag, nag, and cackle, cackle, cackle every time I'm in the house. And now another kid —!'

Fiercely rubbing his face with a ragged towel, he returned to the kitchen, where his wife was sawing at a loaf. She had not yet washed nor combed her hair, and her broad, short fingers, grasping the loaf, were cracked and dirty where the soot had come from the kettle. Slesser, looking at her dirty hands, felt a sudden twinge of pity. Once she had been so careful of her appearance, especially her hands, that she had pleasantly exasperated him with her passion for personal cleanliness. Now that she was soured about him and herself she bothered no longer. She even neglected her once beautiful curly dark hair, taking pains with it only when she was going out of doors or expecting her sister to call. Her inner and outer life, equally harsh, had lined her rather broad face and given to her mouth and eyes a slightly repellent expression which made her look older than her thirty-eight years.

'She's had too many kids,' Slesser thought, watching her cutting the bread. 'And too much worry. It's a hell of a life, this. And it'll never alter, never — as long as I'm out of work. It'll go on just the same, nag, nag, nag, and cackle, cackle, cackle, she at me and me at her until we feel like killing each other. Day after day, month after month, year after year, and it gets worse all the time, like a leaking pipe. And now she's going to have another kid, just because of those tablets... Those blasted tablets!' He rubbed at his face until it smarted and pitched the towel on a chair with a gesture of impotent rage.

"Why must you throw things about like that?"his wife demanded, looking up from the loaf. "You know I've only got to clean it up after you. Why don't you hang it in the scullery, where it belongs, instead of making extra work for me? Eh? Haven't I enough already, with four kids to look after and another on the way —"

"Oh, hell!" Slesser said aloud and hung the towel on a nail behind the scullery door, thinking, 'Anything for peace! Anything!'

He slipped on his jacket and sat at the table, waiting for his wife to bring the two boiled eggs which they managed to afford for Sunday breakfast. In a moment her voice rasped from the scullery.

"Don't sit there doing nothing! Be pouring the tea or

buttering some bread. Why must you leave it all to me? Haven't I enough to do as it is?"

He sighed wearily, picked up the teapot and began to pour. Instantly her voice came again, "How many times have I told you to put the milk in first, or you'll spoil the tea? Eh? Why don't you use your brains a bit, for a change?"

"Oh, all right; you needn't make such a song about it," Slesser retorted, picking up the milk jug. "Where's the milk, anyway?"

"It's still on the doorstep. Where do you think it is? In the lavatory? You know I haven't been out yet. Why don't you get it yourself instead of leaving it all to me? Eh?"

Nag, nag, nag, and cackle, cackle, cackle like God knows what, Slesser thought desperately, as he went along the passage for the milk, her words following in a flood of bitter upbraiding. If only he could get out of it. His eyes lighted on his cap, hanging on a nail in the passage, and a sudden, overwhelming desire to escape from the house took possession of his mind. Without hesitating he grabbed the cap, swung the front door open, struggled with an impulse to bang it shut, and finally closed it softly behind him.

"To hell with her!" he said aloud, pulling his cap hard down over his head. "Let her nag and cackle to herself. I'm fed up with it." And, thus determined, he set off walking along the sun-drenched street with his hands thrust deep in his pockets and his shoulders hunched.

At the bottom of the street he turned left along the dismal squalor of South Park Road. Here there were blocks of trust-owned working class flats, old and hideously grim, and innumerable, dirty little shops with windows stocked haphazardly with cheap but inferior goods of every conceivable description. The litter from the market of the previous night had been cleared away by the dustmen, but the stench of fish and decaying vegetables remained, mingling with the odour of beer that oozed from the frequent pubs. The occasional newsagents' shops were already open, and Slesser, as he headed automatically for the park some little way ahead, glanced at their flaring placards, and wondered why so many referred to a fascist march. This march seemed so important that even the newspapers' favourite themes — seductions, suicides, murders, wars, and sport — had taken second place on the bills. '**Fascist March: Police Leave Cancelled**,' he read. And again: '**Fascist March: Disorder Feared**.' And yet again: '**Reds Oppose Fascist March**.' But the headlines conveyed very little to Slesser. Because he could rarely afford one, he seldom bought a paper. He did not know that hundreds of thousands of people were then waking from sleep and thinking, 'Yes, I must go to that march this afternoon. Those fascists must be stopped. We've let them go far enough.' Indeed that day as yet meant no more to Slesser than any other day when the sun shone brightly, except that he had freed himself from the nag and cackle of his pregnant wife without having eaten his breakfast.

And now he felt ravenously hungry. Thrusting a hand in his trousers' pocket, he carefully counted the coins which lay on his softened palm. 'A lousy tanner,' he thought disgustedly. 'I can't get much with that — and what about fags?' He remembered the boiled egg waiting at home and was momentarily tempted to return. But the knowledge of the row there would be with his wife successfully deterred him. That sixpence in his palm was for cigarettes for the next two days, but fourpence could go on a tea and roll at old Tom Whiteley's kiosk near the park gates. 'Fags'll have to take pot luck,' he said to himself, slipping the coppers away. 'I'll have to make them spin out, that's all. Done it before and can do it again. Ah, what the hell's it matter, anyway?'

Crossing the road he went down a street of clean little houses with neat front gardens and gravelled paths and came to the kiosk near the park gates. An elderly man with weather beaten face and tired eyes rose from his stool behind the counter.

"Morning, Joe!" he called. "What brings *you* out so early? It's barely eight — have you got a job or something?"

"Morning, Tom," Slesser replied. "Me got a job...? Some bloody hopes! Give us a tea and a buttered roll, will you," he added, depositing four pence on the counter.

"Missus kicked you out without any breakfast?" Whiteley asked jocularly, eyeing the coins in surprise. "Ah!" said Slesser, tugging at his cap. "Bloody woman gets on my nerves sometimes."

A fleeting expression of comprehension crossed Whiteley's face, but, not daring to probe for details of the quarrel, he changed the subject abruptly. "Nice day, anyhow," he said, pouring tea from a blue enamel jug.

"Ah," said Slesser, looking about him, as if seeing the sun for the first time. "It's a fine day all right. Soon be winter, though."

"Still, we've had a good summer, so we can't grumble. Heard the news?"

"What news?" Slesser asked, a gleam of curiosity lighting his eyes. Tom Whiteley had a reputation for bits of choice gossip that seldom could be printed in the newspapers. Perhaps this was the news he meant.

"Tart threw herself off the bridge last night into the Thames. You know, the bridge just up the road by the park." Whiteley jerked his thumb towards the grey stone bridge in the distance. "I saw the cops go running up there like hell at about ha'past one this morning, so I thinks to myself, 'there must ha' been a murder' and off I went after them, leaving the kiosk to look after itself. When I got there they'd just pulled this tart out — a cop had dived in just after she jumped, see? — and you should have seen her, Joe.... Head all bashed up where she'd hit the side of the bridge and blood all over the place."

"Was she dead?" Slesser interrupted.

"Was she dead! Dead as a doornob! Nice bit o' stuff, too," Whiteley added, pushing a cup of tea forward. "Same old tale — in the family way, she was."

"Was she now?" Slesser asked uncomfortably. He

24

picked up the buttered roll and began chewing it savagely.

"Yes," Whiteley went on loquaciously, resting his elbows on the counter to ease his aching feet. "About seven months gone by the look of her, and no more than eighteen or nineteen, if that. A blonde, she was, hair permed in them little curls — you know the sort I mean, like sausages —"

"Ah," said Slesser, nodding, his mouth too full to speak further, his eyes straying to a pile of sausages on a plate in front of Tom.

"Well dressed, too," Whiteley resumed. "Seems a pity her going out like that. Same old story, I suppose. Bloke put her in the family way and then vanished. That's not right, that isn't."

"No," Slesser agreed, gulping half-masticated roll. "It isn't. But it takes two to make a baby, Tom."

"Quite right, Joe. Quite right." Whiteley grew thoughtful. "You know," he said presently, "it beats me why she didn't do it a better way than she did — put her head in a gas oven or something like that. Much better that way, don't you think?"

"Never tried it," Slesser answered, grinning.

"Nor have I," Whiteley said hastily, and then laughed hoarsely, "Hor! Hor! Hor!" his fat body shaking all over. "But still," he went on, wiping the tears from his eyes with a greasy apron that was also used to wipe his nose, "if I did have to choose, I'd prefer gas."

"So should I," Slesser told him, finishing off the roll and licking the butter from his fingers. "If I could afford the meter."

"Well, say what you like, Joe," Whiteley resumed thoughtfully, "these days are enough to drive a man to it, sometimes. What with all this unemployment and bad trade about I don't wonder there aren't more suicides than we hear on. Look at me! Here I've been since ha'past ten last night and taken less than fifteen bob. Why, in the old days, when folks had money and work, I'd take over three quid a night, as easy as you please, from off of working folks coming back late from a good time across the water.

"But now —"

"Same all over," Slesser agreed, sipping his tea. "There's no money anywhere these days."

"Except among the bosses — they got plenty. This rearmament's filling their pockets all right. 'Them that has it gets, them that hasn't doesn't.' That's what my missus says, and it strikes me she's right. — What's that for?" Whiteley asked as Slesser dropped twopence on the counter. "Fags?"

"Woodbines," Slesser said. "Must have a smoke, if nothing else. Thanks." He felt in his pockets for matches. "Got a match?" he asked. "I've left mine at home and I haven't another copper."

"Sure! Here you are." Whiteley struck a match and held it to Slesser's cigarette. Pitching the matchstick away, he asked, "Going to the march this afternoon?"

"What march?"

"Fascist march — up in the East End. You've heard about it, haven't you?"

"Oh, that. I've read about it on the placards, but I haven't seen a paper. Can't afford one when you're on the dole. What's it all about, anyway?"

"The fascists are holding a march in the East End this afternoon — but here, it's in the paper," Whiteley explained, producing a paper from under the counter. "I thought everybody knew by now. There! It's on the front page — headlines an' all."

Slesser read quickly, his brow creased in concentration. Presently he looked up. "It seems as if there's going to be some trouble, eh?" he remarked thoughtfully. "I see they've cancelled the police leave for fear of disorders."

"Trouble!" Whiteley ejaculated. "You bet there'll be trouble. But what else can you expect? Decent working folks won't stand for this fascism, and I don't blame 'em, either. Deliberate provocation, that's what this march is, and if I didn't have to get some sleep when the wife comes to relieve me, I'd be there like a shot. I would that. It'll be the event of a lifetime, if I know anything about politics."

"Then you think it'll be worth seeing?" Slesser asked, impressed by Whiteley's earnestness.

"Worth seeing! I should say so! Everybody'll be there! They wouldn't cancel the police leave for nothing, would they?"

"No, I don't suppose they would," Slesser agreed. "Still, I don't see what sense there is in all this opposition business. They're all after the same thing — the money and the best jobs going, no matter whether they call themselves fascist or Labour, so I don't see why they should mess about opposing each other."

"Oh, no! I wouldn't talk like that about the Labour chaps," Whiteley protested, immediately on the defensive.

"Look at the bloody council!" Slesser exploded violently." They're Labour, and look at that lot! If you do manage to get a job with 'em, they go on at you and on at you, about joining their blasted union till you get right sick of it! I know! I've had some! Look what they did to me! Sacked me when the work got slack but left single men on. And here's me got four kids! That's Labour!"

"Well, I suppose everybody's entitled to their own opinions, Joe, but if you ask me, I'm Labour every time. You can't blame 'em for sacking the non-unionists when the work gets scarce, that's what I think. And I'll tell you this, Joe, I wouldn't mind joining a union if it meant a job. And, after all, they do do a lot o' good —"

"Ah!" Slesser interrupted impatiently."All they want is your money. When they get that they forget all about you. Look at the strikes they have without any support! That's trade unionism! The chaps at the top against those at the bottom! Besides," he added, "I wouldn't be forced into a union, not for the best job in London. I'd rather starve on the bloody dole! And so would anybody else with a bit o' pride."

"Well, Joe, as I said; we're all entitled to our own opinion. You believe one thing and me another, and that's all there is to it. But I'm for trade unionism every time," said Whiteley in a conciliatory tone. Looking up, he saw his wife approaching to relieve him of his work at the kiosk. "Here's the missus, Joe. Now I'll have to get home and have a good long sleep. It's a shame to have to lie abed on a day like this, and I did want to see that fascist march, but there you are. We got to live somehow."

"Might as well be dead," said Slesser morosely. "Well, I'll be going, Tom. So long." He tugged at his cap as Mrs Whiteley approached and then turned away, heading for the park. Behind him he heard Tom Whiteley's voice, raised loquaciously, "Heard the news, May? Tart threw herself off the bridge last night into the Thames. You know, the bridge just up the road...."

2

The doubledecker red and white buses were already spluttering into life when Bert Forster hurried through the garage gates. He had run the last two hundred yards to work and now his round, pleasant face and thin fair hair were dewy with sweat. Throwing an anxious glance at the garage warden's clock, he saw with relief that he still had a minute to spare. Nevertheless his hasty movements continued. He scribbled an undecipherable name in the signing-on sheets and, darting into the conductors' room nearby, gasped breathlessly.

"Number five on one-seven-two! And be as quick as you can!"

"Five on one-seven-two," repeated the official on duty in a droning tone. He looked up from his desk.

"Oh, it's you, is it? What's the matter — late?"

"I shall be if you don't get a move on!" Bert retorted, his blue eyes flashing anxiety.

The official smiled, unperturbed, and with irritating

slowness of movement handed out a way bill, ticket box, tickets, punch, and time card for Route No. 172. Thus loaded, Bert snatched up a log sheet and hurried down the lines of buses until he came to the one he was seeking. The driver was there already, tinkering around the engine on routine examination of petrol and water.

"Sleep in?" he asked as Bert hastened past him to the rear of the bus.

"Sleep in? No, no! I never sleep in. I only stopped to cook myself some breakfast and sat over it too long," Bert answered breathlessly.

"The best thing for you to do," remarked the driver, following Bert to the platform, "is to get married, like me, and then you'd have a woman to do the cooking, *and* to get you out of bed."

"Married?" Bert exclaimed, fiddling with log sheet, way bill, and time card. "Hell! I've still got to find a girl to go with me to the pictures, let alone marry me!"

"There's plenty of 'em around —"

"Maybe so, but I can't seem to get hold of one," Bert said with a grin. "I've got the home but no woman. Three rooms all furnished but nobody to live in them. I guess I'm too old."

"What! At thirty! Don't be a fool, Bert! There's thousands of girls would be only too glad to chance it with you."

Bert shook his head. "They're not my sort. I want a homely girl, not one daubed to the eyes with paint and false lashes and what not. I want a wife when I get one, not a beauty preparations advertisement."

"You're too particular —" began the driver.

"Look here!" Bert interrupted. "I'm late. Do you mind opening a few of the windows down here while I'm finishing this? It'll let out some of the fumes."

"Sure, Bert," the driver agreed and stepped on the bus and opened three of the windows. "Still," he continued consolingly when the job was done, "maybe you're better off as a bachelor, Bertie-boy. You don't have to hand the pay packet over as soon as you get it, do you?"

"Perhaps not, but I'd prefer a wife to a pay packet any time. You've at least got somebody to talk to when you get home of a night."

"Cheer up, Bert! You never know what the day might bring, as my old woman says," said the driver encouragingly. He got off the bus, preparatory to driving away. Suddenly he thumped his knee. "Blimey!" he exclaimed. "I've just remembered. The fascist march!"

"What about it?" Bert demanded, still scribbling away on various forms. "I shan't be going."

"I'm not meaning that. It's right on our route! We'll be delayed for hours."

"You're nuts," said Bert. "We turn back at Aldgate, today — short duty turn, so we'll miss it. Buck your ideas up, man!"

"So we do," muttered the driver, recollecting. "Damned good job too. Half London'll be there."

"I shan't," Bert replied firmly. "I'm going to bed when I get finished. — If you're ready to drive off, I am now," he added, his preparations finished at last.

"O.K.," said the driver, and went to his cabin and drove the bus slowly forward to where an inspector was timing the vehicles out on their respective routes. He kept the bus waiting a few seconds and then signalled briefly with his hand. The bus crawled out of the garage, through the gates, and headed east at rapidly increasing speed.

Bert stood on the platform, leaning against the stairs, one hand rattling the coins in his bag, and aimlessly watched the houses fly past as the bus sped along. Here and there bottles of milk were still uncollected on the doorsteps and blinds were still drawn in the bedroom windows of the newly built rows of houses that formed the suburban district. But despite these Sabbatarian signs, life was getting on the move as the sun rose higher, calling the people from sleep with its cheering rays. 'It's true,' Bert thought to himself, staring with unseeing eyes at objects that had long ago become familiar. 'There are thousands of girls around, but I never seem to get hold of them. Now, if I had a wife we could have some real good times together, trips in the country on my off days and a good long holiday at the seaside once a year. Here I have a flat and my own furniture and a steady job with a pension at the end, but no wife. If I don't look sharp I'll be too old!'

The bus halted at its first stop to pick up a solitary passenger. Bert rang the bell, ding! ding! and followed the thickset man upstairs, aimlessly rattling the coins in his bag. The man chose the seat up in front and immediately opened the window, muttering away to himself in ill-tempered tones. Seeing Bert following, he turned round.

"Fresh air don't cost the company anything," he growled. "It's enough to stifle you in here."

"It's not everyone likes the windows open — especially the front ones," Bert explained informatively, used to requests of such a nature. "And as a matter of fact," he added, "it's the conductor that gets all the draught, down on the platform."

"Yeah!" the man snarled. "Pity they don't dress you in woollies for fear you'll get cold, ain't it?" He dug in his pocket. "Here," he said, "give us a penny 'un and then run away out of the draught for fear you'll catch your death."

"There's no need to be sarcastic about it," Bert retorted. "You'd be surprised to know how many colds us conductors get from these windows, even in the middle of summer. And besides," he added, his temper getting the better of him, "sarcasm's the lowest form of wit, you know."

"Is it really now!" exclaimed the man in mock surprise. "I've often wondered what it was. Thanks for telling me."

Stifling a hot retort, Bert punched the man a ticket and hurried below. 'It's all in a day's work,' he told himself. 'And it's no use arguing. They always get the best of it. If they lose an argument they say they've been insulted and report us to the nearest inspector, who reports us to the Board. "The customer is always right." Bah!'

The bus stopped again, this time to pick up a couple of giggling girls, who flopped into seats behind the driver's cabin, ceased giggling, and began immediately to chatter in low, serious tones about a 'boy.' Bert watched them from the platform, studying the expressions on their cleverly made-up faces. One had high, thin, curving black eyebrows that gave her almost a Hollywood appearance. But when her pearly-toothed smile was absent her face seemed curiously hard, as if set in Plaster of Paris. And her clothes were flashy, he thought. He disliked her. She was too artificial to suit his tastes. The other girl, sitting in the inside seat, at first glance seemed more homely; her eyebrows were natural, her expression soft and womanly and she did not smile one tenth as frequently as her companion. Bert wondered what she would say if he were suddenly to approach her and ask, "Look here, what about going to the pictures with me sometime?" Probably call a policeman or slap his face. And then he *would* be in the cart. He went for their tickets, his eyes on the homely-looking girl, ready to converse if she gave him the slightest encouragement. But she treated him coldly, frowning when he stopped beside her, and asked for two twopenny tickets in a surprisingly Cockneyish voice. When he gave her the tickets he saw that her long, pointed fingernails were clumsily daubed with crimson. His interest waned at the sight of them. No, she wasn't his sort, he concluded, as he made his way back to the platform. She wasn't homely; he had made a mistake. What he wanted was a homely girl, a simple girl, a friendly girl with a pleasant voice. She needn't be pretty, she needn't even be brainy, but she had to be homely and gentle and fond of kids, like himself.

Sighing, he took off his uniform cap and with the sleeve of his coat wiped the sweat from his brow. The caps were far too heavy, he thought, pitching his on to a seat. The Board ought certainly to do something about changing them — they got enough profit. What was it? — seven million pounds last year; no, seven and a half million pounds. Seven and a half million pounds! And the chairman of the Board got twelve thousand five hundred pounds a year salary. Two hundred and forty pounds a week!

'And I get four pounds odd for a good week,' he thought disgustedly, but marvelling at some people's fortune.

The bus left the suburban districts behind and entered the grey, crowded squalor of working class streets, where slogan after slogan was chalked, in bold, compelling white letters, urging the public to rally to an anti-fascist demonstration in the East End streets. Still scowling, the thickset quarrelsome man got off, a few other passengers got on, and for some time Bert was busy collecting fares. Then he glanced perfunctorily at a nearby slogan, 'They Shall Not Pass!', resumed his stand on the platform and his absent stare at the streets.

'Yes,' he was thinking, 'if I had a wife we could have some real good times together...' when a sudden thump on the platform broke off his thoughts.

An inspector, breathing heavily after his flying leap at the bus, stood swaying at his side, glaring up at his bare head.

"Haven't you got a cap?" the inspector demanded.

"Yes, and I've got a headache as well!"

"That's no excuse for removing your cap. You know the rules as well as I do. You're supposed to be properly dressed all the time you're on duty."

"Sounds like the army to me," Bert replied recklessly. But he put his cap on his head.

"Never you mind what it sounds like. You know the rules. What's more, I'm going to report you for insolence. Where's your time card?"

Conscious that the passengers on the bus were eyeing the scene with more than ordinary interest, Bert gave the inspector the time card, which was grabbed roughly and studied with extreme care.

"Look here," said the inspector, tapping the card, "you're running three minutes early already —"

"Three minutes my foot!" Bert interrupted, now thoroughly roused. "It's nothing like three minutes."

"I shall report you for running early, as well as for insolence," snapped the inspector, and turned over the log sheet to discover the culprit's name. In his previous haste at the garage, Bert had forgotten to complete the form. "Get these particulars filled in at once," the inspector ordered. "That's another thing I'll have to report."

Snatching the board on which the form was pinned, Bert furiously scribbled particulars. Presently he looked up at the waiting inspector. "I suppose you wouldn't like me to draw some comic pictures while I'm at it?" he asked coldly, not caring now what might result from this encounter.

Grabbing the board, the inspector copied particulars, hastily examined the passengers' tickets and swung himself off the bus without comment. Bert, watching the inspector's irate figure receding, knew now that he would have an implacable foe to face when hauled before his superiors.

'But I don't give a damn!' he told himself. 'They can sack me if they want. I don't care two hoots what they do!'

But, he reasoned, they were not likely to dismiss him. This was his first offence and the Board invariably gave an offender a second chance. Even if he did lose the job, there was only himself to worry; it would be his own funeral. He began to feel sorry for himself. Now, if he had a wife it would be different. He would have to go carefully then. If only he could meet a nice girl and get married. They would have some real good times. On fine days like this they could go to the seaside on a trip, and if she couldn't swim, why, he'd be able to teach her. And what a kick he'd get out of it!

He imagined teaching a girl to swim, a girl with a pleasant voice and a lovely smile who splashed about in the water while he held her under the chin and laughed at her constant splutterings. This girl, who was really his wife, had a slender figure and firm little breasts that she would permit him to fondle, even when teaching her to swim. Perhaps after swimming they would go to a quiet cove where the sand was brown and warm and soft and there have a meal from a picnic basket under the sun. And perhaps later, when the sun had gone down and the moon had come out, turning the sea to silver, they would find a warm, flat rock, black and smooth, high out of reach of the waves, and there remove all their clothes and lie together, with the moon on them, loving as people do. And after that they would get dressed and go to their room, if they were on holiday, or to catch their train, if they were just down for the day, and then home and into bed. Work wouldn't be so bad then. There'd be something to work for...

Ding! went the bell. The bus slowed down. Bert stood back, rattling the coins in his bag, and watched the passengers get off and others get on. He rang the bell twice, ding! ding! collected fares, resumed his stand on the platform and thought again, 'Yes, if I had a girl...'

3

Huddled on the parapet alongside the Thames sat Elsie Lane. Her coat was brown, shabby, and thin, and its unbuttoned top revealed the high neck of a cheap coloured dress. Above the neck was a thin, pale face, with drooping lips that quivered occasionally, and dark, sleep filled, anxious eyes. Above the eyes a head of dark, curled hair, partly covered with a brown, jauntily-worn beret — curiously at variance with her dejected appearance. The girl's ungloved hands were in her lap, restlessly twisting a small grubby handkerchief into a ball and as restlessly twisting it out again. Passers by, chancing to notice the hands, concluded that those restless movements revealed an inner turmoil too strong and overwhelming to be suffered calmly. But none of them stopped. Eyeing her disparagingly, they went on their way without speaking.

Had they stopped, she would not have answered: in fear she would have slipped off the parapet and hurried away. She feared each pedestrian that passed, man or woman, boy or girl. Their approach she watched carefully, though ostensibly looking at the river, and when they had passed a sigh of pure relief would escape her lips. Since shortly after dawn she had sat in that one spot, in sight of a grey stone bridge that spanned the glittering water on her left. She had thought, almost incessantly, of the bridge and what had happened there during the night. The incident was clear in her mind, the whole of it at once, like a painting. She could not suppress its nightmarish details for more than a moment at a stretch. There had been two of them, she and a blonde girl whom she had met by chance in an embankment café shortly after the theatres had closed and the people had headed for home. She and the girl had talked in dramatically desperate tones across the tea-splashed table, until the proprietor, kindly but firmly, had chased them away. They had gone to the bridge and stood in the shade between the lamps, staring down at the water and saying nothing for nearly an hour, immersed in mutual misery.

Suddenly the blonde girl had said, "Look here, kid, I'm so fed up I don't want to live any longer. Not another minute."

"Neither do I," Elsie Lane had muttered.

"There's only one way out for us — and that's to drop over here. They'll fish the three of us out some time or other, I suppose."

"Three of us?"

"You and me and the one inside me."

"Oh, yes, I forgot for a minute."

"He's kicking like hell just now, but he won't kick much when I jump, will he? The poor little fatherless bastard..." And suddenly the blonde girl had started to sob.... Then she had said. "Come on, kid. Let's do it. You're hungry, you've no money and no work and no place to go, like me, so let's do it. Come on. It'll soon be over. Just a splash and

36

you're finished, quick as can be... Come on, kid. Let's do it."

"No, not with you. Not with you," Elsie had stammered. "If I thought of doing it, I'd do it alone. We don't know each other. And if I'm fished out alive and you're under they'll have me for murder. Besides, I don't want to do it, and I don't want you to do it."

While she was talking, the blonde girl had climbed on to the parapet, and there had been no more time for words. Elsie had tried to grip her arms but she struggled free and slipped further over towards the river. Frantic with horror, she had clutched at the girl's flimsy frock and as she had thrown herself backwards the stuff had ripped, leaving some shreds in Elsie's clenched fingers.

There had been a thud, a short, startled cry that pierced the night, and then a sharp splash as the body struck the water. Almost immediately a policeman's whistle had shrilled out its call from the bank of the river near the park. After the first shock had passed, Elsie had fled with the rag of material still gripped in her hand, terrified of being caught and made to account for the blonde girl. When over the bridge, she had stopped and watched the policeman dive from the opposite bank and swim rapidly under an arch. In a couple of minutes he had reappeared, dragging the body through the water, and had swum towards the sound of running footsteps that had answered the whistle. From the shadows of the tree-lined embankment, Elsie had watched the police help the constable ashore and haul out the body; then, in panic again, she had run wildly from the scene.

Until dawn she had wandered, in increasing fear of arrest, through the nearby streets, starting at the least sound in the night's pregnant stillness. With daylight, drawn fascinated against her will to the river again, she had come to this place on the parapet within sight of the bridge. And now she sat torn with doubt and fear — doubt as to what she should do and fear of imminent arrest. In her terror she reasoned that the policeman who had dived must have seen her standing with the blonde girl; she had a faint recollection that he had passed them once on his rounds. The police would be looking for her, wanting to know all about it, perhaps even thinking she had pushed the girl instead of trying to stop her going over the bridge. She didn't even know the girl's name. They had met in the café and talked and then... They couldn't arrest her! She didn't know the girl! She protested to herself passionately. But if they did arrest her, and if they sent her to prison again — but she would rather die than go to prison again! Die the same way as the other girl. Memories of a hateful prison experience crowded out those of the night; her arrest seemed less imminent; she began to think more rationally; her hands became almost steady.

If she only had something to do, instead of having to sit there reliving her troubles... but there was nothing, nothing whatever, and nowhere to go. To sit there was just as sensible as moving away; she was at least resting, and if the police were looking for her — well, this place was as good as any other. They might not think of searching so close to the bridge, and in the last resort she could always jump... With renewal of her old fear she saw the grey clad figure of a man come round a bend of the road. She straightened up, and her fingers clutched the parapet ready to jump down to her feet if the stranger should examine her too closely. She pretended to be absorbed in the birds which circled overhead in a tireless search for food. But all the time she was aware of the rapidly approaching footsteps. Her body was braced, ready for instant action, every nerve strained to catch sinister implications in the on-coming feet.

"Here y'are, comrade," said a friendly voice.

A shiver of apprehension was immediately followed by instant relief. She turned, a deep, guilty flush on her face; with an engaging smile, the man thrust into her nerveless hand a small white leaflet.

"Cheerio!" he said pleasantly.

For a moment she stared with resentful eyes at his retreating back, then, lowering her gaze to the leaflet, she read two bold lines:

THEY SHALL NOT PASS!
RALLY TO THE EAST END!

Who wouldn't pass? she wondered crossly, and read on, frowning at lines that conveyed nothing, absolutely nothing to her. Turning the leaflet, she stared at the blank white reverse, trying to puzzle the message out in the least probable way. At last she turned the leaflet again, and read this time with interest and concentration, noting the time and place of the counter-demonstration to the fascist march which the message urged. After a few moments' thought she reached a sudden decision.

'I'll go to this march,' she told herself, dropping off the parapet. 'It'll help to fill in the time.'

She glanced round, but the long, curving stretch of embankment was deserted again. Greatly relieved, she set off towards the east, in the same direction as the grey-clad man who had given her the leaflet. It would be five or six miles to Aldgate — perhaps more — and she was tired, her limbs stiff and sore through her long vigil on the parapet. Nevertheless she walked on imbued with rising hope, more courageous, taking a less excitable view of the blonde girl's death. She was just being foolish about it; she wouldn't bother any more. Even if the police did arrest her she had done nothing wrong. They would have to let her go immediately,

The sun's warmth and the exercise sent the colour to her pale cheeks and the blood coursing freely through her veins, acting like wine on her spirits. She felt bold enough to walk unconcernedly past a policeman on duty at Westminster crossroads, to saunter casually past Scotland Yard, and then she headed at a rapid pace towards Blackfriars Bridge, determined not to worry again.

'If only I wasn't so hungry,' she sighed, approaching a coffee stall at the foot of the bridge. There was twopence tied in the corner of her grubby handkerchief, but that would not go very far, she thought, as she stopped to examine the tempting wares on the stall with indecisive, hungry eyes.

The stall attendant gazed down at her sympathetically. He could judge that she was down to her last coppers, and undecided what to buy. Lifting a large piece of cake, he said, "Here y'are, Miss. It's a bit stale, but it's fillin'. Y'can have it fer a copper." Without waiting for her answer he thrust the cake in a bag and dangled it under her nose.

With a quick intake of breath, Elsie hurriedly paid him a penny and hastened away. She ate the stale, finger-soiled cake in an alley near Ludgate Circus, ate it wolfishly in the obscurity of a doorway, even scooping the crumbs from the bag in an effort to appease her still unsatisfied hunger. As soon as the cake was definitely finished she wished, contrarily, that she had bought a hot drink instead. But that would have meant parting with her last coin: better, she thought, to have a penny than nothing at all. While she possessed a penny there were still four farthings between her and complete destitution. She tried to dismiss her longing for a warm, refreshing drink, and leaving the alley, turned wearily up the short incline of Ludgate Hill. Something might happen at the fascist march to change her luck; and she looked forward to it with as much excitement as if she were actually interested in its political significance.

Feeling suddenly ill, she was forced to stop to rest in the doorway of a shop. Aldgate, the destination urged upon her by the leaflet, seemed removed by limitless space. She felt she could not go on, and clung to the shop door, trying to quell a slowly rising sickness caused by the undigested cake; and with her low condition the fear of arrest returned, sharper and more real.

Gradually the sickness passed and, on unsteady legs, Elsie left the doorway of the shop and continued on her way. She was determined to get to Aldgate, as stubbornly determined as a patient refusing medicine, and as impervious to the consequences. There she could mingle with the crowd and forget her troubles in the excitement and movement. The police wouldn't find her there. There was safety in numbers. If only her head were better; it seemed to be whirling on an axle, and the pavement billowing in huge, uneven waves. The traffic was like a long, black elevator belt that rushed past on demon wheels, shrieking and groaning and dinning in her throbbing head.

"Here, what's the matter with you?" came a gruff, kindly voice at her side.

The voice acted like magic on her whirling brain. She became aware that someone was holding her arm in a strong though gentle grasp. Her eyes, less blurred, made out the form of a button, then the dark blue of a tunic, and then the round, red, solicitous face of a policeman.

"What's the matter? Feel faint, Miss?"

"I — I'm all right," she gasped quickly, dreading him. "It's — it's the heat —"

"Where do you want to be? Maybe if I put you on a bus you'd be all right, eh?"

She clutched at the straw. "Yes," she gasped. "A bus — to Aldgate."

"There's one coming now," continued the policeman, his grip on her arm relaxing. "Can you stand? That's right. You're all right now. It's this heat. Stuffy street, this. All right afore the war when there weren't so much traffic, but now with all these fumes —"

Unaided, with an immense effort of will, she walked the three paces to the waiting bus.

Chapter II

DING! Ding! Bert Forster dropped his hand from the bellpush and flung it round the swaying girl who had boarded the bus.

"Are you all right?"

"Yes," said the girl in weak, almost inaudible tones. "I'm all right now — I think."

"Let me help you," Bert offered, tightening his grip on her shoulders. "There." He sat her in the nearest seat and stood anxiously watching her. If she were to be taken ill on the bus he would have all the trouble of fetching medical aid, which meant losing valuable running time, and then have to make out a report of the case when the day's work was ended.

"Look here," he suggested, "perhaps you'd be better on top. There's a nice cool breeze up there and it might freshen you up a bit, if you feel faint."

The girl thanked him quickly, and clutching the rail for support, preceded him up the stairs. Taking her arm at the top he assisted her to a front seat, in which she sank in an attitude of utter weariness.

"You'll be much better here," Bert remarked, waiting for her fare. He was sorry for her. She looked ill and pathetically friendless.

"Thank you. It was silly of me really, wasn't it? I mean, coming over faint."

"Passengers often get taken ill on buses, you know," he informed her conversationally. "I had an old lady collapse and die on the platform once. Heart failure. Bad thing, that."

The girl, fumbling with her knotted handkerchief with nervous fingers, managed to release her penny. Bert punched the ticket, but hung about the top deck to be sure the girl had recovered. She intrigued him, stirred his sense of pity towards a human in distress. He had a feeling that she was friendless, and, judging from her shabby brown coat, grubby beret and faded dress, she was down on her luck. She looked seriously in need of some food. Perhaps that was the real trouble behind her faintness! Her face was thin and pale, while her eyes were strangely bright. They were very expressive eyes.

The bus was empty on top, so why shouldn't he say a few words to her?

"I say," he said in lowered tones, bending over her. "If you're in trouble — I mean, if you want any help —"

Startled, she turned her face to him quickly. He saw a flicker of fear in her eyes.

"No, no!" she protested. "I'm not in trouble. It's kind of you, but I'm not. Really I'm not."

"You don't look very well to me."

"I am, really I am. I was only a bit faint, and now I'm much better. Much better, thanks."

"Oh." Bert straightened his back. Her answer non-plussed him. He felt distinctly foolish and half-turned away; but another glance at her dejected figure and the recollection of her pinched face made him hesitate. She was ill — or worried to death about something, despite her denial. In his own friendlessness he was reluctant to leave her. The encounter had jerked him out of his self-preoccupation and gripped his imagination. A voice within him prompted, 'Ask her! Why be afraid of rebuff? She's in need of help....'

Nervously rattling the coins in his bag, he looked down again, and seeing the pathetic dirty handkerchief twisted in her hands, made up his mind.

"I say," he said, bending over her again. "What about you — how would you like to meet me some time — go to the pictures or something?"

She gave a timid laugh. "Well — I don't know about that — you see —" Her eyes dropped from his questioning face to the buttons on his tunic; slowly her pale cheeks

43

went crimson.

"Oh, come on!" Bert urged boldly, feeling that this was something he could manage.

She hesitated, looked up again and smiled.

"Say yes," he begged. "You will? That's fine! When?"

"When would you like me to?"

Courageously, Bert said, "This afternoon if you can. I'm off duty early today. Why not have dinner with me somewhere?" He thought he had done this very neatly, without seeming to hurry her at all. What he had meant all along was that he should give the girl a jolly good feed as soon as possible. He was sure now that she needed it. The girl paused, biting her lip. "All right, then," she said suddenly. "I will if you want me to."

"That's great!" Bert grinned at her. "We can go to the pictures afterwards, eh?"

"But they don't open on Sundays till night," the girl objected pleasantly.

"Lord, I'd forgotten that. What would you like to do?"

"Well." She hesitated, at a loss. Then remembering, she said, "I was going to the fascist march."

"Right you are! We'll go there together," Bert agreed. "Just a minute," he added, as the bus stopped to pick up passengers.

He went below at a trot, feeling full of suddenly acquired vigour, hurriedly collected fares, and returned to the girl, his face beaming. "Can you meet me at Aldgate station at one o'clock?" he asked.

She nodded. "That will do me fine. We'll be near the march, too."

"Yes, that's right. I'll be there just after half past twelve. You will turn up, now, won't you?"

"Of course. Why shouldn't I?"

"Well — you know what girls are!"

"You mean they promise to meet you and then don't turn up, is that it?"

Bert nodded, grinning, and looked down at her with his friendly blue eyes, feeling that he'd made a first rate job of this. She didn't suspect that he was acting out of pity. Nor was he entirely, he realised. She looked a nice, quiet sort of girl. He would enjoy getting to know her better this afternoon.

"You know," he said, "I haven't been out with a girl for ages."

"Haven't you? Oh!"

"I just can't seem to get hold of one," he confessed more seriously, perhaps, than he had intended.

"Perhaps you're too shy?" she suggested.

"No, I don't think it's that. Only — well, I can't take to these girls got up like Hollywood film stars, see? They get on my nerves, always powdering their noses and patting their hair. I like the quiet, homely sort of girls —"

"And am I —?"

"I don't know — yet!"

They laughed together, Bert's laugh a deep, "Hur! Hur! Hur!" The girl's tired face was suddenly transformed. The colour came to her pale cheeks and the strange bright glitter in her eyes diminished. She no longer twisted nervously at the handkerchief. She was better already, he thought, and a good meal should work wonders.

"You will turn up?" he asked. "You're not spoofing me?"

"No, really I'm not. I'll be there just after half past twelve."

"That's fine! Fine! I know you will now."

"Right ho, then." The girl rose from the seat. "I must get off here, my fare's up."

He followed close behind her down the stairs. As she stood waiting to get off the platform he seized her hand and gave it a happy squeeze. She drew away, laughing, and pulled her small brown beret closer on her curls.

"You haven't told me your name. Mine's Bert Forster."

"And mine's Elsie Lane, but I shan't tell you my age!"

"Three guesses!"

"No, no! You might guess right. Ask me again when we meet." She stepped off.

"All right, I will. Don't forget!" he called as the bus

45

moved off. "Half past twelve at Aldgate station — just round the corner there!"

"I'll not forget!" She waved gaily, transformed.

Smiling, Bert hung out and watched her until she was hidden from view by the traffic. Then he propped himself against the steps. 'Well,' he laughed at himself, 'who'd have thought it!'

2

Police Constable Harold Thurgood stirred himself from a deep sleep and fumbled on a bedside table for his watch. But it was still fastened to his wrist. After consulting it, he muttered a faint curse and sprang out of bed. He had overslept by half an hour and would have to hurry.

All round the bedroom were strewn the dress clothes he had worn the night before. He had spent the night dancing, and had reached home — how, he was not quite certain — around five o'clock in the morning. He could remember flinging off his clothes and dropping into bed, but not what had happened before. That was a blank that would have to be cleared up later, when next he met Helen Stroud, he thought to himself. Really she was a fine woman. Getting on in years, but still hiding her age; still ripe and ready for a bit of fun. And Lord, couldn't she drink! More than he could himself, he decided, on his way to the bathroom. 'Lord,' he wondered presently, while the bath was filling, 'did I make love to her?' He may have done! Yes, indeed, he may have done. He slipped into the water and lay back, watching the steam rise slowly to the dead white ceiling and there form tiny drops. If he had made love to her — but no, surely not! Drunk though he may have been, surely he hadn't done that! If so, the, good times he had with her may come to a sudden end. And then... He groaned inwardly. Then life would hardly be worth living. It was only through her that he gained admittance to certain clubs where drink — and other diversions — continued unabated until early dawn. It was only through her that he could hope to escape from his present life in the police force to something, some job or other, where material rewards were greater. In the police force, despite his public school education, his genteel, but impoverished background, the plums were few and very far between. He had been a policeman six years now, and was still a constable. It was these army fellows, appointed to vacancies at the top, who ruined the prospects of the lower ranks and disheartened the best of men. Educated rankers like himself with the background of a public school, expected, on joining, a lot more than they actually got out of the force. Of course, if you had good connections... But he hadn't good connections. His father, who might have gone high in the Civil Service, had been dead for years; and his mother had few relatives to pull any strings, and very few friends.

But just why did Helen Stroud take him around? he wondered suddenly. Why? Perhaps... good Lord, perhaps she *wanted* him to make love to her! The thought staggered Thurgood for a moment. It hardly seemed possible that she should... Yet there were certain things that he had until now overlooked, significant things, he remembered, lathering his great strong chest and muscular arms. Look how often she had told him, in that low thrilling voice of hers, what a magnificent figure he had. That had not seemed to mean much before, but it did now. Of course, he had a good figure; he was as strong as a young bull; but nevertheless, people didn't usually comment about it more than once or twice. Yet Helen Stroud must have said it — dozens of times! Dozens! And what the devil for, unless —? But it seemed unbelievable! Why should she want *him* to make love to her, when she could get plenty of young men from her own set to pay her attention? Still, if she did, *he* wouldn't be unwilling, he told himself happily. No fear! She was all right, despite her age, and that she hid uncommonly well. A woman in a thousand! When he met her next Wednesday at the

47

Grakle Club he would have to try to discover what had happened last night — if he really had made love to her when in his cups. It was quite possible that he had, he reflected, soaping his hair. It was one of his failings, and an embarrassing one on occasions, to make love to the women he danced with when he had had too much to drink. And Helen Stroud — well, he had danced with her nearly all last evening. She had practically made him dance with her by arranging that it should be so beforehand.

Still thinking it over, he climbed out of the bath, and dried rapidly. The appetising smell of frying bacon floated up from the kitchen, where his mother was cooking his breakfast. He threw his dressing gown around him and went below, feeling far less tired than he had done when he first got out of bed. But his head still throbbed painfully and his mouth was dry and bitter.

"Good morning, Harold," Mrs Thurgood greeted him pleasantly.

"Morning," Thurgood answered. "Breakfast not ready? I'm late."

"Yes, in just a minute." Mrs Thurgood went as fast as her prematurely aged legs would permit to the gas stove in the scullery. She was a little woman with grey hair and heavily wrinkled face, and suffered from rheumatism, about which she seldom complained.

"What time did you get in?" she asked, returning with bacon and eggs.

"Just after five, I think."

"I didn't hear you, though I was wide awake until very late. Did you enjoy yourself?"

"So so."

Mrs Thurgood handed him his plate and poured tea. He noticed that she looked worried about something. Bills, he thought. There always seemed to be a pile of bills, mostly for repairs to the house and drains. If he'd had his way they would have sold the house and got a more modern place. It was far too big for the two of them, with its eight rooms, large front garden and even larger back. Besides, the district may have been 'select' in his father's time, but it wasn't now. It gave him a shudder to enter the road and to see the dilapidated fronts of houses long ago converted into working class flats. Even the trees that lined the road seemed dilapidated. But his mother would not hear of moving. To her the house was alive with memories of her married life and better times, when the Thurgoods had entertained guests and kept a maid. Mrs Thurgood, having seated herself, continued the conversation.

"Was Lady Stroud with you?" she asked, with a pretence of idle curiosity. But Thurgood knew at what she was hinting.

"No," he said sharply. "She wasn't."

"I don't much like that woman, Harold. A person in her position —"

"— doesn't mix with policemen for nothing," Thurgood ended for her.

His mother flushed. "Well, does she?"

"I don't know. In any case, it doesn't matter to me. I can look out for myself, you know."

Thurgood laid down his knife and fork. He was in the mood to argue this grievance between them. "If her husband hadn't bought his title she'd have been plain Mrs Stroud, and then I don't suppose you would have objected?"

His mother parried the question. "It isn't so much her position, or her title, Harold. But she is, after all, considerably older than you, and a widow into the bargain. Her reputation —"

"You can't judge people by their reputation."

"You can judge that kind of person."

"What kind?"

Again Mrs Thurgood parried. "When I was a young woman we kept ourselves to ourselves —"

"Yes, and are you any better off for it? Dash it all!" Thurgood added impatiently, "I have been brought up as well as anyone in her set, as you call it. I did go to a public school, didn't I?"

He stabbed viciously at his bacon, his temper rising. He could not understand his mother's hostility to Lady Stroud. Several times lately they had argued heatedly about her, so that he had decided not to tell his mother more than was necessary about where and with whom he spent his evenings. He wished he had preserved secrecy from the start, but he had been proud to make a society woman's acquaintance, and had told his mother — with this unexpected result.

"I could understand your dislike more if you had met her," he said. "But you haven't met her."

"No, but you have told me enough about her for me to form an opinion. If you are not careful she'll be the ruin of you."

"Don't be silly, mother, don't be so silly! For the Lord's sake —"

"Very well. Say no more about it, Harold."

The meal continued in silence to its end. Then Mrs Thurgood got up and cleared away, while Thurgood went upstairs to dress. On his dressing table, in a silver frame, was a photograph of Helen Stroud. He picked it up and gazed at it, thinking how lovely she was, how desirable, and how worthwhile. He set the frame carefully in its place and went below again. His mother was old-fashioned, and rather silly, and maybe a little jealous.

"You're on duty in the East End today, aren't you?" she asked.

Thurgood nodded. "Why?"

"It certainly seems as if there is going to be some trouble."

"Trouble!" Thurgood grinned. "You mustn't always believe the newspapers. They're out to sell copies."

"I know what these demonstrations are. When your father and I were in India — that was in nineteen-seven, I think — but you will take care, won't you? Keep calm and everything will be all right —"

"I must hurry," Thurgood interrupted her. "You'll be staying in tonight, won't you?" she asked, showing him to the door.

"Yes, I expect so, Mother."

"I'll have a hot meal ready for you — about seven — and your slippers warmed, and then we can have an evening by the fire," his mother said in happy anticipation.

She watched from the front door until Thurgood had turned a bend in the road, and then went smiling into the house. The thought that he hadn't spent last night with Lady Stroud had cheered her.

Chapter III

THE paint-blistered door of Slesser's home stood open to the sun, which shone remorselessly on the finger-stained wallpaper and the bare, tiled passage with its skirting boards rotted with age and many mouse holes. From the flat above came the noisy blare of a gramophone, which, twenty times a day, played a brass band version of 'The Rosary.' The record was on now, and as he walked along the passage it dinned so loudly in Slesser's ears that he winced. When he had closed the kitchen door and stood blinking in the vault like darkness, the tune sounded less raucous, though still maddeningly insistent.

Slesser pitched his cap on a chair, looked up, and saw his wife glaring grimly from the scullery door. She had been preparing the dinner and her face was red from the heat. Long before she spoke he guessed what she wanted to say. 'Ah, well, let her nag and cackle and get it over with, then there'll be peace,' he thought resignedly, dropping on the sofa near the window and feigning indifference.

"Oh, so you have managed to find your way back," she observed in a heavily sarcastic tone. "I was thinking you'd got lost or something, looking for the milk you went to fetch off the doorstep at eight o'clock this morning. Or did you have to go to the country to fetch it?"

Slesser realised with a pang that this was something else she could tell to her sister Rose, to his own humiliation. But he remained silent, trying not to listen to his wife's loud words.

"One of these days," she went on, no longer attempting sarcasm, but in a threatening tone, "you'll go out in one of your sulky moods and come back and find me missing.

52

Don't think I'm dependent on you, Joe Slesser! Because I'm not! My sister Rose'll keep me any time I like to go, and don't you forget it! And one of these days I shall go, you lazy, good for nothing —"

Slesser leapt to his feet. "Damn your sister Rose!" he exploded. "Tell her from me she's a bloody whore! Tell her that!"

"You daren't tell her yourself —" his wife began.

"Daren't I! You wait and see! I'll tell her if she comes in this house this afternoon. I'm the boss here, not her! I'll throw her out, neck and bloody crop — *and* that nancy husband of hers on top of her."

"I'll —" she tried to interrupt. "You too," Slesser stormed. "The whole bloody lot of you — neck and crop. Anybody'd think I was a lodger in this house, the way you go on! Nag, nag, nag all day long. I'm sick of it, sick to death of it!" he shouted in desperation.

She turned pale at his fury, and said nothing, fearing him. He had never been like this before, never in all their married life. He stood perfectly still, glaring at her savagely, his fists clenched hard as if to strike her. Then nausea swept through him in a sickening wave. He gulped as if choking, and, fearful of vomiting, pushed her aside and let himself out to the backyard. One hand ready to close over his mouth, he tugged open the lavatory door, and leaned, gasping and spitting, over the bowl; his stomach rolled and heaved in a sickening, deceptive manner, and pain tore at his bowels. But nothing came up except a spoonful of bile which left him more miserable than ever. He groaned and retched and spluttered so horribly that his two young children, who were watching from near the dustbins, ran screaming into the house.

When the worst of the attack was over, Slesser wiped his lips on his hand and staggered back into the house. His wife shot him a sharp, querulous glance and immediately turned away, apparently indifferent. The two young children, gathering courage, clamoured round him anxiously; but he pushed them roughly aside and dropped on the sofa, where he lay back, depressed and miserable. Dimly he heard his wife call the two children into the scullery, whisper something inaudible and send them quietly off along the passage.

A few minutes later they returned, breathless but quiet, and rejoined their mother in the scullery. Slesser, hearing the chink of coppers, thought they had been for change for the gas until he heard his name, and, opening his eyes, saw his wife standing patiently beside him.

"You'd better take these," she said in non-committal tones, holding out three aspirins and a glass of water. "You've had a bilious attack through getting excited on an empty stomach, and I don't wonder either, the way you behave. Take them and lie quiet and you'll be all right by dinner-time. It'll only be ten minutes. The Lord only knows," she added as he silently accepted the tablets, "we can't afford to have you on the panel. The eighteen bob they give you wouldn't hardly pay the rent, let alone buy food. If you hadn't gone off like you did this morning, this wouldn't have happened. You know that as well as I do."

Slesser made no attempt to reply. He did not blame himself for the quarrel, or for anything else, but he felt too weak and miserable to contradict her. It was better to keep quiet, he thought, and lay brooding and dozing alternately until a sharp question from his wife awoke him.

"Do you think you can manage to eat any dinner?"

Rising cautiously to his feet, he was surprised to find that the weakness had passed. Except for a throbbing head he felt almost himself again. "Ah," he muttered. "I'm all right now."

"Your headache'll soon pass off," said his wife as he rubbed his brow. She turned to one of the children, "Jackie, run out and tell Sally and Frankie that dinner's ready. And don't stop to play about!" she called as the child ran off along the passage.

Slesser took his habitual seat opposite his wife, at the end of the table near the sofa; and soon the children

54

swarmed into the kitchen and clambered into their chairs, squabbling like monkeys. They all ate in hungry silence the meal of stewed rabbit, potatoes, and peas which they had had every Sunday for weeks. They had rabbit, not only because it was cheap at sixpence a pound, but because it made excellent gravy. Had Slesser not been brooding over the quarrel he would have remarked, 'Rabbit again! We'll all be growing long ears at this rate!' and the children would have laughed with delight, despite their hunger. But today they knew very well that their parents had quarrelled, and they gave no thought to joking, fearing to disturb the heavy oppressive silence.

The dreary meal ended after a quarter of an hour and Slesser, who rose first, went out to the backyard while his wife cleared away the pots. Soon, he thought gloomily, sister Rose would appear, and then there would be tea and cake, domestic discussion, and the more spicy titbits of local gossip for three long hours. Slesser himself would figure largely ('What! No work again!' 'No, no work again.') and the thought filled him with a feverish longing to escape. But there was nowhere to go to avoid those chattering tongues, unless — unless he went to the fascist march, he thought hopefully. That would mean fares, he remembered with a sigh, and he had no money left. Unless he asked his wife...? No, that would mean explaining what he had done with the cigarette money; and she would assuredly have something pretty nasty to say if he told her he had spent it at the coffee stall.

He sat on the dustbin top, smoking a Woodbine, thinking over the problem. Suddenly his wife called him loudly from the kitchen, "Joe, come here! Come inside!" He went in, wondering what was the matter, unprepared for Rose, who was sitting, overdressed, scented and huge, in a small cane chair which cracked beneath her spreading bulk.

"Hullo!" she greeted him in her deep, booming voice. "I've got some news for you. That's why I've come early."

"What news?" Slesser asked suspiciously, glancing round for his wife, who was busy making tea in the scullery.

"Aha!" Rose exclaimed. "I see you don't believe me." A grin of delight spread over her face. "But you will," she added mysteriously, nodding.

"What do you mean?" Slesser demanded roughly. "What's it all about? It's not a secret, is it?" He felt his temper rising, as it always did at the sight of her these last few months.

"That's just it!" Rose exclaimed, unaware of his resentful demeanour. "It's a secret!" She lowered her voice to a conspiratorial whisper. "You mustn't tell anybody, mind you, or you'll not get it!"

"Tell who what?"

"Anybody. It's like this. You know that plot of ground near the railway?"

"Well, what of it?" Slesser demanded frostily. Damn her! Why couldn't she spit it out, whatever it was, instead of all this mystery and whispering. The fat fool!

"Ah! I thought you would!" Rose went on. "Well —?" and here she paused dramatically.

He was supposed to guess what she tried to infer with wide open eyes and expectant grin; but he refused to try. He looked at her steadily for a moment, then turned deliberately away and sat on the sofa and waited resignedly. Some silly stupid gossip! he thought contemptuously. Not worth bothering his head about. Why didn't she get on with it, instead of all this messing around?

"Can't you guess?" Rose queried in a disappointed tone.

"No, I can't."

"Oh, dearie me! You are the dullest man —! I can see I'll just have to tell you. It's like this." Her voice dropped to a whisper again. "The council start building flats down there on Monday week — direct labour. Now do you see?"

"You mean —?" said Slesser, crouching forward on the sofa.

"Yes, exactly!" Rose cried triumphantly. "Go round to the council tomorrow afternoon and you're almost bound to get a job."

"No bloody fear I don't!" Slesser retorted violently. "Not

on your life!"

"Wh-a-at!" came two startled shrieks, so close together that they sounded like one — and Mrs Slesser rushed in from the scullery, flourishing the teapot and spluttering with rage, while Rose gaped like a floundering fish.

"You heard what I said. I'm not going back on the council, so that's that!"

Mrs Slesser turned appealingly to Rose. "What did I tell you? You heard him. Now you know what he is. Now you know what I've got to live with. Is it any wonder I'm going grey? I ask you, Rose, would you put up with it? No, I should just think you wouldn't," as Rose shook her head in emphatic denial. "Nor would I," she added bitterly, "if it weren't for my kids. No, not another minute would I stay with him. And he knows there's another one on the way —"

"Another!" Rose gasped. "Another baby!"

"And that's your bloody fault!" Slesser jerked out.

"What does he mean — my fault?" Rose asked immediately of her sister.

"You take no notice of him," said Mrs Slesser. "It just shows what I've got to put up with, Rose. First he turns down the chance of a job because he won't join a union — yes, *that's* why! — and now he's trying to blame somebody else for what's his own silly fault. Nobody can say that I'm a bad mother or a bad wife, and that's what I get. I ask you...? Only this morning I sent that there man," pointing at Slesser, "to fetch the milk off the doorstep, and do you know, Rose..."

"Christ! Let me get out of it!" Slesser cried, "I'll go stark staring mad in a minute!" He sprang to his feet, rushed into the scullery and shut the door with a bang. He grabbed his shaving tackle and took it out to the tap in the yard and shaved in the ice cold water. Then he washed, polished his shoes, combed his hair; and all the time their voices drifted to him from the kitchen, now a shocked exclamation from Rose, now a flood of complaints from his wife. And suddenly he smiled. Let them tear him to pieces with their poisonous tongues! Let them nag and cackle like vultures over his sins!

He could get out of it for once. He could go to the fascist march, as old Tom had seemed so keen about it. To hell with the naggers and cacklers in the kitchen! And he wasn't going to walk; no fear! He was going to ride — by tram. Useless to ask his wife for the fare. Well, then, he'd have to take it himself. From her purse, tucked away beneath the mattress in the bedroom — for fear of burglars. Burglars! Well, there *would be* a burglar, only it would be his own money he was taking. Yes, his own money. He could do as he pleased with it. He wasn't like other men — drinking and gambling and dogs — so why the hell shouldn't he take a shilling when he wanted it? Take it, instead of having to go on his knees and beg for it — and then most likely not get it? Why not? Who could stop him? Neither of those old hags in the kitchen! Just let them try! Just let them... Then there *would* be a bloody row! Thus, grimly silent, he stalked his way through the kitchen, pausing only to snatch up his cap, and then went to the bedroom and took a shilling from his wife's purse where it lay under the mattress. Whistling cheerfully, he passed out into the sunshine — a giant of resolve.

2

Bert Forster emerged from the hot, subterranean depths of Aldgate station and halted, looking for Elsie. He was early, and he half doubted if she would be there, but presently he saw her a little way down the road, staring at a huge anti-fascist slogan chalked in the gutter at her feet. Her dejected manner, as she stood unconscious of being observed, struck him once more, and he felt interest in her and curiosity. He approached quietly, taking stock of her, noting for the first time that she carried no handbag and that her shoes were down at heel so badly that she seemed to be falling outwards, in both directions at once. She *was* a bit of a mess!

"Hullo!" he called cheerfully, tapping her shoulder from behind. "Wake up, Elsie!"

She wheeled round as if stung. "Oh — you!"

"Made you jump, did I?"

"Y-yes." She gulped visibly. "I didn't see you coming."

"A thief in the night, eh?" Bert laughed. "Come on, Elsie. I know a quiet little café near here where we can get a good meal without having to wait for it." He took her arm and led her away with friendly familiarity.

Bert had changed his conductor's uniform for a brown sports coat, and flannels, baggy at the knees, and a thin, white open-neck shirt which showed a considerable stretch of his sunburned, slightly hairy chest. To complete the picture of progressive youth, he was hatless; his fair hair, parted at the side, lay untidily scattered on his large round head.

Elsie, glancing up at him furtively, was pleased that he had dressed like this. She herself did not look so shabby by comparison when he wore those appallingly baggy trousers. It was because of her clothes that she had hesitated when he first asked her to meet him, but now, she noted gratefully, she needn't particularly worry. Bert didn't seem to care about clothes, as so many men did.

"We're nearly there," Bert announced cheerfully, turning a corner into a narrow street in which the houses looked as if they would soon collapse for want of repair. "It's not much of a place, this street isn't, but the café's good — I've been here before. Besides, we'll be near the scene of the march. I suppose you still want to go?"

"Not unless you do."

"There isn't much else we can do on a Sunday afternoon, is there?"

"All right, then. We'll go to the march."

"We'll have a jolly good dinner now and take our time over it, eh? I'll bet you're twice as big when you come out — that is, if you eat as much as I do," he added, with a laugh that was almost a guffaw. "I'm a one for grub, I am. You wait till you see me eat!" (Good for him to put it like that, he thought.)

He stood aside for Elsie to precede him into the small,

clean café. Near the hatch leading to the kitchen, tall, sallow, and profoundly bored, lounged the Cockney proprietor. His eyebrows lifted the briefest trifle in answer to Bert's cheery greeting.

"Silent Sammy," Bert whispered to Elsie as they sat down at a table in the window bay. "But he takes everything in... What'll you have? I'm having roast beef, Yorkshire, baked potatoes, and cabbage for a start, and then there's a choice of..." He read right through the menu without pause. "What'll you have?" he repeated.

"I — I don't know," Elsie said timidly. "You see, Bert, I don't eat much —"

"What's the matter? Aren't you well?"

She sobbed but made no reply. Bert hastily glanced round the café. Thank God it was deserted, except for the proprietor, who appeared oblivious to Elsie's weeping. "Look here," he said, desperately concerned. "Shall I fetch a doctor or something?" ('And where the hell shall I find a doctor?' he wondered.)

"No, no! I'm all right — honest I am." She dabbed her eyes. "I'm sorry, Bert. I — I just don't know what came over me. Let's — let's get on with the dinner, shall we?" she suggested, by an effort of self control ceasing to cry.

"All right."

Bert sat down, but continued to stare at her in pardonable amazement. He began to wish that he had never asked her to come out with him; her behaviour to cry like this without apparent cause, seemed ridiculous. But no. That wasn't fair, he told himself. She looked ill. She probably was ill — something she didn't like to tell him about.

Still considerably flustered, he ordered two dinners, and when the attendant had gone to the hatch he bent over the table, and whispered, "how do you feel now, Elsie? Better?"

"Yes, thanks. I'm sorry, Bert. Perhaps I oughtn't to have come."

"Oh, that's all right, Elsie. Don't you bother. Here's the grub!" he added with assumed jocularity as the proprietor noiselessly approached with two huge plates of food. "One landlady I used to live with," Bert continued," said I ate her out of house and home! I had to leave there — she said she wanted five shillings more a week on account of my appetite!"

Elsie smiled. She looked better already, Bert thought, starting to eat in a more confident frame of mind. The food would do her a world of good. Poor kid, she certainly looked as if she needed it.

They ate almost without speaking. Bert had to urge her to have a sweet; her first refusal he put down to nervousness. He was becoming increasingly more at ease with her, and noticed with satisfaction that colour was returning to her cheeks. She was certainly more alive and less self-conscious by the end of the meal.

"Now," Bert said, pushing away his empty plate, "what about a coffee to finish off with?" He waved to the proprietor without waiting for her answer. "And have a smoke," he offered, pulling out a packet of cigarettes. "These are what I won at the pin tables. You know, those places in the West End where you put a penny in a machine — and sometimes win."

"Yes, I know what you mean, but I've never been inside one."

"Haven't you? I go there nearly every day. It's a racket, really, but there's always a bit of excitement, like playing cards for money. You keep on playing in the hopes of having some luck, losing all the time. This packet of five cost me half a crown!"

"To think I'm smoking a cigarette that cost sixpence!" Elsie cried, suddenly amused and eager.

"That's one way of looking at it," Bert agreed, grinning. "Here's the coffee."

After a pause during which he racked his brains to think of something pleasant to talk about, Bert, with many divagations, recounted the incident of the inspector who had boarded his bus that morning. His jocular treatment brought both smiles and a warning from Elsie.

"But you might get the sack," she said. "And then what?"

"Oh, I don't think so. It's my first offence and they usually let you off. But even if they did sack me," he added, "I think I'd soon get another job. I seem to be lucky about getting work lately — I dunno why. Years ago though—" He waved his hand in an expressive gesture and shook his head. "I had some hard times."

"*I* can't seem to get a job," Elsie said.

"So you're unemployed?" Bert was beginning to understand. "Then I suppose you have to live at home —?"

"No, I haven't a home, either."

"Then — then —?" Suddenly a horrible suspicion assailed him. He blurted out, "you're not on the... on the —?"

Her glance was steady upon his anxious face. She smiled grimly. "No, I'm not on the streets, Bert, if that's what you mean. No. To tell you the truth," she added bitterly, "I'm worse. Far worse." She paused a moment and drew at her cigarette, trying to make her voice even and controlled, "Perhaps when you know you will wish you'd never met me."

Bert leaned forward and placed his arms on the table. His face was close to hers, "Go on, Elsie. Tell me. It'll be all right. I knew you were in trouble when I met you, and you can rely on me. I trust you, and you can trust me."

Elsie, to gain time, sipped her coffee before answering. She was not quite sure what to say. It was all very well for him to talk like that, but he didn't yet know all about her. Perhaps when he did — she glanced at his honest blue eyes, bent seriously on her face, waiting for her to speak, sympathetic and encouraging.

"All right, I'll tell you. It's like this." She lowered her voice to a whisper. "This morning, about two o'clock, I was with a girl who threw herself in the Thames and got drowned. I tried to stop her going over, but she was too strong for me."

"Phew! What a ghastly experience!"

"Yes, but let me explain. I didn't know a thing about her. I met her in a café last night, and we got talking, and then afterwards we went along to this bridge, and she jumped over. I couldn't stop her, Bert. I swear I couldn't stop her!"

"But it's nothing to do with you, is it? I mean —"

"Oh, but don't you see! The police might think I *pushed* her over. One of them saw us together on the bridge just before she did it." Elsie explained at length her fears of arrest.

"But look here," Bert consoled her when she had finished. "They can't pin anything on you. And they've got to find you first —"

"Do you really think it will be all right?"

"Sure, Elsie! Don't you worry about it. I shouldn't. Is *that* all you had to tell me?"

"No," said Elsie, slowly shaking her head. "It isn't. But that's what's been worrying me —" She broke off, and drew nervously at her cigarette. "You see," she confessed. "I — I've — well, I've been in prison already."

Bert's amazed stare disconcerted Elsie further. At last, to her great relief, he laughed and said, "oh, well, that's nothing. So have lots of us. My old man was in once — for getting drunk and assaulting a copper!" He laughed again at the recollection, a deep gurgling laugh, 'Hur! Hur! Hur!' which Elsie found comforting and kind. "What were you in for?" he resumed, lowering his voice.

"Stealing," she said, brazening it out.

"And did you?"

His tone, free from condemnation, disarmed Elsie. She looked at him... timidly, like a child owning up, but begging for understanding. "Yes, Bert, I did."

He was silent, contemplatively stubbing his cigarette.

"I didn't want to! But there was nothing else! I swear there wasn't! I was terrified all the time, down and out and terrified. Where I was in service they wouldn't let me keep my job. I didn't know where to turn for help — Bert," she entreated, "please don't hate me. I haven't had

63

anyone to talk to for so long — you've been kind — I —"

He touched her hand, which was rigidly gripping the table edge. "You don't have to tell me anything you don't want to, Elsie. And of course I don't hate you. You can say anything you like to me, you poor kid. I've been around a bit and I'm no prig. Now see here, you just take it easy —"

She was dabbing at her eyes with the hopelessly inadequate handkerchief. "Take mine," he said.

"It was hell in there," she said. "They treat you like cattle, and even when you come out you've still got to be punished one way or the other. I've had no work since I've been out — nearly a month now."

"I know it's tough," Bert said. "I've seen fellows like that when I was in the States. It must be a damn sight worse for a girl."

"Bert," she said, lowering her voice as a party of customers sat down at a nearby table. "I'd like to get it off my chest — I'd like to tell you. It's so awful being alone and having to hide things all the time —"

"Then tell me. I can stand it."

She gave a watery but grateful smile. "It's all pretty bad, like a nightmare. You see, I got into trouble —"

"You mean —?"

"Yes, I was going to have a baby. As soon as Lady Stroud knew, she sacked me. I begged her to let me stay another month till I could see my way a bit clearer — but she wouldn't hear of it."

"Who was this Lady Stroud?" Bert asked, feeling at sea.

"I used to work for her as housemaid. I used to iron her dresses and help with her hair and everything. She found plenty for me to do outside my usual work. Always gadding about, she was, with men and that, and I thought she might be a bit sympathetic when she knew the fix I was in, but not her!"

"But," said Bert diffidently, "wasn't the man —?"

"He was killed," Elsie said. "They were loading his ship and he was knocked in the hold. He never even knew about me... He died before he got my letter."

Bert mumbled inadequately.

"So, you see, I was quite alone, Bert. Without a job, I just couldn't manage. So I tried to get away with a fur from an Oxford Street store, thinking I could sell it —"

"And they caught you?"

"Yes, they caught me. It's a horrible story, I know. I'm ashamed it should be about myself, but I've told you the truth. Funny!" she added thoughtfully, "I don't feel any different from what I was before it all happened — really I don't — except older, maybe. I feel a lot older."

Bert was regarding her solemnly. He was keenly interested and sorry for her too; but chiefly interested. This was the kind of thing you read about. Hell, and he'd thought *he* knew the world! What this girl had been through!

"What happened to the baby?" he asked suddenly, his eyes bright upon her.

Elsie met his gaze. "It was born dead — in prison," she said. "A little girl, it was." She added, "I suppose all this seems queer, but it's true, every bit of it. You do believe me, don't you?"

"Yes, yes. I believe you, Elsie," he said. (It was true. Strange though her story sounded he believed it. She had spoken honestly, he was prepared to swear, at a moment when off her guard.)

"I wouldn't lie to you, Bert," she exclaimed with feeling. "You've been too damned good to me. If it hadn't been for you I'd have starved today, like I did yesterday — and the day before that."

"You mean you haven't had any food for two days?" he asked in a shocked whisper.

"Honest, Bert, I haven't — except a cake this morning. And now you'll understand why I cried when I came in here. I was so weak and I just felt like — well, you know how it is."

"I know," he said gently, laying a large, comforting hand on hers and squeezing it sympathetically. "You poor kid! You'll have to let me help you, somehow."

"You've already helped me. If it hadn't been for meeting you today, God knows what I'd have done. Maybe the same as the other girl."

"Nonsense! I've done nothing that anybody else wouldn't do. And you don't want to think of that way out. Something always turns up in the end, you know. Promise me you won't."

"I promise. Actually I wouldn't — I was only pitying myself. No, I shouldn't do that — not after what I've put up with already. And meeting you has made all the difference — having someone to talk to —"

"I know. It helps to get it off your chest, doesn't it? Well, if you've finished your coffee, shall we go? Silent Sammy's beginning to glower at us!"

While Bert paid the bill, Elsie hurriedly tidied her hair and adjusted her beret before a small mirror on a nearby wall.

3

From beneath the rumpled sheets Helen Stroud stretched forth a slim white arm and rang the bell for her maid. Her lips showed her mood more clearly than the glint in her pale eyes. She felt physically depressed this morning, and her head ached painfully after a hectic late night. She longed to stay in bed, to sleep on for hours, but that unfortunately was quite impossible, she remembered. She had to lunch with the Carstairs, and it was a long drive out to their house beyond Rainham. And after lunch, she reflected, she had to return all the way to town to visit the truly dreadful Banks in Kensington. That was the worst of being almost penniless. One had to cultivate the most atrocious people. Still, if old Banks made good his boast, if he could, indeed, live up to his reputation for 'cert' investments that brought a quick return, her visit would be made tolerable. She hoped he would not fail her.

If he did, she would in the near future be bankrupt. Already she had difficulty in facing her creditors, and if the pile of unpaid bills and threatening letters which reposed in her dressing table drawer were not paid soon...

"Good morning, my lady," a modulated voice cut through her thoughts. The maid had entered silently and deposited the breakfast tray beside the bed. She crossed the room and drew the curtains, letting in the too powerful sunlight. Lady Stroud, blinking in the sudden light, reached for her tomato juice and sipped it cautiously. The girl entered the bathroom and turned on the taps and added bath salts in a generous quantity.

Soon Helen Stroud resisted the claims of laziness and left her bed, to relax once more in the comfort of her bath. But not for long, it was already late in the morning. She must hurry. As she dried herself she glanced appraisingly at her reflection in a pier glass on the opposite wall. Despite her forty years, her body was still as firm and slender as a healthy young girl's. Her breasts were firm and small, her limbs pink, smooth and shapely — she was one of the few women of middle age who could wear a backless evening gown with genuine success. But her face, now undisguised with cosmetics, was the face of a woman of fifty. It was lined; crow's feet were scored under her eyes; there was the beginning of a dark moustache on her upper lip. These symptoms of her age in no manner disturbed her. She knew that, with a few deft touches of cream, rouge, powder, lipstick, and eyebrow pencil, she could reduce the age of that face to thirty-five — and sometimes even to thirty.

Humming gaily to herself, for the hot bath had worked a miracle, she went back to the bedroom, where the maid had her clothes and cosmetics prepared. Together they reduced the age of the face, this morning to thirty, and combed and waved the silky brown hair, and dressed the slim, girlish body in perfect clothes, that had still to be paid for — alas! And then Lady Stroud, very well pleased with their efforts, rose, and pulled on a close-fitting hat, and asked if the car was ready in the street below. Assured that it was, she snatched up her gloves, her handbag and, with a final glance in the mirror, hurried from the room to the lift. The liftman touched his cap respectfully when he came gliding up from below; she stepped inside, gave him one of those rare, dazzling smiles which made her seem beautiful, and they went down, without words, to the bottom floor. A few minutes later she was sitting back in the limousine, on her way to Rainham.

Passing through Hyde Park she glanced at her wrist-watch. It was far later than she had thought. "Faster, please," she said to the chauffeur. "I'm late." He nodded and obediently accelerated to forty miles an hour. He knew that, if he refused to exceed the limit, she would promptly dismiss him. 'You silly old fool!' he thought contemptuously. Still, she paid the fines...

The car swept down Grosvenor Place, turned left along Buckingham Palace Road, whirled round the Victoria Memorial outside the Palace, and shot up the tree-lined Mall. It slowed to circle Trafalgar Square, where the pigeons fluttered in swarms, and then down the Strand, on into Fleet Street at gathering speed, until halted abruptly in a traffic jam at Ludgate Circus. Two precious minutes were wasted before the car was released; it breasted Ludgate Hill without effort and dashed along Cannon Street towards the Bank. Here the chauffeur turned along Cornhill, heading for Aldgate.

When the car passed out of Leadenhall Street into Aldgate High Street, Lady Stroud was considerably surprised to find, a few yards farther on, a surging crowd of people and vehicles blocking the road. There were scores of policemen, mounted ones too — why couldn't they keep these crowds in order? It was a positive disgrace that one could not have a free passage in one's car when one was hastening to keep an engagement.

The chauffeur was forced to bring the car to a standstill behind a long line of stationary traffic. Lady Stroud sat patiently for a moment and then, jerking open the window, beckoned to a nearby policeman.

"Constable —" she began. And then she gave a sharp, amazed cry of pleasure. "Why! It's you, Harold!"

"Yes," said PC Thurgood, feeling uncomfortable. "It's me all right." He bent his head down to the window.

"I'm so delighted to see you," Lady Stroud went on, in an instant recovering her composure and speaking in low tones to avoid being overheard by the chauffeur. "How remarkable to meet you here. It is the very first time I have ever seen you in uniform, and you look splendid! Magnificent!"

"Do I?" Thurgood laughed. "I return the compliment," he said gallantly.

She laughed roguishly. "And how do you feel — after last night?"

"Oh, not too good. Rather a thick head," replied Thurgood, apparently at ease, but inwardly still flustered by this sudden meeting, and aware that it would be better to avoid any intimacy in front of the chauffeur.

"I believe you enjoyed yourself?" she suggested.

"Immensely! Thanks to you, Lady Stroud."

"I'm so glad." She let her long lashes down over her eyes for a moment.

"Well, you must come along and have a chat with me when you can find the time," she said. "And, by the way, I'd almost forgotten why I called you! Do you think you can get a way cleared for my car?" she added in louder tones. "I shall be fearfully late for luncheon."

"I'll try," he promised, still staring at her.

"Just why are all these people here?"

"It's a political affair. The fascist march, you know."

"Oh, yes! I had completely forgotten it. What a bore for you."

"It is rather." He laughed and added, "but one's life has compensations. Am I going to see you on Wednesday?"

"Of course, Harold," she said and gave him a queenly smile.

She watched closely as he drove back the crowd with the assistance of other policemen. How strong he must be, she thought as the car edged forward. Yes, and so amusing. It was a pity that he had to be a policeman. She would have to try to do something for him. He must not be allowed to waste himself at this sort of work. He was too good for it, the dear boy. And he really had shewn himself interested in her last night.

Her thoughts could not wander for long. The crowd was in an obstinate mood. As fast as one batch was driven back to the pavement another broke through the cordon, pushing the constables forcibly into the centre of the road among the vehicles. On the air resounded a slogan, shouted with maniacal intensity, 'They Shall Not Pass!' From the shuttered shops anxious faces watched the surging throng in the road below. Women in the crowd repeatedly screamed as the police threatened the struggling people.

Lady Stroud began to get afraid. The crowds were dangerously close to the car, shaking their fists at it, she thought. She raised her handkerchief to her mouth, and held it there, fighting her fears. She thought she would faint. She had stretched out a hand to get out of the car, into the sunshine, when a shadow loomed before the window.

"Oh, thank heaven you're back! This is dreadful! Simply dreadful! I dare not sit here a moment longer. Can't something be done about it?"

She opened the door and stepped out, in order to gain more strength from his proximity. Also she felt that she could speak more intimately if they could have a moment's conversation by the car.

"There's nothing to be afraid of, you know," Thurgood said, rather excited and almost amused at her concern. "I'll stay beside the car," he added gallantly.

"Thank you so much. Really, I thought they would attack me."

"Oh, no!" he laughed. "They wouldn't do that. They've

only got their blood up over these fascists. We'll have them in hand in a minute."

"I sincerely hope so," she replied. "This is dreadful."

They were both silent, pretending to be absorbed in their surroundings. But Lady Stroud was thinking of what he had said while dancing at the night club. "You're nice, Helen, awfully nice. I'd like to kish you, Helen. You're a darling. I love you, Helen...." Tipsy, of course, but —?

"Harold," she said softly. "You drank a lot last night, you know."

"I hope I didn't make a fool of myself?"

"Not exactly. But you said some very surprising things to me."

"Good Lord!" he exclaimed. "I hope I haven't offended you, Lady Stroud. I'm dreadfully sorry if —"

She smiled mysteriously, but he dared not look at her.

"I shall be quite alone this evening," she said. "Perhaps you would like to call on me and — shall we say — apologise? Over supper?"

He stared at her for a moment, surprised.

"Will you?"

"That's most awfully kind of you," he stammered at last, still not able to give her his full attention.

He must get her car away as soon as possible, for although the excitement appealed to him, he was aware of the many dangers of the situation. Thank the Lord! there appeared to be more of the force at the end of the street.

"At nine o'clock?" she asked.

"I shall be delighted. I'm off duty at seven," and he turned to open the door for her, as it really seemed that the car could leave.

"Then I'll expect you at nine. I shall want you to soothe my nerves after this shocking outrage. Goodbye again — Harold."

"Goodbye," said Thurgood, feeling on top of the world.

He left her to join the newly arrived force of police.

Lady Stroud watched them successfully drive back the crowd. The long line of vehicles, first slowly, then at gathering speed, got on the move as the route ahead was cleared. She looked back, hoping to catch a final glimpse of Thurgood, but he was indistinguishable from hundreds of other policemen. She glanced down at her watch. She would be late for lunch, certainly, but that troubled her no longer.

4

At half past one Claire Rentner climbed from the dark basement of one of the houses in Belgrave Square and paused at the top of the steps to inhale the fresh air before walking away to the bus stop in Grosvenor Place. She wore a flaming red silk blouse, a dark tweed skirt, and a pair of heavy, flat-heeled shoes. Her sleek fair hair, framing her large and intelligent face, was bared to the sun and wind. She walked quickly, and soon her expectant eye picked out a tall, grey clad figure smoking patiently under a lamppost. Her expression immediately changed; her eyes became tender and a soft smile curved at her lips. When the two met, the smile changed again to the intimate smile of a lover.

"I'm not late again, am I, Dick?"

"We've heaps of time," Dick Calvin answered. "We should be there by two o'clock. By the way," pointing at her blouse, "where did you get that abomination? Woolworths?"

"This?" Claire fingered the red silk blouse. "It was the reddest I could find in Knightsbridge! And what's more," she added, "if I could have got you a tie only half as red I would have done. That pink thing you're wearing must have been made in the year dot!"

A bus drew in at the stop and Claire mounted laughing to the top deck, which was deserted. Dick followed her rather plump figure and sat beside her.

"Joking apart, Claire, today's going to be a pretty serious business for all of us."

"You mean the fascist march?"

"Yes." The conductor came for the fare. "Who's paying this time? Is it my turn?"

"It is. Besides, I haven't brought any money out with me. Pay up and look pleasant!"

Calvin paid. "In a perfect system of society we shouldn't have to pay to go to a counter-demonstration, should we?"

"In a perfect society we shouldn't have any need for counter-demonstrations," Claire pointed out.

"What do you think of that?" she asked, indicating a large anti-fascist slogan chalked in bold white letters. "There are some on the walls of Buckingham Palace gardens."

"That's a beauty," Calvin agreed. "I haven't seen so many slogans in London before. They're everywhere."

"You won't go and get pinched at the march today, will you? You had a bad enough time trying to get out after the hunger march, remember?"

"I didn't get pinched on purpose," he said with mock sarcasm.

"You know what I mean," she said. "Anyway — *don't!*"

"I'll try not to. But it's a serious business, this march. It's the first time the fascists have really set out to show their strength in this country. They're importing drafts from provincial towns to make a better show. But if what I saw in the East End last night is any indication — they're going to be in for a rough time. Slogans everywhere, scores of meetings, protests, and what not. But chiefly, there's unity against fascists, and that's what's going to count. London, generally speaking, is on our side. I've been out this morning with leaflets, along The Embankment and round Chelsea and Westminster, and everywhere I got a good reception. For once the newspapers have done us a good turn by advertising the counter-demonstration. Almost democratic!"

73

They sat looking out of the window at the slogans. In Parliament Street, Whitehall, and Trafalgar Square the slogans were less frequent, but from Ludgate Hill onwards they appeared again, bold and compelling until, near Aldgate itself, hardly a single road end or wall had escaped the chalkers.

Such persistency had had its reward, for Calvin and Claire were forced to get off the stationary bus long before Aldgate itself was reached, since the road ahead was blocked by a mass of people. Long lines of tightly-wedged traffic stretched far away in the distance. Tramcars stood end to end, forlorn and empty in the middle of the road, while the buses stood nose to tail beside the pavement, their engines silent, but a few of them still containing a handful of optimistic passengers. Continually adding to the turmoil and congestion came more buses and trams, more cars and bicycles and lorries, and more and more eager, excited people to swell the enormous throng and lend their voices to the common voice raised in thundering defiance, 'They Shall Not Pass! They Shall Not Pass! They Shall Not Pass!'

"Good God!" Calvin exclaimed. "Did you ever see such a crowd!"

"Never," said Claire happily. "Never! It's like a Red dream."

"But how are we going to push our way through there to Gardiner's Corner?" Calvin demanded anxiously.

"We don't stand an earthly," said Claire. "But come on! Let's try to get down to Royal Mint Street where the fascists are supposed to assemble, or we shan't get anywhere, by the looks of it. Come on, Dick!" She tugged at his arm.

"All right," he agreed. "We might as well be there as anywhere else. Lead on. You know this district better than I do."

They threaded their way across the road and joined in a stream of people hurrying towards the river. And following them came that defiant roar from the thousands

74

assembled at Aldgate, 'They Shall Not Pass! They Shall Not Pass! They Shall Not Pass!' until the ground itself seemed to tremble.

Chapter IV

S LESSER was hopelessly jammed in a vast excited crowd, and he was considerably perturbed. He had not intended to get there. He had got off a tram determined before he reached the scene of the march to keep at a respectable distance from the threatening cordons of police, and had stood at the back of a crowd to watch with critical eyes. But he had become so absorbed in the tumultuous events up in front that he had not noticed the throng that had gathered at his back, hemming him in. If anything should happen now, if the police charged and there was fighting, he would be right in the thick of it. Perhaps he would get a whack on the head with one of those murderous batons. He looked round again for a way of escape, but to right and left, in front and behind, there was none. The ranks of anti-fascists stood solidly protesting, roaring out their challenging slogan and shaking their raised clenched fists in angry defiance. Oh well, he thought to himself, he would just have to stay where he was for a while until the pressure eased, and then make his way to the back. But just where was he? The street was wholly unfamiliar. It was wide, but not very long, and flanked with dull grey buildings which echoed the deafening roars. He was somewhere near the river, true, for he had walked over Tower Bridge and then... He couldn't exactly remember. There had been hundreds of determined people swarming past the Tower, and he had joined them, hoping they would take him to the scene of events. For all he knew the fascists themselves might be miles away. They wore black shirts, or something like that, but so far as he could see there weren't any black shirts in sight. There was a black van moving slowly through the crowd ahead, escorted by policemen, and the crowd were getting nasty, as if they were going to attack it; but no fascists. Suddenly curious, he raised himself on his toes to get a better view of the van. And instantly a devilish roar of fury rose up from the people around him. He dropped to his heels, turned to get away, but was swept forward in an irresistible rush, as helpless as a leaf in a storm.

Events occurred with bewildering rapidity. First he saw, away ahead, the doors of the black van open, and two black clothed figures alight, strutting jauntily. Next, the figures fell, battered to the road as the crowd swept unitedly forward. Then fighting round the van, then hordes of police, then more fighting, and shrieks and groans and blood and blows. Then the crowd scattered, still fighting, sweeping him along with them, smashing him breathless against a wall, a smarting pain in his legs and his cap knocked crooked on his head from a sudden blow. There he stayed, gasping, until a further rush knocked him flat on his back. He struggled to his feet, found he was alone, and ran, suddenly afraid, along by the wall. A policeman stepped across his path, truncheon swinging at the ready. He stopped, looked wildly round, saw with a sick heart the litter and blood in the road, and darted madly to the right. The swish of the weapon sounded wickedly close; he ducked, swerved, and the blow missed his head by an inch. But it grazed the bone of his shoulder and left a pain like the thrust of a knife. He shouted a curse that was drowned in the loud sharp clatter of horses' hoofs, and ran on, following a woman with a bleeding head who screamed continuously. He heard the horses clattering immediately behind him and put on speed, terrified lest they should catch him. His lungs were like fire, his heart beating like an engine, there was a dull roaring in his ears, and he felt he couldn't carry on much longer. Soon those devilish horses would reach him and batter him down. He could almost feel their snorting breath on his neck. With a last desperate effort he tore ahead and reached the fringe of the fleeing crowd. He felt safer immediately. They wouldn't ride down a fleeing crowd. They couldn't do that. But he kept on, running with the others, panting and gasping, the sweat rolling down his face in salty streams. Then he heard with horror a shrill long scream away on his left. His head jerked round automatically, and he saw a youth go down beneath a horse's hoofs, his arms thrust despairingly upwards. The devils! There was no need for that! No bloody need at all! He slowed his pace and saw that others were doing the same; they were shouting and urging the crowd to stand fast. One man stopped altogether, turned, and flung an object at a galloping horse that was riding him down. The animal reared, pawing the air with its iron hoofs, while its rider dug in the spurs, urging it on and sawing away at the bit in baffled rage. Almost everybody near him yelled and cheered and booed as the policeman fought to hold the horse. Slesser thought that now they would stop, to fight again, and make a stand to the end; but the police on foot and horses came at a rush, batons and truncheons rising and falling, driving the people back with blow after blow until the street was cleared.

Gasping for breath, Slesser stopped with the rest, took off his cap and wiped the sweat from his steaming brow. He was angry now, like the people in the crowd around him. He hated to have had to run away; it was undignified and made him feel like a mouse instead of a man. Men shouldn't have to run like that, like mice from a cat. He wouldn't run again, he vowed heatedly. No bloody fear he wouldn't! He'd stay and fight and to hell with the bloody cops! He shook his fist defiantly in the direction of the mounted cordon, longing to get at them.

A man at his side shouted, "Cossacks! Cossacks! Down with the dirty Cossacks!" Emboldened by the man, Slesser shouted as well and swore like a drunken trooper. Let them start again if they dare! Just let them start! They'd feel the weight of his fist — wallop! — right in their fat red clocks! *He* hadn't caused the rotten trouble. He was neither a Red nor a Black. *He* hadn't charged at the van and tried to bash up the fascists, but they'd tried to get him for it just the same as if he had. And that showed what they were, if anybody needed any telling. Just let them start!

Gradually his temper cooled, and with it his limbs became steadier, though his shoulder still ached where the policeman's blow had struck him on the edge of the bone. He was proud of the blow and stared about him with slightly arrogant eyes. Not everyone had stopped a copper's baton! But wait... away on his right he saw the woman with the bleeding head. She was quiet now, and very pale, and a man was tying a handkerchief over the wound and knotting it under her chin. And not very far from her there was a youth with a bloodstained face: he was laughing to a girl at his side. Strange, Slesser thought. They didn't seem to bother about their wounds, though they'd suffered far worse than himself. But maybe they were Reds and used to trouble with the police? Of course they were! Reds were always fighting, as nearly all the newspapers told you, and if they fought for the love of the thing, or for politics, they only deserved what they got. And by the way they were shouting, loud and embittered, they were longing to fight again. Blockheads! Perhaps it would be wiser if he tried to get to the back, in case there came another charge. After all, it was no use getting mixed up in somebody else's quarrel. Let them fight it out among themselves.

Slesser pushed his way to the back and climbed on a jutting piece of wall at the foot of a building. From here he could see right over the heads of the crowd to the black-clothed procession beyond the cordons. Now he guessed where he was. This must be Royal Mint Street, for that procession up there was surely that of the fascists. Nearly all wore black, and some of them, far down the line, were women and girls.

There were hundreds of cops on guard, nearly two to every fascist, as if the fascists were precious stones and the crowd all thieves. He chuckled to himself at the thought and shifted his gaze to the crowd. They were getting worked up again, shouting and hooting and whistling and waving their raised clenched fists at the cops. They looked funny from the back — flushed red faces when they turned; bald heads, covered heads, slim or brawny shoulders; and their red and white fists thrust up in salute. And what a motley of colours! Blonde hair, dark hair, no hair at all; red hats, black hats, grey hats, and brown. And then the suits and dresses, all manner of suits and all manner of dresses, but a lot of them with red — a hell of a lot of them with red. And the sun on the angry faces staring ahead... Reds all right. You couldn't make any mistake about that. They were longing to get at the fascists away down the road behind the police.

How they were roaring! Again and again, 'They Shall Not Pass! They Shall Not Pass!' — loud, fierce, challenging. And sometimes 'Down with Fascism' or that communist *Internationale.* You'd think they were going into battle, the sun shining, weapons in hand and red flags flying and all. Serious they looked, and grim, ready to resist another charge, when they weren't shouting and waving their fists — which wasn't very often. Surely they weren't all communists! There couldn't be so many as that or there'd soon be a bloody revolution, like the papers told you about. Then there must be Labour as well, and some of those Co-op people who were always on about dividends. But even so, a lot of them couldn't be either — then what the devil were they? People like himself, just there to watch? But there was hardly a soul hereabouts that wasn't shouting or giving that communist salute, so they must all be plain anti-fascist. That was it — anti-fascist. But whatever they were, they made you feel like one of themselves, which was comforting. And most, he noted, were poor working men like himself. Some still had on their working clothes, stained and muddy, as if they had come straight from work to add their voice to the opposition. There were Jews too, as well as the Gentiles, and even an angry little parson, yelling as loud as the rest and raising his small white fist as if he thirsted for somebody's blood...

Something was happening up in the front. The police were bunching together round a smart-looking cop on a horse. Slesser strained as high as he could, clinging for support to the wall. Yes, the cop on the horse was giving instructions and pointing his gloves at the crowd. Were they going to charge again? he wondered. It looked as if they were, and the crowd seemed to know that too, for the slogans and jeers and cat calls had doubled in intensity, splitting the ears. But nobody tried to get away, though they knew well enough what a police charge meant. They seemed determined to resist to the last and to give not an inch without a struggle.

Slesser felt his own blood quicken in his veins and his limbs begin to tremble with excitement. He strained higher on the jutting piece of wall, watching the police intently. He saw them leave the cop on the horse, spread out in a long blue line and join their fellows in the cordon. Now they were six or seven deep and pushing at the crowd for all they were worth... His heart gave a sudden leap as the short dark truncheons came out and descended in an endless, murderous rain. He saw the people fight back, their bare fists opposed to the whirling batons; and some of them fell and others dashed madly to escape. A few stayed and fought to the last, to be battered or arrested or both. He heard the scream-pierced din rise louder and louder as the mounted policemen came at a gallop and charged at the thick of the throng. He saw the people in the front go down, and vanish from view; and reappear as the crowd retreated, leaving the victims exposed in the road in queerly unhuman shapes. He was far too excited to move, and clung to the wall, staring with distorted eyes as the people swarmed past him in headlong flight, seeking escape from the batons. "Come on, you fool!" yelled a man as he rushed by. Slesser laughed a reply. He felt perfectly safe where he was and had no intention of leaving. The cops were getting closer, driving the people along at ever increasing speed. Now they were only fifty yards away, and laying about them like madmen. He could see their red, sweating faces twitching and jumping as they landed their heavy blows. They must like it, he thought. The crowd was thinning into scrambling, scattered groups. He saw a girl in a flaming red blouse leave one of the groups and dart towards a nearby doorway. She ran right in the path of a galloping horse, glanced up, and froze in her tracks. His heart missed a beat with apprehension. What the devil did she think she was doing? She'd be ridden down! She'd be killed! She must be mad! He hardly paused a moment to think. He leapt from the wall, ran at the girl, dragged her from the path of the charging horse and rushed her along to the door. The horse continued at its reckless pace as if they didn't exist.

"Holy smoke! That was a close one!" Slesser gasped, and turned to look at the girl.

"Yes, thanks," she said breathlessly. "It was... Phew! I don't know what came over me. I was petrified. But we'd better not stay here," she added hurriedly.

"They wouldn't touch us here —" Slesser began.

"Wouldn't they! That's just where they'd like to get us! In a doorway! Come on! Let's make a dash for it. Now. Quick!"

She ran out before he could answer, and he followed reluctantly, thinking it foolish and simply asking for a whack on the head. What's more, she began to run the wrong way! "Hey!" he started to shout, when she cut him short, "Down here!" and darted down a passage which led between two tall buildings. Now what? he wondered. This was madness! They might be arrested for trespassing. He quickened his pace and puffed along at her side, intending to protest.

"There's a wall at the bottom," she panted before he could speak. "We'll have to get over it. Then we'll be safe."

They came to a six foot wall. Forgetting his fear, he said, "Let me help you over," and bent, and seized her round the legs and heaved. He caught a glimpse of a gartered thigh before she dropped to the other side. Blue knickers, he noted; and he scrambled over and joined her, feeling as if he would burst after so much exertion.

"It's not far now," she informed him breathlessly, and began to run on again, along another dark passage which he guessed ran in line with the road, for he could hear the muffled roar of the crowd coming over the buildings.

"Is there any need to run?" Slesser gasped in a minute, catching up to her. "My side —"

Instantly solicitous, she slowed her pace to a walk. "What's the matter, Comrade? Stitch?"

"Ah!" said Slesser between his teeth "I'm not so young as I was."

"Keep walking and it will pass off quicker," she said. "We haven't far to go. This passage leads into a street adjoining the one we left, and we'll be able to get back in the crowd. I know, because I used to work round here at one time. Isn't it awful? The march hasn't started yet and there's all this trouble already. I shall have to try to find Dick — my companion. Heaven knows where he is now. The last time I saw him he was fighting those cops... How's that side of yours, Comrade?"

"It's nearly all right," Slesser answered, rubbing his side. "Nasty thing this stitch. Gives you gyp for a minute."

"Yes, I know... Here's the street now," she added as they turned a corner and came suddenly into a street that was packed to the walls with people.

2

At the crossroads further north, where five roads met, the counter-demonstration that had gathered since shortly after noon had reached such vast proportions that the police were very nearly powerless. They charged the throng repeatedly in attempts to clear the roads for the almost stationary traffic that stretched for miles from east to west; there was fighting, and there were scores of injured and arrested, but still the people stood their ground. And ever and again rang out the threat, 'They

Shall Not Pass!' from the thousands on thousands of people packed in the sound torn streets.

Bert Forster and Elsie Lane were pressed against a hoarding that enclosed some excavations close to where the five roads met. From there it was difficult to see what was happening, but they knew that in front there was fighting and occasionally they saw the batons whirl down through the air. After these passionate outbursts they would see the white tops of ambulances and the black tops of police vans crawl through the crush to pick up their respective cargoes, and then disappear again in the distance.

Bert was thinking that this was a damned queer way to spend a Sunday afternoon. Still, today had been queer in more than one respect. Here was this Elsie, almost a stranger to him, hanging on to his arm, her cheeks flushed and her eyes excited as she strained on her toes to get a better view. Once she had even raised her small clenched fist and shouted aloud with the others, 'They Shall Not Pass!' as if she knew what the trouble was about. But that she didn't know. He had asked her, and she, confessing with a smile that she didn't, had explained that she loathed all cops and was having revenge on them. And no wonder, he thought. She had had a pretty rough passage. She would have still. Her future would be black as hell, unless she got help. And it wasn't fair — she should have a chance, for she was really a fine sort of girl who had been peculiarly unlucky. And despite her very shabby clothes, she had an air about her that appealed to him. Since the meal in the café she had altered so vastly that it was hard to believe she was the same Elsie Lane who had boarded his bus.

The more he looked at her, the more he felt himself drawn to her, and liking her. And it was good to be with a girl again.

He thought of Lola, whom he had known in America, Lola who had fired his senses and whose defection had left him diffident with women, suspicious of their painted beauty. Lola had been hard and grasping, though he hadn't realised that till he lost his job and she threw him over. He had thought of her so long with bitterness... but now that was fading. He'd been a sap to fall so hard for Lola...

There came a sudden lull in the surrounding storm of sound. Breaking the train of his thoughts he said in Elsie's ear, "You seem to be enjoying yourself, Elsie."

"I am!" she cried honestly, turning and facing him. "This is great! Don't you think so?"

"It's exciting, I admit," Bert replied. "But it would be better if we knew what was happening, wouldn't it? We can't see much from here."

"No, but it's interesting all the same. At least, I think so. But," she added, "if you don't want to stay, let's go."

"Go? Oh, no! If you're all right, so am I. Besides, I've got my eye on this hoarding. When somebody gets off it we'll make a rush and try to get on, then we'll have a better view."

"It doesn't look very safe to me," Elsie said doubtfully, glancing round at the hoarding, which was swaying and creaking alarmingly under the weight of the spectators perched on the top.

"I'll look after you," he said, superior before her fears. "Look! There's somebody getting off now! Push along!"

In a minute, breathless but happy, they were up on the hoarding with their arms round one another's waist.

"It's safer like this," Bert said needlessly.

"And nicer," Elsie whispered with a quick, flashing smile.

Staring over the heads of the crowd, Bert felt uncommonly happy.

3

P.O. Thurgood occupied a space in the cordon that was stretched across the end of Leman Street, down which the fascists were eventually expected to march. He had been there an hour, an hour of incessant and ugly conflict, of sweat and blows and sound. He was wedged between two heavily-built policemen, who toiled and sweated like himself as they sought to withstand the pressure of the constantly increasing crowd. He couldn't get a moment's respite. He had to be continually alert, ready to forestall any rush that the crowd might suddenly make, and the strain was beginning to tire him. When they rushed, they never gave any warning. They rushed suddenly, spontaneously, a solid, united mass that would seem for a time irresistible. He watched for a rush against his will and tried to sense it. He was always ready to forestall it but he always failed. It came without warning, and when it happened, he had to fight it, truncheon in hand, for that was all that he could do. If only they would stop that damnable, horrible, everlasting shouting! But they never did, not for even an instant. They seemed to thrive on it. They were at it now, as fierce and loud as they could, 'They Shall Not Pass! They Shall Not Pass! They Shall Not Pass!' as if they had gone stark mad. It was the same all round — opposite in Commercial Street, on his far right in Whitechapel Road, on his near right in Commercial Road East, and on his left in Whitechapel High Street. And then again at his back, in Leman Street, where they were seldom still for longer than a minute at a time, always surging and pushing in the hope of reaching the space at the centre of the crossroads. That space was their objective. Once they got there in force they could stop the fascists' march by the sheer weight of their numbers. Nothing but bullets would ever be able to remove them.

Thurgood pulled out his handkerchief and rubbed the sweat from his face. With the crowd pushing at his back, the constant struggles and the dry heat of the sun, he felt like a furnace. To make matters worse his tunic was tight at the neck and chafing his skin unbearably. He wished for the hundredth time that he had not reported for duty, had 'swung the lead,' and for the hundredth time remembered that if he hadn't reported he wouldn't have met Helen Stroud. He managed a smile at the thought of her. She was older than himself, without question, but she made up for that with her charm, her smile, and her wonderfully youthful ways. He could picture her now as she had sat in the car when he went in answer to her signal... her surprise... her undoubted pleasure... her mysterious smile, the moving magic of her eyes... and her words, 'Harold, you drank a lot last night,' in her soft and seductive tone... and his own reply, 'I hope I didn't make a fool of myself?'... and her answer, 'not exactly. I shall be quite alone this evening. Perhaps you'd like to come and — shall we say — apologise? Over supper?'

"Share the joke," said a voice, and Thurgood was jerked from his thoughts, back to the world of sound that had momentarily receded. It was the paunchy policeman on his right.

"What joke?" Thurgood asked, not in the least comprehending.

"The one you were laughing at," replied the other. "Was it smutty?"

"Was I laughing?"

"Laughing like hell, but to yourself. What's it all about?"

"I didn't know I was laughing," Thurgood said truthfully. "I was thinking —"

"Thinking! I don't know how you manage it with all this bloody row! I'll be glad when it's over."

"I should say I would, too," said Thurgood, grinning all over his face.

And suddenly the crowd behind him rushed. They took the cordon by surprise. They swept through, fighting, heading for the centre of the crossroads. The grin vanished from Thurgood's face. He tried pushing the people back, failed, and whipped out his truncheon. He swung it to the right and the left, striking a head here and a shoulder there with deadly mechanical precision. But they wouldn't be stopped. They retaliated and rushed on, on past the shattered cordon, on towards the centre of the crossroads. Somebody leapt on his back and clung like a monkey to a pole, trying to gouge at his eyes. He reached upwards with his free left hand and tugged at the person's hair. There came a high, thin, feminine squeal and the monkey-like grip relaxed. What devils these women were! They'd tear you in a thousand pieces!

"You're under arrest!" he shouted, turning and grabbing at a feminine arm. But she fought him like a raging demon. She kicked and screamed and struggled as he tried to drag her along. She cursed and howled and scratched at his face with her razor-sharp finger nails. She bent her disordered head and sank her teeth in his wrist. She was absolutely uncontrollable.

"You're under arrest!" he shouted again, twisting at her arm. But she wouldn't desist for an instant. She fought him harder than ever, with fury flaming in her eyes. Very well, he thought, and lifted his truncheon to stop her. He felt a devilish kick in the groin, groaned, went suddenly weak as the pain spread up in his loins, and was forced to let her escape. "You dirty little bitch!" he gasped after her, and fell, unable to stand on his feet.

Two constables picked him up and carried him along to an ambulance. They were putting him inside when he managed to say, in a voice that was almost a whisper, "I'm all right, you chaps. Just a kick, here...."

"Oh," said one. "Nasty place, that. We thought you were dead, buddy. Just lie quiet a minute and it'll soon pass off."

"Thanks," Thurgood muttered weakly, and lay back, listening to the sounds of the struggle outside until the pain had eased. Then, infinitely weary, he went back to his place in the cordon, which had closed again across Leman Street, wondering if ever this crazy day would come to a peaceful end.

Chapter V

"**Y**OU see," Claire said to Slesser, "we have a system. It's Dick's idea, really. If ever we get separated at these political meetings — and we often do when there's trouble! — the arrangement is that I stand on the fringe of the crowd, near the front, until he finds me."

"What if he gets arrested and you don't know about it?" Slesser asked.

"We've allowed for that," replied Claire, hitching her red silk blouse at the waist. "If he doesn't turn up within twenty minutes or so I just carry on without him. Likewise if he can't find me in the same time he concludes that I've been arrested. I do hope he got away from the cops," she added.

Though she spoke in a cheerful tone, Slesser guessed that she was badly worried about the absent Dick. Ever since their frantic dash through the alley she had constantly fidgeted and scanned the crowd with apprehensive questing eyes. They stood in Cable Street, across the narrow end of which was drawn a strong cordon of police. From where they were they could see, directly ahead, a considerable stretch of Royal Mint Street itself, now cleared of all anti-fascists by the police. The fascists themselves were still lined up in the hope of proceeding with the march, although the streets for half a mile around were packed with an angered opposition of at least a quarter of a million people.

"Should we push a bit closer to the front?" Slesser suggested after a time. "Maybe he's up there somewhere, near the cordon."

"Perhaps he is," Claire answered with some apprehension. "Anyway, let's go and see."

Slesser followed her red-bloused figure through the

dense, resisting throng. He hardly believed they would find the man of their search among those thousands on thousands of people. She had said he was a youngish man in a grey suit and a trilby hat, but there were hundreds dressed like that in the crowd. It was like looking for a needle in a haystack, he thought to himself as he followed her, and no mistake.

Claire halted suddenly outside a heavily-shuttered shop and seized his arm. "Look!" she cried excitedly." I wonder if that's him over there?"and pointed across the street, near the cordon. "It looks very much like him. I believe it is him. If he'd only turn! There! He has! Yes, that's Dick all right. He's looking round for me." Strangely excited, she clambered on a window ledge and hung there perilously, waving her hand above her head. Presently Slesser saw a man wave back an acknowledgment. Claire dropped breathlessly beside him.

"He's seen me!" she said triumphantly. "He's on his way over. Thank God he hasn't been arrested! You see," she explained, "he's been pinched before for political offences — several times — and he'd get it really hot if they got him again."

"So that's why you were worried!" Slesser exclaimed.

"So you noticed?" She laughed. "Yes, that's why. Here he is," she added, as Calvin pushed his way forward. "Oh, Dick! I thought you'd been arrested!"

"Not this time," Calvin said grimly. "Nearly though." He glanced at Slesser. "Hullo, Comrade!"

"Hullo!" said Slesser.

"They nearly got me too," Claire said. "Only this Comrade here came to the rescue." She recounted the incident of the galloping horse and their frantic rush through the alley.

Slesser stood apart, hands in pockets, cap pulled over his eyes, pretending to watch the crowd. But he was wondering if he now ought to leave these two to their own resources. He guessed they were something far more than ordinary acquaintances. Courting, he thought, glancing furtively at Calvin. Not a bad chap, either, by the looks of him. You wouldn't think he'd been in prison.

"Thanks for what you did," Calvin said warmly when Claire had finished her account of what had happened to them both.

"Oh, that was nothing!" Slesser protested, but inwardly pleased, feeling a somebody. "I just happened to be there, that's all."

"Well, what about having a smoke while it's quiet round here?" Calvin suggested, and handed round cigarettes. They lit up and pressed back against the shop, and smoked in silence, watching the crowd milling in the narrow street.

"What do you think of it?" Calvin asked presently of Slesser. "Fine turnout, eh?"

Slesser nodded and blew circling smoke in the vibrant air. "I don't know much about it, but I suppose it's like this everywhere else?"

"I'll say it is!" Calvin exclaimed. "Claire and I were up at the crossroads before we came down here — you should have seen the crowd there! But," he added, and his voice rose and his hands gesticulated forcefully, "what else can you expect? It's been coming all along. Everybody with any gumption realised as soon as this march was announced that it was a challenge to the organised working class, and especially to the large Jewish population of the East End. Slogans such as 'Kill the Jews' were chalked all over the place by the fascists in the hopes of starting a pogrom, the dirty rats! But they failed, and I don't wonder. Think of those hundred thousand signatures —"

"What hundred thousand signatures?" Slesser asked.

"Why, didn't you know — a petition was sent to the Home Secretary about banning this march," Claire told him.

"Was it? Well, I never heard of it," Slesser confessed. "You see," he added apologetically, "I don't read the papers much."

"In addition to the petition the mayors of five East End boroughs personally went to the Home Office about it — about having the march banned."

"Besides which," Calvin continued, "the newspapers have been running scare stories about the Reds all this last fortnight. Surely you know something about it?"

"No," Slesser said uncomfortably. "I only read the placards this morning — saw it for the first time —"

"Anyway," Calvin said, grimacing at Claire behind Slesser's back, "since the Home Secretary wouldn't ban the march, this turnout you see here —" he waved at the surging throng — "is the result, the reply, if you like, from the workers. And by the look of it, if they try to hold the march in the face of all this opposition there'll be holy hell in the streets today! Absolute holy hell!"

"The joke is," Claire interposed, smiling, "nearly all the Labour leaders and the Liberals have been urging the workers to stay away. You can see for yourself what they think of that advice! This turnout is the result of propaganda by the Communist Party and the I.L.P. and other small organisations, so you can guess what it would have been like if the Labour leaders had also urged a counter-demonstration, can't you?"

"Well —" Slesser began, intending to state his views on Labour. But the crowd around them let out a roar which seemed to make the very houses tremble. He glanced ahead to where, beyond the cordon, a group of policemen were struggling with a hatless, bald-headed little man who appeared to be resisting arrest.

"The swine!" Claire shouted indignantly. "There's no need for that!"

Immediately following her words came an angry, overwhelming rush on the part of the crowd. Slesser and the others were swept from their position near the shop like straw before the wind, carried along in a maelstrom of humanity. Next to Slesser a burly man with a scarf wrapped tightly round his thick red neck bellowed repeatedly in stentorian tones, "Come on, men! At the sods! Knock their bleedin' 'eads off!" The police cordon was swept aside by the sea of infuriated people, and a deafening concatenation of shrieks, blows, groans, yells, and curses reverberated in the air as fists and truncheons clashed in embittered onslaught. For a moment the crowd were driven back, then, rallied by a score of brawny men, they surged forward again, a desperate, revengeful army. On they swept, on towards Royal Mint Street, charging like demons at the lines of police that came rushing forward to stem the rush at the column of fascists ahead. Then the loud sharp clatter of horses' hoofs rose high above the turmoil, and a score of mounted policemen charged recklessly at the crowd. Long batons swept wickedly to right and left. The crowd stopped, scattered, fled; were rallied, fought for a while, and then were scattered again in headlong retreat. A few men stayed to brave the horses, and were beaten down, inevitably, smashed and bloody in the road.

Slesser pushed his way back to the shop where he had been before the rush began. Except for a slightly scratched knee, caused when he'd fallen in the first wild scramble, he was unhurt. But the shock of the rush, coming as it had without warning, had temporarily shattered his nerves. With fingers that shook from the shock, he lit a cigarette and leaned, trembling, against the shop, looking round for Calvin and Claire.

Presently he saw Claire's flaming red blouse moving slowly through the crowd towards him, her face angry and hot, her sleek fair hair, glinting in the sunshine as she moved, scattered all over her head as if a whirlwind had struck it. She saw him watching from the shop, and waved, but her face never changed its fierce, angry expression.

"The dirty swine!" she cried hotly as she came up to him. "Did you see what they were doing to that man?" She meant the man who had been resisting arrest, the original cause of the rush.

"But he got away," Slesser told her. "The crowd got him free as the rush started. Didn't you see?"

"No! Did he? That's fine!" Claire cried, and her expression changed instantly to eager approval. "That's one thing we achieved, at any rate. For a minute I thought we'd get right through to Royal Mint Street, but those horses — if we had done —"

Slesser saw her lips tighten grimly on words that needed no uttering, and there was a strange, cold glint in her eyes that told of implacable hatred for the distant fascists. 'I wouldn't like her for an enemy,' he thought. 'No fear, I wouldn't!'

At that same moment Calvin returned and pushed between Slesser and Claire without a word. But on his face there was that same grimness and in his eyes that same implacable hatred that Slesser had seen in Claire's.

"You didn't get hurt then," Slesser said.

"No," Calvin replied brusquely, and bared his teeth in a hard, fixed grin.

"Of course," Slesser went on, "it's these police. They're responsible for all the trouble —"

"No! You've got it all wrong!" Calvin interrupted impatiently. "It isn't a case of workers versus police. It may seem so, but it isn't. It's democracy versus fascism, aided by the Government."

Slesser frowned with annoyance at the other's brusque, didactic tone. "How do you mean, democracy versus fascism?" he asked.

"I mean this," Calvin retorted, and his voice rose again to a higher pitch, and his hands gesticulated forcefully, as if he were addressing a meeting. "The Government's no longer democratic — never has been, for that matter — it's as near fascist as it dare be. And you know what fascism is. There's Germany and Italy to show you, besides Abyssinia, and now Spain at this very day. Good God! Just look at what's happened over Spain this last few weeks!" he exclaimed hotly. "You can't call the Government's action democratic, can you? Like hell, you can't! No, the Government leaders are doing their damnedest to help Franco and the fascists, because they

94

don't want a solitary smell of democracy in Spain, nor in any other European country. Nor in Britain, either. They want fascism. They've got to have fascism as the only means of bolstering up capitalism by suppressing the workers, cutting wages and so on. That's why this march hasn't been banned. They try to tell us that they allowed it because it's a question of free speech for everybody, but if it was a workers' march, by Christ, then it would be a different story! They'd soon find an excuse to stop it! I shouldn't be a bit surprised," Calvin added excitedly, "to know that the police had been given instructions to get the fascists through the East End today at all costs, even if it means calling out the troops. Because the Government, this National Government of ours, is behind fascism all the time, all over the world. Never mind wars in China and Spain, and Abyssinia, never mind casualties in the East End streets today, get the fascists through — that's their motto, their slogan, even if they don't chalk it on the streets for us to see."

"That's right," Claire said, nodding encouragement.

"Of course it's right!" Calvin exclaimed, and turned again to Slesser, seizing him by the lapels of his coat. "But we workers have got our slogan as well. We say, 'They Shall Not Pass!' and we mean it. We've gathered our forces, the people you see here" — he waved at the crowd — "the people in every other street in the district, and we're just as determined as the Government. Every damned bit as determined! We're pitting ourselves against the Government and we'll fight them on this issue — somehow. We're not afraid of their police, nor their soldiers — if they dare to call them out — though it's neither police nor soldiers who are our enemies. That's where you make the mistake, Comrade," he said, poking Slesser in the chest. "That's where a hell of a lot of others here today make a mistake. These police and the soldiers are just the hired mercenaries of the ruling class, and I daresay many of them sympathise with us, only they've got to do the dirty work for the bosses — or starve on the dole, like yourself. So just don't think it's a simple case of workers versus police," Calvin ended breathlessly, releasing Slesser's coat. "Because it damned well isn't quite so simple!" This long, informative speech left Slesser filled with resentment. It reminded him forcibly of the trade unionists on the council, who were always giving him lectures, and he bridled.

"Whether it's workers versus police or not," he said testily, "what about all the poor folks who've been injured and arrested? Arguments won't help them any."

"You've got to think of Spain to get that in the right proportion," Calvin replied quickly. "Think of the Spanish people, not just getting injured, but killed in the struggle against fascism! Think of our own men! They're there, besides men from all the other countries in Europe, and they're not grumbling. They might get killed in the fight against fascism, but we won't — yet. Why should we baulk at getting a whack with a baton, or arrested? In comparison to what they're doing, our part is trivial. And besides, we might just as well risk a bash on the head now as have to face the bullets later on because we didn't try to stop this fascism in time."

"Ah! Violence!" Slesser exclaimed angrily. "It never gets anybody anywhere."

"Violence? Hell! Who starts the violence? Us? Not on your life! They start it, not us! They want the violence — so long as we aren't organised to resist it, and then, by God! it's a different matter."

"The trouble," Claire butted in, "is simply this. They know we're not organised as we should be. They know that only one in four of the working class is in a union. They know that we're split in our own ranks, instead of being united against them, so they are trying this on today. If we all stand together, if me, you, and Dick here were all organised with everybody else in a common front against them — why, they just couldn't stand against us, not even with the backing of their police and army."

"That's right," said Calvin. "Take yourself. You're not

in a union, are you?"

"No," Slesser snapped aggressively, feeling they were singling him out for an especial lecture on trade unionism. "What of it?"

Calvin was about to plunge into another long explanation when Claire cried suddenly, "Look, Dick! Look down there! Look what they're doing!"

The two men turned and followed her eagerly pointing finger. Slesser could see nothing except a sea of angry heads which stretched far down the narrow street.

"Well, what is it?" he asked, still in a snappy tone.

"Can't you see?" Calvin yelled. "Right at the back! They're building barricades!"

2

Right in the front of the enormous crowd which blocked Commercial Street at Aldgate, Bert Forster and Elsie Lane stood as part of the serried ranks which stretched, dense and protesting, into the distance as far as the eye could see. Police standing shoulder to shoulder, three lines deep, were engaged in a desperate attempt to keep the crossroads clear for the slow moving lines of traffic, which, having been held almost stationary for nearly an hour, were at last beginning to move. Two long red lines of trams stretched right down Whitechapel Road and Commercial Street, their indicator boards stowed away inside for fear that the crowd would use them. Already, under the pressure of the crowd, the hoardings round the excavations had fallen with the noise of guns in the heat of battle, and the spectators who had remained had been cleared from their positions by the police, for fear of yet a heavier casualty list than the batons had caused. Cameras whirled and clicked as delighted newspapermen, from the security of cars and lorries, feverishly recorded the ever-recurring combats. Pale, anxious faces peered out from the windows of the motor cars which threaded their slow way through the surging, restless throng. A little black dog, parted from its master and bewildered by the uproar, ran in and out among the police who occupied the centre of the crossroads, snapping and snarling like a wolf at bay.

Laughing at the terrified dog, Bert turned to Elsie and said, "I've never seen anything like this in all my life."

"No, neither have I," Elsie retorted. "But I wish this fat copper would move and let me see what's going on. He would have to plonk himself in front of me."

"You'd better not let him hear you," Bert warned her. "They just seem to be waiting for an excuse to start trouble. Look at the way they chased us off that hoarding! Just as if we were dogs!"

"That's right," said Elsie, nodding.

"We've been lucky so far," Bert resumed, "but there's no telling how long it'll last. Maybe we oughtn't to have come right to the front, because if they do start, we'll be right in the thick of it."

"But we can't go back now," Elsie said, glancing at the solid mass behind them."Besides, why should we? We've as much right to the streets as anybody else."

"What I'd like to know," Bert said presently, "is when these fascists are supposed to come." Standing on tiptoe, he peered in the direction of Leman Street, down which the fascists were eventually expected to march. "There's no sign of them yet," he continued, lowering his heels. "And by the looks of it there never will be. They're playing bloody hell over there — excuse my French, Elsie! — I shouldn't be surprised if there isn't another baton charge in a minute. It looks as if the cops are getting ready... yes, they are! They're drawing truncheons! By Christ! The rotten swine! They've rushed right into the crowd and are lashing out right and left! Look at them! Good God! Look at them! It's bloody murder! They're —"

His next words were drowned in a deafening roar of protest which rose from the watchers in an evergrowing volume, shattering the air. For several minutes it was impossible to speak above the uproar, then the noise died to a low growl when it was seen that the fighting in Leman Street had come to an end. And again the ambulances and the police vans crawled through the crush to take away the victims.

"It's nearly as bad as America!" Bert said disgustedly. "And that's saying something if you like."

"Were you really in America?" Elsie asked.

"Me? Yes, I've been all over the States in my time. And I've been in riots, too. They use tear gas over there, and it smarts like hell and makes you cry like a baby, but I don't know as it's any worse than a truncheon. You don't have to go in hospital after it, anyway," he added as the ambulances drove off with the casualties. "I used to think America was bad enough, but it seems as if England's as bad."

"What were you doing in America, Bert?"

"Anything that turned up. All sorts of jobs. But there wasn't much chance — there was ten million unemployed out there. So I came home and got on the London buses about four years ago. Yes, four years ago next month."

"It's supposed to be a good job, isn't it?"

"Well, it's not bad, but when you get all these different shifts it's above a joke. One time you've got to get up at three o'clock to get to the garage in time, another you're on so late that it's two o'clock in the morning when you get home. If it wasn't for the wages I wouldn't stick it another week."

"I wish I could get a job," Elsie sighed, his talk of work reminding her of her own predicament. "But it's hopeless when you've been where I have. Honest, Bert, nobody cares a hang whether you get work or not when you've been in there."

"I just don't see how you've managed this last month," Bert said.

She smiled bitterly. "This week I've been sleeping out on the benches and living on fourpence a day. I even had to get what I could for my handbag."

"Haven't you any relatives or friends?"

"No, none at all — not in London, anyway. I've a few friends at home, but mother and dad have been dead for years now, since I was sixteen. I wouldn't like to go back there, after all that's happened."

"No, I don't suppose you would. My parents are dead too, so we're both in the same boat. But what are you going to do? You can't live on nothing, can you?"

"There's nothing I can do, is there?"

"I don't know... there might be... I've been thinking.... Maybe I could do something, that is, if you — you —" He broke off in confusion. It was a ticklish job helping this girl. He must take care not to offend her. Looking away, he added inconsequentially, "There's some more trouble over there."

"Where?" asked Elsie excitedly, straining on her toes.

"At Leman Street, opposite. See? Cops are starting their old tricks, trying to drive the crowd back to let the fascists through."

"Yes, I see them!" she cried. "The beasts!"

"Stop that!" commanded the fat policeman in front of her, turning his fat red face and scowling heavily. "Let's have no more on it, see?"

"Hey!" Bert protested, "aren't we allowed to talk in this bloody town?"

"You shut up, too," said the policeman, giving him a shove.

The crowd pressed forward ominously. Bert tried to get back, found there was no escape, and stood his ground.

"Look here —" he began, when the policeman pushed him again.

"Let him alone!" roared a man in the crowd, waving his fist at the policeman. "I'll knock your bleedin' 'ead off!"

"Come on!" Elsie screamed, tugging at Bert's arm in a frenzy. "Let's get back!"

"To hell with them!" he shouted recklessly. "Let's stay and have it out!"

"No, no!" she cried. "Come on! That cop'll arrest you!

100

Come on!"

He shook her off, charged at the fat policeman and was knocked flat on his back beneath a struggling mass of legs. He fought his way up, gasping and spluttering in his rage, feeling nothing of the blow that had felled him, and found himself being carried along before a charge of mounted policemen. He ran back, afraid of the pounding horses, until he came, breathless, to the broken down hoarding, where he stayed, trying to recover his wind. Now where was Elsie? he wondered anxiously. Had she been hurt? If she had — by Christ! If she had! He rubbed his smarting shoulder, looked round for her, saw her at last, behind him, looking for him. "Hey!" he shouted. "Hey! Elsie!" She waved back and began to push her way through the crowd.

"You're not badly hurt, are you?" she asked fearfully. "Oh, Bert, if you are! It was all my fault — bringing you here —"

"No, no! I'm not hurt. Just a smack on the shoulder, that's all!" he cried excitedly, clutching his shoulder. "By Christ, but that was a scrap!" he added, his blue eyes flashing with delight. "I didn't think I had it in me!"

"I'm ever so glad, Bert. I was afraid you'd get arrested and then —" He smiled at her fears.

"I'm all right now," he said, looking over the heads of the crowd that had gone forward again to fill the gaps that the charge had originally made. "It seems to be all over. Where's your beret got to?" he asked, suddenly noticing her bare head.

"I lost it — and it's my only hat! Do I look a mess?"

"No, no. You don't look a mess, silly!" He laughed happily, breathlessly, still feeling keyed up after the fight.

"You don't happen to have a comb on you?" she asked. "I know I look a mess, no matter what you say!"

"Here you are then." He fumbled in his pocket and produced a worn old comb. "But you don't need it, really you don't. You look all windswept as you are —"

"Go on with you, Bert!" she said, blushing. She began to

101

comb her dark, wavy hair into shape. "You'll have to tell me if it's all right," she said. "I haven't a mirror. How's that? Is the parting straight?"

"Well, that's funny," Bert exclaimed, staring at her boldly. "You look quite different without a hat. Why, you're darned pretty —!"

"Am I? Well —!" She blushed again and silently returned the comb. It was too bad of him, here in the crowd, to say things like that. She glanced furtively at the people next to her. They seemed indifferent. They were all staring ahead, watching the police at the centre of the crossroads.

Bert's eyes were still on her face and hair, admiring her.

"I wish I had some make up," she said. "I'd feel much better then."

"You don't want any make up. You're better without," he protested. "Besides, I don't like it."

"Don't you? Then I'm glad I haven't any," she said, patting her hair. It was good of him to say that. He was fine, was this Bert. Really fine. If only she had some decent clothes to be out with him in...

"I'm glad you got on my bus this morning," Bert said, slipping his arm within hers. "If you hadn't, I should have been moping about on my own —"

"And me on my own!"

"Yes. When you come to think of it, it's amazing how many people there are in London, yet so many never seem to make friends. Look at me. I've been here nearly four years now — as I told you — and I know only about half a dozen people!"

"I don't know many either," Elsie said, "and it's over five years since I came here. And since I came out I've hardly talked with a soul — except that poor girl last night." Her face grew serious.

"What surprises me," Bert said frankly, forgetting they stood in the centre of a crowd that was milling and shouting itself into a frenzy, "is that you didn't go on the streets."

She shuddered. "My God, Bert! I may be bad but I shouldn't do that! Men pawing you about — ugh! I'd rather die of starvation." Somehow, this answer pleased him. At that instant a deafening shout of triumph broke from the crowd across the way. People, eager to discover the cause, began to press forward against the cordons. The police, who had been having an easy time for the last five minutes, straightened up, on the alert, looking for signs of impending trouble.

"There's something in the wind," Bert said to Elsie, straining on his toes. "Some news or other. Maybe the fascists are coming at last."

Elsie clutched at his arm and tried to raise herself up. "Here," he said, and seized her round the waist and lifted her. "Can you see anything?"

"No," she said, "but there must be *something* happening. The crowd opposite seems to be shouting something —"

In front of them a tall man in a red tie cupped his hands to his mouth, drew a lungful of air, and shouted in tones that all within range could hear, "Comrades! The dockers have built barricades in Cable Street! Three cheers for the dockers! Hip, hip —!"

"Hooray!" roared the crowd.

"Hip, hip —!"

"Hooray!"

"Louder, Comrades. Hip, hip —!"

"Hooray!"

Then, his clenched fist raised in salute, he led the singing, his face shining like a star, "Arise, ye starvelings from your slumbers —"

Chapter VI

STILL smarting with resentment at Calvin's lecture, Slesser stood in Cable Street and moodily watched the building of the barricade. In his present temper the project seemed to him to be immeasurably foolish. He condemned it utterly. He would have no part in it, he told himself. The police would never allow the barricade to remain. There would only be more fighting, more blood, more arrests, and all because some silly fatheads were looking for trouble. One wasn't allowed to build barricades in England and get away with it.

Claire and Calvin, toiling with the rest, should know better than to get mixed up in it. Claire especially, he thought. She wasn't the hooligan kind, but that Calvin, with his fancy talk about Labour and Capital, and fascism and democracy, and standing together and trade unionism, had obviously gone to her head. There she was now, next to Calvin, working away as red-faced and sweaty as a navvy.

And how the hell much more were they going to bring for that barricade? Hadn't they enough already? There was a lorry and a cart, and scaffolding and boards, and oil drums and barrels, and wire and bricks, and boxes and bottles — all piled up in a tangled heap that stretched across the road from one grey wall to the other. Surely they had enough? They must all be mad, mad as hatters, he thought contemptuously, glowering at them from under his cap. It was all right to stand in a crowd and do a bit of shouting, but this sort of thing, building barricades, as if London were in Spain, was just simply asking for trouble.

Claire beckoned across to him to come and give a hand, but he shook his head savagely in reply. He would stay where he was, close by the wall, and watch. It was safer to watch and far more sensible than getting mixed up in this hooliganism. They would have to pay for it soon: the cops at the end of the street were already preparing to charge, and they had the horses ready as well. He would wait until they were closer and then shift off down the street, out of the danger, he decided.

But when the police at last came charging down Cable Street, Slesser's legs refused to carry him away. Instead, he dashed forward involuntarily, his fists clenched and his jaw set in defiance — right to the foot of the barricade, joining with the others who were already there to resist the oncoming police. He was there when the police rushed up, truncheons drawn, their round metal buttons glinting in the sun, their bodies arched forward as they ran, as if bent by the force of a storm. And there he stayed, hurling the stones and the bottles which darkened the sound torn air, and then, seizing a plank in frenzied hands, he lashed out again and again until the police ran back faster than ever they had come, sorely battered by that volley of stones and bewildered momentarily by that grim and ferocious resistance. They then reformed, while the crowd behind the barricade yelled their defiance, and came cautiously on again, dodging the stones that were flung, and reached the barricade, and began to fight their way through it and over it, their truncheons scoring heavily on the dense mass of heads below. There was no quarter, for none asked for it and none gave it.

Frantic exchange of blows thudded and cracked on heated flesh amidst the yells and groans and screams that rose high above the common din. And then the police were suddenly over, wave after wave of them, and steadily advancing, and attacking the crowd, as they broke and fled to escape the revengeful truncheons. The people rallied further down and faced the police again, weaponless now, their bare fists opposed to the whirling truncheons, until it was the police that retreated, driven desperately back to the barricade.

Immersed though he was in the battle, Slesser saw

things there that he would never forget. A policeman catching a woman in a vicious grip, hitting her head against a wall, and kicking her down in the road... and then the policeman pounded senseless by a hail of retaliatory blows from a trio of brawny dockers. And he himself, seized in powerful arms, kicking at blue-clad shins and sinking his teeth in the sweaty flesh of a hand that groped for his throat. And there a man with a blood-spattered nose, flattened on his face by a baton's swing. There another with both eyes closed by a punch, staggering along in a sightless attempt to escape. There a girl, screaming in a high-pitched voice, her dress torn off at the shoulder, revealing a dull red welt on her pink-white skin. Flashes, momentary visions, each seen for a fleeting second, but imprinted on his mind ineradicably as he fought in that bitter battle.

The fighting was over at last, and the narrow street, littered with glass, wood, stones, wire, bottles, bricks, and pieces of planks, was wet in places with darkening blood. Patches of brown dry earth gaped nakedly where the paving stones had lain before being used to grimmer purposes. The police had captured the barricade, but it would stay there, serving its purpose, until long after dusk had fallen. The fascists could not march that way, no matter what number of police toiled to clear the road; and Slesser, Calvin, and Claire, together again in the crowd, watched their laborious efforts with amused contempt.

"I bet we've shown them we mean business, eh?" Calvin remarked with satisfaction. "There'll be no march down Cable Street this fine day."

"No," Slesser agreed, thinking of the part he had played and proud now that he had not run away when the police first charged. "That's a fact they won't!"

"We've been quiet far too long," Calvin went on. "It's about time we made a stand. We've been on the retreat since the war, letting the ruling classes drive us to the gutters without a protest. But now we're on the defensive — at last. You'll soon see, Comrade! Cable Street's the starting point. We've put up that barricade together, we've fought over it together, and there'll be no more retreats after this, not if we stand united. After all, what's the use of going on in the old way? We've never gained anything by it — not a thing! We've had to fight for everything we've got. And we've got to fight more than we have done. Fascism won't just fade away like a bad dream. It's got to be smashed!" He uttered his pronouncements in that didactic tone which had previously riled Slesser, but which now left him unmoved.

"Yes," Claire said, "and when we smash that we smash capitalism, the Government and the ruling classes all in one blow — as they did in Russia in nineteen-seventeen. They're all in the same boat, sailing for the same end. That's why the Government's been so keen to get the fascists through the East End streets today. But this is one street they won't get through," she added, turning again to watch the policemen in the distance struggling to remove the barricade.

"No, by God!" Slesser exclaimed, laughing his sudden barking laugh and rubbing his hands together in glee. He felt a giant, a somebody, and everybody here in this vast milling crowd was his friend. The resentment he had felt towards Calvin was gone. He cocked his cap back jauntily on his greying hair and let his eyes rove over the crowd in happy contemplation. They looked astonishingly cheerful now, knowing they had done a job of work that would hamper the hated fascists and their police protectors, and were laughing and chattering together in little groups, sometimes bursting into chorus, 'They Shall Not Pass!' or singing the *Internationale*.

Calvin handed round cigarettes, and they smoked for a while in silence. Then Claire, shaking grey ash from her blouse, suggested they should move.

"There doesn't seem to be much to do here now."

"No," Calvin agreed. He turned to Slesser. "What do you think, Comrade?"

"Well, since you ask me," Slesser replied, "I'd say let's go somewhere else."

"Up to the crossroads," Claire suggested. "We can dodge through the back streets and along Commercial Road East, and then get in the crowd at Gardiner's Corner."

"There may be some more fighting," Slesser added, grinning with relish at the thought.

Calvin looked at him swiftly. "Do you like fighting?" he asked. "Physical combat, I mean?"

"Well, not exactly," Slesser began.

"Neither do I. I hate it. But at this stage of development it's sometimes necessary —"

And as they moved out of the crowd Calvin expounded his views on force, both moral and physical; and Slesser listened intently, while the discourse changed slowly back to fascism as an evil that had to be eradicated or democracy would perish from the face of the earth. And the more he spoke the more Calvin's hands waved, the more his fists thumped down on imaginary tables with impassioned emphasis.

"The other day," Slesser said when he had finished, "I heard a chap speaking on politics at the bottom of our street. He said there wasn't much danger of fascism coming in England."

"Oh! isn't there just!" Calvin ejaculated. "It's growing up all around us, like jungle weed. That talk about England being different is just tripe! Sheer tripe! England's no different from Germany or Italy or Spain or France. Saying it is different is just an excuse for staying idle and doing nothing but chant the old mumbo jumbo of wait and see. And even if fascism weren't a menace in England itself, isn't it menacing us from outside? In Germany and Italy and Austria — and now Spain? That's fascism for you! Franco kills off every man that holds a trade union card, shoots them down in batches with machine guns... ties the cards on their legs... terror..." His voice choked off with emotion. Then he thumped his hand a blow that cracked like a wielded whip. "That's fascism for you."

"This chap," Slesser said as they walked on, "this chap at the meeting said Spain was different to England in nearly all respects, a backward country of peasants or something. Mind you," he added hastily, seeing Calvin's lips curl, "I'm only saying what *he* said."

"Different!" Calvin snorted. "He ought to read Lenin and Stalin —"

"*And* Palme Dutt's *Fascism and Social Revolution*" Claire added. "Plus the *Daily Worker.*"

"The *Daily Worker?*" Slesser repeated. "Isn't that a communist paper?"

"That's right," said Claire. "Why, haven't you heard of it before?"

"Ah, I've heard of it," Slesser answered. "Chap I once worked with used to read it. Say, are you two communists?" he asked in a wondering tone as a sudden thought struck him.

"We try to be," they answered together.

"Ah!" said Slesser. That explained things. But just fancy *her* being a communist!

They turned a corner into Commercial Road East, and their pace quickened. Half a mile of empty trams and slow moving lines of assorted traffic stretched up to the distant crossroads. The people up there were packed solidly, as at a football match, but even more noisy. Their cry came down the road, 'They Shall Not Pass! They Shall Not Pass! They Shall Not Pass!'

2

"If you arsk me," an old woman wearing a black hat and black coat was saying to Bert, "if you arsk me, there'll be no fascist march through 'ere this day, no, that there won't."

"How do you mean?" Bert asked.

"Look fer yersel'," said the old woman, waving a fat arm at the crowd. "D'yer think they'll get through that lot? Not if I knows anythin' about t'workin' class! They're roused, that's what they are. Roused." She nodded vigorously. "They don't like these 'ere fascists wi' their dirty tricks an' ooliganism an' whatnot. 'Tain't yuman, it ain't.

109

I bin on this 'ere earth nigh on sixty year, I 'ave, an' I ain't seen nothin' like this afore. I ain't that."

"Neither have I," Bert agreed, glancing at Elsie, who winked a reply and smiled.

"But just wait till there's t'revolution," the old woman resumed. "Then there'll be sights, there won't 'arf!"

"You don't think there'll be a revolution in our time, do you?" Bert asked conversationally.

"Well, that's a differcult one, that is. It depends. It depends 'ow long it'll be afore t'people says, 'ook 'ere, you wi' all the money, that's ours, that is. We earned it for yer, so it's ours. Give it back ter us.' Then there'll be t'revolution, 'cos they won't give it back, see? They'll fight fer it, fight like 'ell they will. I knows 'em."

"A man on my bus was telling me something like that about Spain," Bert said. "He said the government there was going to take the money from the rich and give it to the poor. But the rich started fighting before it could happen."

"That just proves what I said!" the old woman exclaimed. "I know what I'm talkin' about, I do. Yers, an' what I'm goin' ter tell yer's true as well. I'm goin' ter tell yer these 'ere fascists ain't goin' ter march through 'ere today. Deny that, if yer can!" she challenged.

"Well, we don't know yet, do we?" Bert said. "We can't tell yet. They might bring more police out and do it that way."

"They ain't got no more bloody police ter bring out, see? They're all out now. Besides, you just feel in my pocket. Feel there." Bert put his hand near her thigh, where something hard bulged beneath her coat. "That's a stone, that is," she said in a grim whisper, "an' I'm goin' ter use it, see? I said ter my Milly, I said, 'Milly, there's only one way ter stop these 'ere fascists an' that's ter throw things at 'em. Hard things.' An' my Milly says, 'Don't yer get yersel' arrested, Ma,' an' I says, ' 'Ell, whassitmarrer s'long's these 'ere fascists get stopped.' I says. An' she says — she's a cute 'un, is my Milly — she says, 'Ma, yer a hero.' "'Ero!' I says, taken aback, like. 'Don't yer talk daft, our Milly. You go out an' get me a stone.'"

"I wouldn't risk it," Bert said anxiously. "You might get pinched."

"Nor me," said Elsie fearfully. "That's just asking for it."

The old woman snorted, and said, poking Bert with a wrinkled finger, "Mind yer, I ain't bein' personal, like, but it strikes me some folks're too scared ter stick up fer 'emselves. That's what it is. Take me, I'm an' old woman, I am, nigh on sixty year an' a widder inter the bargain, but I believe yer've got ter stick up fer yersel' if yer wants any thin' really bad. An' what I want is ter stop these 'ere fascists afore it's too late, an' 'ave a revolution like they Russians did." She began to cough violently, her face and neck turning crimson with the effort.

"Have a cough lozenge," Bert offered. "I've got some in my pocket somewhere. Always carry them about in case I get a cough when I'm working. Here you are," he said, producing the lozenges. "Take one. A stitch in time saves nine, you know."

"Thanks, I will," said the old woman. "Ta. My chest's not what it was, it ain't. Too much scrubbing, that's what it is."

"You have one as well," Bert said to Elsie. She took one to please him. He had one himself and stuffed the packet away, and they stood sucking lozenges, gazing at the swaying heads that blocked the crossroads. Around them mouths opened redly to shout out the slogan; fists rose clenched and quivering in the air; the traffic moved slowly along; gesticulating, red-faced, tired policemen shouting the drivers to hurry and what the hell —? And the drivers sat taut, tense, and fearful, fearful of hitting a vehicle in front and being hit by a vehicle behind as they crawled and jerked and stopped and crawled and jerked and stopped again.

"Are you getting tired of standing?" Bert asked Elsie.

"No, I'm not tired," Elsie said in a bubbly voice, sucking

at the lozenge. "But I wish there was a lav. handy," she whispered.

"So do I," said Bert. "But I don't want to leave just yet. Something might happen soon. Let's wait another ten minutes, then if they haven't come we'll hunt round for one."

"All right, Bert. But you'll have to lend me a penny."

"Here you are."

"No, no! Don't give it me now! It looks bad! Later on!"

"Righto!" Bert let the coin slide down in his pocket and slipped his arm round her shoulders, squeezing her gently against him. She looked up, gave a slow smile, and looked away again.

"Look over there!" said the old woman suddenly. "Look over there! I arsk yer, is it yuman?"

Two policemen were marching a struggling girl towards a Black Maria which stood in the cleared space. She was screaming, but happy because she was being arrested because she was a socialist, and perhaps because a cameraman had stopped to photograph her as the police dragged her along.

"Is it yuman?" the old woman repeated.

"No, it's a disgrace!" Bert said indignantly, blue eyes flashing.

"I'm goin' ter get ter the front, I am, so's I can use this." The old woman tapped her bulging pocket. "Come on, let's get ter the front an' show 'em who's who."

"We've been up there already, and nearly got ourselves arrested," Bert objected.

"Let's go, Bert," said Elsie, following the old woman through the crush. "We might see more than we can here."

They squeezed through the tardily-yielding ranks until they reached the second row, within arm's length of the cordon, and only a few feet from the slow-moving stream of traffic. Behind them and opposite the slogan rose unceasingly, 'They Shall Not Pass! They Shall Not Pass! They Shall Not Pass!' and sometimes 'Down With

Fascism!' The blazing sun shone on the windows of the buildings and on the policemen's buttons and the polished cars. Like writhing silver snakes the tramlines glinted in the middle of the road, where the police officials moved about, protected by horses. When one of them happened to slip the crowd began, 'Yah, Cossacks! Yah, Cossacks! Yah, Cossacks! Ride 'im, cowboy. Who-a there! Yah, Cossacks! Mind you don't slip, Sergee-aa-ant!'

"Isn't it about time they came?" Bert asked the old woman presently. "They're an hour late as it is.

"If they *are* coming, then they won't be long now, an' when they *do* come —" The old woman patted her pocket and winked. "They won't get through 'ere, not if I knows anythin'," she added grimly. "Say! What's goin' on over there, by Leman Street?"

"They're all shouting and pushing about," Bert said, standing on his, toes. "Maybe, it's the fascists coming." He placed his hands on Elsie's shoulders and hoisted himself higher, staring over her head. "No, I don't think they are. It's somebody been arrested... three men... they're fighting like hell... crowd's rushing forward... police can't stop 'em... Why! The bloody swine! Those bloody Cossacks 've rushed right into them lashing out right and left... people all over the place. My God! I've never seen anything like this before, never," he said, getting down.

"I wish they'd start somethin' round 'ere, I do. I'd show 'em," said the old woman grimly. "I'd Cossack 'em."

"It's all over now," Bert said. "They've arrested about six — no, seven. They're pushing them in the van now. One chap's got his head cracked open. Here's an ambulance coming... It's just like a war, just like a bloody war," he ended.

The commotion subsided. The two long lines of cars and buses and lorries and cycles got on the move again, creeping forward a few inches, stopping, creeping forward, stopping... *Down with fascism. They shall not pass. The people's flag is deepest red. Arise, ye starvelings from your slumbers. They shall not pass —* the words were thrown

113

up tumultuously from the thousands of throats of those who waited in the streets, waited for the fascists beneath the sun, certain of victory, ready to resist to achieve it when the time came. And the police shouted all round that bulging cordon, 'Get back there! Hi, you! Get back there!' and nobody took any notice.

The old woman and Elsie watched the traffic as it passed some six feet away. Buses filled with people who stared from the windows, some of them waving their raised clenched fists. Boys on bicycles. Baby cars with fat round faces peering from the windows. Private cars, taxis, a fruit barrow, a man with ice-cream in a basket. Then a polished black limousine with an angry-faced lady sitting bolt upright on the cushions, staring at the crowd.

"Look!" cried Elsie. "Look!" Bert and the old woman looked. "See that car! That black one! See that woman in it!" cried Elsie.

"Yes, I see," said Bert and the old woman together.

"That's Lady Stroud — the one I used to work for. Sacked me without a moment's notice, she did!"

"What, 'er?" said the old woman scornfully. "She looks like she'd sack 'er own mother. Hard-faced bitch!"

Excitement was working in Elsie. The sight of Lady Stroud, luxurious, sheltered, aroused her hatred. She saw her as the author of all her troubles, the woman who had turned on her ruthlessly in misfortune. She gave a sobbing cry, and then she screamed hysterically, "it's all her fault — the bitch! She turned me out on the streets — sent me to prison —"

"Sent yer ter quod, did she?" said the old woman in a curious, trembling tone. "The thin-gutted, staring cow!"

"Yes, she did," Elsie screamed, losing all self control. "She threw me out — into the gutter. She did! The bitch!"

"Then I'll send 'er ter bleedin' 'orspital," said the old woman, and flung the stone.

Chapter VII

A POLICEMAN in the cordon saw the stone leave the old woman's hand and crash into the car. He and another rushed and seized the woman by the arms. The police in the area, anticipating a rescue, lashed out. Fists rose and fell where a minute before there had been a quiet throng. A girl shrieked as a blow descended on her head; a man cursed horribly in pain; roar followed angry roar.

The old woman battered at the policemen's faces as they dragged her away. One struck her. She kicked him on the shin, yelling with pain in a frightened voice, "Lemme go! Yer dirty cowards! Lemme go!"

Bert and Elsie were driven right back when the cordon got to work. They helplessly watched the old woman being dragged away to the van.

"The dirty swine!" Bert cried.

"I wish it had killed her," Elsie said, as if in a trance.

"I didn't think she'd throw that stone, or I'd have stopped her. It was a good shot though..."

"I wish I hadn't told her what I did, then it wouldn't have happened. Why did she throw it, Bert?"

"Worked up. Had to throw it somewhere. She's got some guts. More than I have. I wouldn't have done it, worked up or not. That's wilful assault. I hope they don't send her to prison."

"They're sure to," Elsie said. "Sure to. Like they sent me. They ought to send that bitch in the car instead!"

2

"They needn't treat her like that," Calvin said. "She isn't struggling now."

"They're just getting their revenge," Claire said. "If it had been a fascist stoning a little Jewish shop they wouldn't have caught anybody."

Lady Stroud had got out of the car and was addressing a policeman in plain clothes. She was obviously very angry. "I'm sorry this has happened, your ladyship," the policeman said. "Very sorry indeed."

"Sorry! You ought to be ashamed of yourself. It's a positive disgrace! A positive disgrace! What do you think we pay taxes for? That stone could have injured me for life! Besides, it will cost four pounds at least to replace the glass in the car."

"You'll be preferring a charge, your ladyship?"

"Certainly I shall prefer a charge. I shall also complain to the Home Office. One ought to be safe in the streets of London."

"We're doing our best, your ladyship."

"Then it seems you are not very capable. If the police are insufficient we shall have to rely on the troops for protection, as they do in India." Lady Stroud put one quivering foot on the running board. "I have to keep a very important engagement," she snapped. "I'm late as it is. How much longer shall I be detained by this — this howling mob!"

"If you step inside and tell the chauffeur to pull out we'll get you through right away, your ladyship. I'm really very sorry about this."

"Very well."

She got inside and slammed the door. She barked at the chauffeur. The plain clothes policeman beckoned a group of constables in reserve, and together they drove back the crowd. Followed by envious glances, the car pulled out of the line, glided forward, and vanished in the crowd to the west. The people booed and laughed when they saw the shattered glass and the hard-faced, angry lady. And the chauffeur thought, 'Pity it didn't brain you, you silly old cow!'

"That's the best of having a big car," Claire said when

the car had gone. "Now, if it had been a baby car..."

"Wonder why she threw the stone, anyway?" Slesser asked, tugging at his cap to shade the slanting sun from his eyes.

"I suppose the old woman just couldn't help it," Calvin said. "She just felt she couldn't let that woman pass in that car without having a smack at her. I don't suppose for a minute that she had the stone purposely to throw at the car. Do you, Claire?"

"It's not likely," said Claire. "More likely she had it for the fascists."

"But when are they going to come?" Slesser asked, peering over to Leman Street. "Surely they ought to be here by now."

"If they ever get as far as this," Calvin said, glancing at the crowd, "there's one thing certain. They'll never get any farther."

"But there's a hell of a lot of police, mounted as well," Slesser pointed out dubiously.

"Yes, but look at the streets! Look opposite at Commercial Street! Look at Leman Street! Look at Commercial Road! There's only High Street and Whitechapel Road left, and they're both blocked with traffic, so where the hell can they march?" asked Calvin triumphantly.

"Maybe," said Claire, laughing, "maybe they'll march them into the excavations opposite and take them underground to wherever they want to be!"

"That's about all they bloody well could do!" They all laughed heartily together, and then all fell silent, watching the crowds in the streets around them.

The people seemed to be listening, listening for the fascists, even when they were shouting, and wondering when they, would come. Faces were strained, eyes staring unnaturally, and limbs rigid as they watched. Just like the calm before a storm, Slesser thought, and groped for a word to describe them. Ominous. Yes, that's what they were. Ominous. Funny word, an ugly word with an ugly meaning, but that's what they were. Ominous. They weren't shouting so much now, but this impassive staring, this peculiar attitude of listening, never lasted very long. Something would be sure to happen, and then they would start again — fighting, groaning, shrieking, yelling, taunting, cursing, and shouting that slogan, 'They Shall Not Pass! They Shall Not Pass! They Shall **Not** Pass!' — loud, long, defiantly. It was grand to be there, among those thousands, to be one of them, standing together against those fascists. 'I'm glad I came,' he thought, his lips framing the words. 'It's been an eye opener. Must have been for others, too. I can't be the only one who didn't know anything about it. Wish I knew as much as Calvin and Claire. Funny they're communists. You wouldn't think they were to look at them. Well, I mean, you wouldn't think *she* was. He stole a glance at her. Ordinary? Well, she *was* ordinary, just like any other girl. Not a bad looker either, with that yellowish hair of hers and that sensible face. Bit too fat in the breasts though...' He looked away from Claire, over the heads of the crowd towards Leman Street. No sign of the fascists. Not a glimpse. He hoped to God they would come. It was almost unbearable to think that they would not come now. All these people, all these thousands on thousands of people, had been here for hours, waiting, each to do his share when the time came. And if they didn't come...

The heavy intolerable silence was broken by the sudden back-firing of a car which startled a policeman's horse. The animal reared, pranced on its hind legs, slipped, and crashed on its side in the road. The policeman went sprawling on his belly, but still clinging to the reins, and the crowd yelled. 'Hurrah! Ha! Ha! Ha! Serves yer right! Cossack! Ha-ha! Cossack! Cossack! Ride 'im, cowboy! Who-a there! Ride 'em! Yah! Cossack!' And the fighting started again, followed by baton charges, and then the ambulance and the police van came to take the casualties away.

"I wish I knew what was happening at the other end," Calvin said when the din had died to a murmuring roar.

"I suppose it's like this," said Claire.

"It's worse, mate. A bleedin' sight worse," announced a man just beside them. "I've just come up here from Mansell Street and it's hell down there. It's the same in Leman Street — the bottom end — and the Minories and all the other streets. Fighting like hell, they are! Them fascists won't march *this* day, I'll warrant. Too much opposition and not enough bloody cops!" His information delivered, he turned away and lent his rough deep voice to that of the crowd.

"I'd hate to think we'd stood here all this time for nothing," Slesser said, stamping his aching feet.

Claire laughed. "You're a bloodthirsty monster!" she cried. "I'm surprised at you! Why, earlier on you didn't seem very interested, and now —!"

"If they don't march at all then our victory's complete," Calvin explained.

"Ah!! I see what you mean," Slesser answered. "Still —" He rubbed his fists together and grimaced.

"What's happening over there?" Calvin cried suddenly, pointing to the corner of High Street and Leman Street, where the crowd were particularly noisy. "Now what are those cops up to? I wonder —? Are they making a last attempt to get us out, or what?"

About a hundred policemen, brought from reserve, made towards the crowd on the corner. Other groups supplemented the surrounding cordons, and they began persuasively, saying, "Get back there! Back, please! Clear the road! Get back, back on the pavement! Out of it! Back please!" But it was no use; no-one would go back now. No-one could go back for the pressure behind. Next sheer weight was tried; the policemen packed ten deep and pushed as hard as they could, shouting at the crowd. And that was no use, so all around the cordons, without apparent reason, the truncheons came out and the police charged and the fighting started again.

At those five crossroads the police in the end lost the struggle. The people knew by instinct that the authorities were making a final, desperate attempt to clear the streets for the march. And in all the neighbouring streets, in Mansell Street and Leman Street and Minories and all the little side streets leading off them, the people resisted with a greater grimness than had ever been shown before. Nothing, short of troops and murder, could have shaken those solidly united ranks from their fixed determination to block the streets to the fascists. And when the worst of the fighting had ceased and the injured and arrested had been carted away, the jubilant roars which rose between the buildings defied heaven itself to intervene.

"It takes some believing," Bert said, his blue eyes glowing with battle. "I'm glad I met you today, Elsie, or I'd have missed all this."

"I'm glad I've done something for you, Bert," retorted Elsie. "You've done a lot for me, you know."

"Now don't keep saying that, Elsie, because it isn't true!" he protested.

"All right, then. I won't if you don't want me to. But you have all the same."

"Here, have a cigarette and stop gassing," Bert said. "We might get a chance to smoke now it's quietened down a bit."

They lit cigarettes and puffed contentedly, staring ahead. Except for the traffic and isolated shouting it was calm all round. Everybody seemed to be waiting for something to happen, wondering if the fascists would come.

Then a ripple ran through the crowd, herald of excitement. Heads craned forward eagerly towards the High Street. There the crowds were breaking up at the back and running west in little groups, then in greater numbers, anxious not to miss a thing that might be happening. The wildest of rumours spread through those still held fast by the cordons. Some said that the fascists had crossed the High Street and were heading for Shoreditch through the back streets. Others said they had gone towards the docks, and were marching unmolested to Limehouse. One man arriving from the Minories pushed to a stand near Elsie and Bert and swore with the utmost conviction that the Guards were out, with bayonets fixed at the ready. A woman immediately denied the bit about the Guards and said it was the Tanks, brought specially from Aldershot the night before and hidden in Hyde Park in case they should be wanted. The man promptly called her a silly bloody fool and offered to bet her a fiver that she, and not he, was in the wrong. Whereupon, drawing herself to her full height, she silenced him by asking in tart tones if he happened to be a fascist, using such disgusting language to a working woman and as good as calling her a liar?

"I wonder if it's true?" Bert whispered to Elsie.

"What?" she asked.

"About the soldiers being out."

"It might be —"

"No, I don't think it is," he amended. "No, it's not likely."

"Still, it might be," Elsie repeated, watching the rush of people from the High Street, and longing to join them. "We might stay here and miss something."

"Well —" Bert began.

But a man at Gardiner's Corner opposite suddenly cupped his hands to his mouth and bellowed, "Stand fast, comrades! Don't be fooled by rumours! Stand fast!"

"That man's right," Bert said. "Let's stay here. We might miss something if we leave. Are you tired, Elsie?"

"No, no! I'm not tired. I'm fine. Only — well, I'd like very much to spend one of your pennies somewhere!"

Claire fidgeted with her blouse, patted her hair, shuffled her feet impatiently and said, voicing the thought of thousands, "When *are* they going to come? This suspense is beginning to get on my nerves. It's nothing but false alarms."

"There are sure to be false alarms," Calvin said. "Sure to be. Half of what you hear at a time like this is simply nonsense. Our place is here, right in this crowd, despite all the rumours."

"Are they expected to march through here?" Slesser asked, for the sake of something to say to relieve the suspense of waiting.

"Well, they are and they aren't. At times like these the police often alter the route at the last minute, to fool the crowd. But I don't suppose we'll see them today," he added. "It must be getting on for half past four and they were supposed to leave Royal Mint Street about three. No, there isn't much chance of them coming now."

"I think we've won," said Claire.

"Yes, I think we've won," said Calvin confidently.

They were right. Even as they spoke, the fascists were marching to the west instead of to the east — forlorn, crushed, without spirit or bravado, animated only when a prominent nose was seen in the passers-by.

An hour before, amidst terrific opposition — fighting, booing, jeering, shouting, and the singing of workers' songs — the fascists' leader had been escorted into Royal Mint Street by hundreds of police and there told that the march could not take place. Only a march to Blackfriars, to the west, could be allowed — rather, only a march to Blackfriars was possible. But this news was slow to reach the thousands to the north. When questioned, the police professed to know nothing of the fascists' whereabouts. They were concerned to keep the people cordoned in the East End streets until the fascists were safely away. And the first symptoms that the march had failed came when the cordons, with the exception of those guarding the lines of traffic passing slowly from east to west, suddenly relaxed and began to urge the people home.

Wondering, asking each other questions in an endless stream, the released crowds milled into the roads over which they had recently struggled, still scarcely able to credit the evidence of victory. Had the fascists really marched — by another route? Had all their endeavours been in vain? Was this police action a trick to get the people home by means both peaceful and cunning?

Doubts, worries, apprehensions, momentarily swept the crowd. And then the news came at last, and spread, sweeping like a flame through that vast assembly. The fascists had marched — but to the west. The workers of London had won. United they had stood in a common aim against a common enemy. United they had fought; united they had dared; united they had cursed and laughed and joked; united they had suffered to united purpose; and united they had won.

Storm after storm of cheering thundered in the teeming streets. Eyes gleamed, limbs tingled, faces shone with a strange new joy. Hearts beat quicker in sturdy breasts. Fists clenched tightly shot quivering in the air. Victory! Fruits of Unity! Flung to the darkening sky the chant of triumph thundered, 'They Did Not Pass! They Did Not Pass! They Did Not Pass!'

Chapter VIII

THE tired policemen cajoled the jubilant people who packed the East End streets. They foresaw the end of their strenuous day and urged, "hurry along, please! Hurry along. It's all over now." Hardly any one took any notice. There was too much excitement to heed the law. The fascist enemy had not passed. The East End streets belonged to the working people, and for most of them, though the sun was sinking and the lights were twinkling on in the windows, the day was not yet done. For, released at scores of points in the area, leaflets urging the people to flock to Victoria Park Square to hold a meeting had fallen like snowflakes on the rejoicing throngs at the moment when victory was announced. Hands had seized them, eyes had scanned them, heads had nodded in appreciation; and now, from all those streets in the area the people were converging on the Square, singly or in pairs, in batches of a dozen or in vast long columns of some hundreds strong. And as they marched they flung proudly to the reddening sky their new and inspiriting slogan, 'They Did Not Pass! They Did Not Pass! They Did Not Pass!'

Slesser, seated on a bus that nosed its cautious way along Whitechapel Road, likened the surrounding scenes to those that had followed the Armistice. But now there were no ten million dead to remember, and, remembering, mar this hour of triumph. Instead, everywhere there was unrestrained, infectious happiness. From the packed vehicle itself rose excited triumphant cheers, and through the open windows were thrust clenched fists in happy salute to the passers-by. Answering cheers and Red Front salutes came gladly from the pavements, from the windows above the shops, from the people inside the shops, from the slow moving buses and trams, and even from the passing cars. Far too young to realise the real cause of their elders' excitement, but nevertheless determined to share it, little groups of children yelled and screamed and cheered and ran wildly through the crush, happy to return a salute or to join in the shouting of the slogan. Flushed, triumphant faces glowed everywhere unrestrained beneath the newly lighted lamps that flanked the pavements. Such sustained, united, mass enthusiasm could not have been witnessed in the streets before.

Slesser himself was the willing participant in this mighty and glorious festival. He was witnessing an outburst of emotion which hitherto he would have scorned as impossible. The happily excited faces, the spontaneous gestures, the confident, victorious words of those around him, were those of a new people, a people who had cast off a shadow. And he was there among them, going with them, as one of them, to their victory meeting in the Square.

When he and Calvin and Claire scrambled off the bus at Bethnal Green Road, they found that that mass enthusiasm still prevailed. They got off the bus into a hurrying swarm of people who swept them along to the Square, where, beneath the street lamps, an enormous gathering had already arrived, carried there by bus and tram and underground: or they had come on foot, marching along in batches of upwards of a hundred strong, singing their songs and shouting their slogan in the new, united voice of victory.

But they were silent now, except for murmurs of excitement from the newcomers, for the meeting had begun and attention was fixed on the speaker, who stood, barely discernible in the gloom, in the far centre of the throng, reviewing the events that had led up to the calling of the counter demonstration. His voice flowed evenly in the still night air to the furthermost fringes of the listening crowd. Then, his speech finished, he climbed down amidst a prolonged outburst of applause.

"Who was that?" Slesser whispered to Calvin when the

clapping had died away.

"I don't know his name," Calvin replied, "but this is a communist meeting."

"S-sh!" Claire warned.

The chairman of the meeting announced, "Comrades! Before I introduce another speaker, I want to remind you that after this meeting there will be a march to Shoreditch Town Hall, where we shall hold another meeting as already arranged. We shall form up here and march through the East End streets — and we shan't need five thousand police to protect *us*. Let our march be an expression of the people's will. Let every one of us take part in it. Let us show to the ruling classes, to the fascist hordes and their masters, the National Government and Hitler and Mussolini, that those who uphold the principles of democracy can march through the East End streets — or any other streets, for that matter — entirely unmolested, with the full support of the East End people — aye, with the full support of democratic peoples throughout the world!" He stopped, waited for the applause to end, and resumed, "So, Comrades, don't forget. After this meeting, a march. A people's march!... And now, Comrades, Comrade B— will say a few words."

Comrade B— climbed on to the platform. The crowd clapped long and heartily, for he was popular. He plunged straight into his speech, his voice starting low and then rising gradually until his words were distinctly audible.

"Comrades! The fascists have bragged for weeks past that they would march through the East End streets today. In that aim they have had the full support of the National Government and the full support of the police. With that support they thought nothing could stop them in their foul campaign of filthy abuse of the Jews and all democratic liberties. But they made one serious mistake, Comrades — one *very* serious mistake — they underestimated the temper of the working class, and all lovers of liberty." He cleared his throat and resumed, "We know very well what the fascists are, what fascism stands for.

126

Fascism aims by brutal force to tie the workers to the bosses, to smash trade unionism, to smash all democratic institutions, to deprive us of everything that we hold dear, to make us slaves to a bestial creed which glorifies, not peace, but war — as Mussolini and Hitler glorify war."

His voice rose to a higher key. "Comrades! The fascists said they would march through the East End streets today. They boasted about it for weeks. They said they would wipe the Reds off the map... But, Comrades, the working class rallied unitedly together. The workers said, 'They Shall Not Pass!' and, Comrades, they —"

His words were snatched from his lips and flung thundering skywards in a mighty volume of sound, 'They Did Not Pass!'

And when the thunderous noise had died the speaker went on, his voice sometimes touching emotion when he mentioned the victory; and Slesser, Calvin, and Claire listened, and all the people about them listened, oblivious of their aching limbs and empty stomachs, forgetting these in the common cause which held them together in the Square as the dusk darkened slowly to night.

2

Helen Stroud thanked her host and hostess and entering the car told her chauffeur to drive home. She then opened a small white envelope. By the car's interior light she read a list of stocks and shares. Strange, she thought. Mr Banks' 'red hot certs' were all in armaments.

3

In a stuffy café off Whitechapel Road, Bert and Elsie sat hunched together at a tiny table, waiting for their order to be served by the two dark-haired bewildered girls who rushed hither and thither among the hungry, chattering customers. Behind the cake-speckled counter the Italian proprietor toiled like a Trojan to fill the cups with the thick, hot liquid which squirted frothily from the glittering urn. In the kitchen beyond the hatch his wife cracked eggs by the score and sliced potatoes in a futile attempt to catch up with reiterated orders. The babel of excited, eager, triumphant voices rose loudly above the clatter of crockery, the chink of knives on the glass-topped tables, and the intermittent scraping of chairs on the worn linoleum. Pale blue columns of smoke from cheap cigarettes held in brown-stained fingers rose mistily in the foetid air. Fat, shining globules of steam snaked rapidly down the distempered walls to halt at last in widening pools on the dusty floor.

"My God!" Bert exclaimed, wiping the sweat from his brow and neck. "It's like an oven in here!"

"It's bad enough," said Elsie. "But we're lucky to have a seat. If we'd been five minutes later we'd never have got in at all."

"I'd like to know when we're going to get served," Bert grumbled. "They've had our order long enough."

"Still, we're getting a good sit down. I was tired out. I couldn't have stood another minute."

"So was I. It's funny, but you never notice how tired you are until the excitement's all over. It's like being at a football match. When the game's on you don't notice anything, but when it's over all you want to do is to rush back home and have a rest."

"Do you like football, then?"

"I used to, but on my job you never know whether you'll be working or not on a Saturday, so I've stopped going. Ah! Here she is with our grub! At last!"

One of the girls hurriedly placed their egg and chips before them and then went back for the tea and bread.

"It's tea I want most," Bert said. "My throat's parched. It's that shouting. If you'd told me this morning that I'd go to a political meeting and shout myself hoarse, I wouldn't have believed you. But I've learned something today, say what you like." He nodded his fair head emphatically.

The waitress returned with the tea and bread. Bert pushed the tea towards Elsie. "Here, you pour it. It's a woman's job."

"Sugar?" she asked.

"Two," he said. "I've got a sweet tooth."

Elsie smiled.

"Well," he said, "let's eat for today for tomorrow we may die."

"There's a lot of truth in that," Elsie said with a trace of bitterness.

"Oh, cheer up, Elsie!" he protested. "Look on the bright side! Things aren't going to be so bad. You'll see."

She made no reply. She began to eat, following his example, her head bent over her plate, so that he shouldn't see her eyes.

"I wonder what's happened to the old woman?" Bert pondered presently, dipping a square of bread into the oozing yoke of an egg.

"The one who threw the stone?" Vivacity came back to Elsie's drooping face. "What a shame she got arrested! And the way they knocked her about..."

"It wasn't necessary," Bert mumbled with his mouth full. "I hope she gets off."

"She won't. She'll get six months."

"A bloody shame. She was only excited." He dipped some more bread in the egg yolk. But there, we can't do anything. We don't know her address, or her name even."

"No, we can't, poor thing! I only wish we could."

Elsie ate quickly, thinking of the old woman, of Lady Stroud and the smashed glass of the car, thinking of prison, the river, and Bert. A good sort, Bert. You didn't meet many like him. But what was going to happen after they left the café?

As if he had read her thoughts he said, "I've been thinking about you, Elsie. We haven't decided anything yet, have we?"

"How do you mean?" she asked.

"Well, you've no work and no money. You can't just wander about the streets, can you? Besides, you might do something daft..."

"I shan't do that, Bert. It'll be all right. Don't you worry. I'll get a job, somehow."

"You haven't any references," he objected. "Nobody will take you without references. You said that yourself, didn't you?"

"But I'll manage, Bert. Here, have some more tea." She picked up his empty cup and began to pour from the teapot.

"You haven't put the milk in," he said reproachfully, in the tone one adopts to a naughty child. "You should always put the milk in first; the tea tastes better."

"Oh, I'm so sorry, Bert," Elsie said in confusion.

"If you were my wife I'd stop your allowance," he continued jocularly, taking the cup.

"But I'm not your wife. You'd want somebody better than me..."

"How do you know that?"

"Of course you would! Don't be silly!"

"You're as good as any other girl I've met," he said earnestly, suddenly reaching across the table and laying his hand on her own. "And in many ways, Elsie, you're better. I know what most girls in your position would have done — gone on the streets..."

"S-sh!" Elsie warned, blushing fiercely.

Bert, startled, looked round. A ginger-haired man in a khaki shirt and flannels was standing behind him, an amused smile on his freckled face. "Hello, Bert!" he said. "I didn't expect to see you around here — and with a girl."

"Hello, Ginger!" Bert answered. "I didn't recognise you at first. Fetch a chair and sit down with us, if you can make room. We're just finishing." He moved the crockery and left a space at the end of the narrow table.

Ginger fetched a chair and flopped down heavily. He

stared hard at Elsie with his bold, grey green eyes, then stared at Bert, his brows lifted inquisitively.

"Meet Elsie," Bert said, divining the other's unspoken question. "Elsie, this is Ginger, one of the busmen."

"Pleased to meet you," Elsie said politely.

"I didn't know Bert had a girl," Ginger said, his eyes roving over Elsie's clothes.

Elsie coloured deeply. Bert chuckled.

"Why shouldn't I have a girl?" he demanded.

The waitress arrived for the order, cutting off Ginger's reply. He wanted only a tea and a buttered roll. "I'm too tired to eat," he explained when the girl had gone. "Been on my feet since twelve o'clock, chasing the fascists. Phew!" He mopped his heated forehead with a large khaki handkerchief.

"So have we," Bert told him.

"Been what?"

"Chasing the fascists."

"You! My God! What's happened? You're not feeling bad, are you?"

"Don't be sarcastic, Ginge. I know I don't bother much with politics, like you do, but today's been an exception."

"I should just think it has! Anyhow, what did you think of it? We stopped 'em, eh?" Ginger cried.

"You bet we did," Bert answered, nodding approval.

"That's unity for you," Ginger said. "It just shows. With unity you can go forward, without it you go back. It stands to reason. If you're split among yourselves you can't beat the bosses. You've got to stand together, the same as the ruling classes."

Ginger's tea and buttered roll arrived. He began to stir the tea, forgetting he had not sugared it. "Where would France be without unity?" he demanded. "Nowhere! Germany'd just walk in whenever Hitler wanted to. And if we don't buck our ideas up we'll have fascism in England before we know where we are. I can't understand some of the Labour leaders being all against unity. They're blinking the facts. But I hope they get a unity resolution passed at the conference next week. If they don't..." He sighed, and drank a large mouthful of tea. "Damn it!" he spluttered. "I haven't sugared it!"

Elsie, smiling, passed him the sugar. He glanced at her sharply with his keen, grey green eyes. "You interested in politics?" he demanded.

She shook her head." I don't know anything about it," she confessed.

"It's time you did. You and Bert can study Karl Marx together!"

"Who's Marx?" Elsie asked.

"Blimey! Haven't you heard of Marx. *Karl* Marx?"

"Women aren't interested in politics," Bert said to defend her. "You can't expect them to be."

"You haven't been to a working class meeting," Ginger said bluntly. "If you had, you'd know better." He swilled some more tea down his parched throat and took a huge bite of the buttered roll.

Bert wiped the last traces of grease from his plate with a piece of bread and glanced across at Elsie. "What about some cakes to finish off with?" he suggested. "Well, I'm going to have some. I'm as hungry as a hunter." He looked round for a waitress, but both were busy serving, their faces red and hot and angry since they were not yet able to cope with the rush. "I'll fetch them myself," he announced, and went off to the counter.

"Bert's a deep one," Ginger said to Elsie, talking with his mouth full of roll. "I didn't know he was courting." Elsie opened her mouth to deny it, but Ginger went on, "He's always made out he couldn't get a girl, but it just shows..."

"Shows what?" Elsie demanded, determined to defend the absent Bert. "What do you mean?"

"Oh, nothing! That's just an expression, that's all. I don't mean any offence," Ginger replied hastily. "Bert's all right. A bit lazy minded, that's all — if you get my meaning. It beats me why working men with intelligence, like Bert, for instance, don't try to help themselves against the bosses. You'd think they'd be the first to come forward, but no..." He shook his head sadly and finished off the buttered roll at a gulp.

Bert came back with the cakes. Ginger, looking up from the table, said informatively, "Bert, I've been telling what's-her-name here, that the only thing I've got against you is that you won't join the working class movement. Isn't that right?"

"But I'm in the union," Bert objected as he sat down.

"Yes, but you never go to a branch meeting, do you?"

"Oh, what's the use! Neither do a good many others."

"What's the use! Hell! If some of us didn't go there wouldn't be any union at all, would there? That's non-sense!" Ginger gulped down the remains of his tea. "Isn't it?" he appealed to Elsie.

"Well, I suppose you're right, but everybody isn't the same," Elsie said, glancing at Bert, who was unconcernedly eating a cake.

"Let's put it this way," Ginger went on, producing a packet of Woodbines. "All the working man really wants is bread, peace, and security. But he can't get them. Why? Because our economic system's all wrong. On the one hand you have a few thousands of capitalists who never want for anything, and on the other you've got millions and millions of workers who just manage to live at starvation level all their lives. Is that right?" he appealed to Elsie.

"No," said Elsie. "It isn't. But —"

"Of course it isn't!" Ginger snorted. "There's enough for everybody, really, but it isn't shared properly, the factories don't work to capacity and so on, because the rich don't want them to. The rich get the best of everything, while people like you and me often have to go without even a bite of grub. The rich are just parasites. And that's where the trade unions come in, that's where the working class political parties come in. They're the organisations of the working class that function to protect the interest of the working man —"

"Oh, dry up!" said Bert.

"No, I won't dry up!" Ginger retorted. "I'm telling this girl of yours, Comrade Elsie what's-her-name, not you, so get on stuffing yourself with that cake and don't interrupt... Well, Comrade whatever-your-name-is," Ginger resumed, stabbing the table. "It's like this. There's only one way you'll ever get rid of the rich, and that's to build up powerful political parties and powerful trade unions and dictate to the ruling class instead of letting them dictate to us. In other words, we've got to seize economic power by mobilising every single working man there is against the bosses and the Government. So when I say to Bert that he ought to take an active —"

"That's all right in theory," interrupted Bert, who had heard a similar discourse from Ginger on innumerable occasions. "But in practice most people won't do anything except moan about it."

"But you've got to set an example," Ginger persisted, striking the table with his fist. "Take today, this fascist march. What would have happened if somebody hadn't set the example and issued a call for a counter-demonstration? Why, the fascists would have been strutting about here tonight probably throwing bottles at you and me or coshing us with a knuckle-duster. But as the lead was given, they're skulking about the West End somewhere, where their bosses are. Now do you see?"

"I think I do," said Elsie vaguely. "We all ought to do our share all the time, instead of only sometimes."

"Yes, but Bert here doesn't see that."

"Today's a special case," Bert argued.

"In a way, it is," Ginger admitted. "But doesn't it show what could be done if everybody pulls together? Think what a difference it would make in the Government's attitude to Spain, if only the working class would demonstrate as solidly as they've done today! Think what else could be accomplished!" His eyes glowed with a vision of socialism and a free and happy people.

"I suppose you're right," Bert agreed finally. "But I

can't see it happening in our time."

"It would happen if people only bothered. It would be inevitable. Still," Ginger pushed back his chair. "I can't stay here jabbering all night. I'm going to that meeting in Victoria Park Square. What're you two doing? Coming along later?"

"We haven't decided where we'll go yet," Bert answered, glancing at Elsie. "Maybe we'll go to a funfair."

"You and your pin tables," Ginger growled. "Why don't you come to that meeting and learn something?"

"I'm too tired, and I'm sure Elsie is. Aren't you, Elsie?" Bert asked, winking at Elsie.

"I am a bit," she admitted.

"Bah!" Ginger snorted disgustedly and got to his feet. "Tired! Pin tables! Why don't you buy a bag of marbles!" He went to the counter, paid his bill and left the café in disgust.

"It's a wonder he didn't try to get me to join some party or other," Bert remarked. "He usually does."

"He seems clever," Elsie ventured.

"Oh, he's clever all right. But he's always in trouble at the garage for agitating. He's in the I.L.P., you know. Well, shall we go to a pin table place? Or are you too tired? Maybe you'd like to go to the pictures instead?"

"I don't mind which," Elsie answered indecisively.

"Then let's go to the West End and try to win some cigarettes," Bert said. "We can go to the pictures some other time."

"Anything you like, Bert," Elsie said as they got up from the table.

Chapter IX

"FORM up for the march, Comrades! Form up for the march!"

"Form up! Form up! Form up for the march!" The meeting in Victoria Park Square was at an end, and the march to Shoreditch Town Hall was forming up in the road amidst constant exhortations from the organisers. So long had the people been standing that their limbs had stiffened with inaction; and now they moved tiredly into position in ranks of four where they shuffled about, discussing in loud, eager tones the events of the day as they waited for the signal to start.

Slesser stood on the inside of the column, near the pavement. On his right was Calvin, silent and thoughtful, and next to him Claire, talking to a woman whom she knew about the fighting round the barricade in Cable Street. Slesser himself felt nervous; this was the first occasion that he had taken any part in a public procession, and the staring, though friendly eyes of the watchers, seemed all to be directed to himself. He tried keeping his eyes on the thick broad back of the man in front, but those eyes to his left still seemed to be picking him out for especial attention.

'Oh, hell!' he thought miserably, and had almost decided to leave when the two mounted policemen allotted to lead the procession gently dug their spurs into the smooth flanks of the horses and started off at a brisk pace. Slesser saw the column behind them shake itself into a more purposeful activity and follow eagerly. Then the man ahead was marching and he was marching; that nervousness had gone with the first step forward. He braced his shoulders, stuck out his chest, and swung his arms like a soldier.

The idle chatter of the marchers gave way to shouting,

and hands dug deep in pockets became clenched fists thrust in the air. Small fists, large fists, white fists, brown fists; fists that had toiled in mines and quarries and docks and washtubs, and fists that had penned and typed or done nothing at all. Everywhere he looked Slesser saw those fists, no longer grimly challenging, but joyfully saluting. There were thousands of them — above the heads of the marchers and above the heads of the watchers who packed the pavements as far as his eyes could see. They were everywhere — up at the lighted windows and in the buses and the trams and motor cars which crawled their slow way along the teeming streets.

He remembered the words of the speaker, 'we shan't need any five thousand police to protect *us.*' That was true, he thought warmly. The widely-spaced policemen escorting the procession were just a formality. Nobody here was hostile. They were all friends. He saluted them constantly, glowing with pride to be with them.

'We don't need any police,' he thought. 'They ought to go home. They're spoiling our march. We're not fascists. We're anti-fascists. We're Reds. We stopped the fascists today and we can stop them again. They can't march here like we can. These are our streets, not fascist streets. Let them all go to Germany if they want to march. Let them all go to hell. That's where they belong. Hot place, hell. Wonder if there is a hell? Really, I mean? No, can't be, really. But if there is, that's where the fascists ought to be — in hell. Wish I were the devil, ha! ha! I'd show 'em! Fascists — Bah!'

The procession stopped and bunched up in the road. Now what's up? Slesser wondered. Why have we stopped our march? What's happening over there? Good God! Fighting! What for? Who's fighting who? Why?

"What's the trouble?" he asked Calvin breathlessly.

"I think it's some fascists," said Calvin. "Crowd must have spotted them —"

"Fascists!" Slesser repeated. "Here?" Surely not, he thought. Not here.

"Yes, Comrade. They'll be out looking for revenge tonight. They always do that trick when they've suffered a setback. And they'll be pretty sore after today."

"Ah, I see!" said Slesser.

He fell silent, watching the milling crowd that had gathered at the crossroads ahead. The police led off a couple of youths, the crowd booing heatedly after them, and then, the incident over, the procession moved on again. When he reached the scene of the trouble, Slesser looked across at the crowd, but they were all in a merry mood now and saluting the marchers as if nothing untoward had occurred. They'd soon got over it, he thought, and marched on, shouting the slogan.

The column swung sharply to the right, passed under an iron bridge which intensified the deafening roars and cheers, and entered a long straight road at a brisker pace. The slogan-shouting and the singing went on as before, drowning the tramp of the marchers' feet in the thunderous volume of sound.

"What do you think of this?" Slesser heard Calvin say above the uproar.

"Bloody fine!" Slesser retorted enthusiastically. "I've never seen anything like this before!"

"No, nor have I. Is this the first time you've been on a march?"

"Yes, but it won't be the last!"

"I've been in God knows how many marches," Calvin said, "but this is the best of them all. Easily the best. I thought the hunger marches would take some beating for the welcome they had from the public, but this surpasses the lot."

"What's that?" Claire demanded suddenly, breaking off her conversation with her woman acquaintance. "Did I hear something about hunger?"

"Hunger marches," Calvin corrected her.

"This is a hunger march, surely!" Claire protested, grimacing. "At least, it is for me, for I'm positively starving after all this time! Every time we pass a café I feel like dashing out of the ranks and gorging!"

They laughed at her words, Claire and her friend in high-pitched, feminine tones that resembled shrieks, Calvin silently, shaking all over, and Slesser his sudden, barking laugh that ended in a pleasant grin. Then they shouted their slogan again, 'They Did Not Pass!' and marched over a crossroad that was packed with a cheering throng that had gathered there to greet the marchers.

Glancing back over his shoulder, Slesser saw that the marching column was even longer than he had imagined. In addition to the thousands in front, it stretched right down the long straight road they had recently left to beyond the dark arched bridge in the distance. There seemed no end to it. How many thousands were there? he wondered, and tried judging each hundred with his eyes. Impossible! He gave it up and turned again to the front.

The street ahead was narrower than the one they had left and flanked with towering red blocks of working class flats. Draped from the lighted windows of the flats, as high up as the topmost storey, were scores of crimson flags and pieces of dark red cloth, fluttering in the cool night breeze. The tenants leaned out, family by family, cheering and waving and shouting their welcome to the marchers below. And then the flats were gone and they were in another little street, this time of shops with curious Jewish names and peculiar signs. But still the same greeting, the same salutes, the same cheers, and the same reiterated slogan.

On still, into a very wide, brightly-lit street that was so full of traffic that the marchers had to squash close in to the pavement. In this street the watchers began to fall in beside the procession and to march along, at first in pairs, a boy and his girl or a husband and his wife, and then more and more, in steadily increasing numbers, until the ranks of the marchers swelled five deep, then six deep, and then on to eight and twelve deep — a great solid band of marchers who half blocked the road, forcing the traffic to a standstill as they swept proudly along together.

Knowing their conquering mood the police left them alone and went along with them, some in their midst, the late bitter feelings now forgotten in the common rejoicings. And as that immense parade went on, more and ever more joined the swollen ranks, until it seemed that the whole population was swarming forward to a vast common meeting somewhere in the night ahead. They were irresistible, stopping for nothing that could move. Thousands of the watchers went along with them, adding their voices to the common voice that triumphantly roared and echoed in the East End streets, 'They Did Not Pass! They Did Not Pass! They Did Not Pass!'

Thus Slesser came to Shoreditch Town Hall with Calvin and Claire; and found the building full to the doors already with those who had marched on ahead. He was smitten with sudden dismay. He had looked forward to getting inside to listen to those stirring speeches, and now the thing was impossible. Fatigue and hunger assailed him as his spirits sank. His feet felt as if they would burst asunder in his dusty shoes; his legs were trembling after so much unaccustomed exercise, weak from the exertion; his belly was hideously hollow, crying for food; his shirt was stuck to his back where the braces crossed on his spine; and even the cap on his head seemed unbearably heavy. Fiercely he snatched it off and glared at the Town Hall doors. But not even a general's glare could have altered the fact that the hall was already full to the topmost step.

"So we can't get in," he cried to Calvin in a disappointed tone. "It's a bloody shame, after marching all this way!"

"It's just our luck," Calvin replied, seemingly in no way disappointed. "But there's sure to be an overflow meeting in a couple of minutes."

"Where?" Slesser growled.

"Here, outside the Town Hall. Look, there's the loud-speaker car coming now," he added as a small black car nosed its way through the crowd that had gathered in the open space outside the hall.

With renewed hope, Slesser watched the car cruise to a standstill beneath a lamp-post. A man climbed up on the car's roof and began immediately to urge the crowd to remain where they were. The speakers inside the hall would all address the meeting outside in due course, he announced, and in the meantime, Comrade J would be pleased to say a few words. The police in the vicinity began to walk away in twos and threes, since their services were plainly superfluous. And Comrade J appeared, slim, straight, tall, and obviously greatly excited, and began to speak in a fast, emotional voice into a microphone.

Slesser listened intently for five minutes, then a sudden, insistent pain smote at his bowels. He squirmed, shuffled in the crush, tried to concentrate again on the speaker's words, but the interest was gone beyond recapture. He hated to have to leave now.

He had wanted to stay to the end, to make it a day, but his body cried out for ease and rest and food. He would have to go, he told himself. He wasn't so used to standing about for hours at a stretch, as were Calvin and Claire, who stood together nearby, absorbed in the speaker's words, apparently unexhausted by the tiring day. Slesser sighed, regretfully, wearily, and whispered his decision to Calvin.

"I must go now," he said.

"Oh, are you off, Comrade?" Claire asked. She shook his hand. "I'm glad you came along today. What did you think of it?"

"I wouldn't have missed it for anything," Slesser answered sincerely.

"Well, so long," Calvin said, and offered his hand. "Don't forget the lesson."

2

As they jumped on the platform of the bus, Elsie said, "Inside, Bert?"

"No, on top. At the back if you can," Bert replied.

The bus was half-full, but the back seats were empty.

Seating herself, Elsie was arranging her hair with the aid of the window as a looking glass when she noticed Bert's eyes upon her in open admiration. Blushing a little, she turned to him, but at that moment the conductor trotted up the stairs. Bert produced his pass, paid fourpence for Elsie, and, when the conductor had gone below again, asked, "Tired, Elsie?"

"No, I'm all right," she said.

Bert diffidently slipped his arm round her waist, and they sat close together for almost five minutes, silent and thoughtful. Suddenly Bert withdrew his arm and fumbled in his pocket.

"Take this," he said gruffly, pushing a note in her fingers.

"No, no!" she cried instantly in a hurt voice.

"Take it," he insisted. "Get yourself somewhere to sleep tonight. Go on. I can afford it."

"No. Please, Bert —"

"Go on!" he insisted again. "Don't be silly about it. Why shouldn't you?"

"You don't understand," she said miserably. "You don't understand what it means —"

"Look here. Answer me this. Do you want to see me again?"

"Yes, Bert, but —"

"And I want to see you again, so you've got to take it and be sensible. You've got to have somewhere to sleep, haven't you?"

"Yes, but —"

"Then stop being foolish," he said harshly. "Stop being proud. For God's sake be sensible!"

"Now you're angry —"

"Of course I'm angry! Who wouldn't be? Here I am trying to help you and you behave like this. Now take it. You can get a room at a YWCA place for tonight, and tomorrow I'll help you find lodgings. It'll be cheaper."

"All right," she said meekly, chastened. "But I've got no pockets, so you'll have to keep it till later, in case I lose it."

"Now that's being sensible," Bert said, putting the note back in his pocket.

"I'm sorry if I offended you, Bert. I didn't mean to."

"You didn't offend me, only it makes me wild when people won't let themselves be helped. I know what it is to be without money, believe me. I had some rough times in America, when I was glad to be given a crust of bread or a bit of cheese once a day. What you need is some good food and a few clothes, and then you'll stand a chance of getting a job. And I'm going to help you until you do get a job," he added firmly.

"But why should you do this for me?" Elsie asked. "You hardly know me."

"Because I like you," he said shortly. "Here," he added, offering cigarettes, "have a smoke before we get off."

Thoughtfully they watched the lights and the traffic that streamed past. The bus crossed Ludgate Circus and went steadily along Fleet Street and into the Strand. At Charing Cross they got off into a thick mass of people who were waiting at the stop, and pitched away their half-smoked cigarettes, uncommonly extravagant.

"Shall we walk up?" Bert asked, taking her arm. "Or shall we wait for a bus?"

"Let's walk," Elsie suggested. "We'll save twopence."

"A penny," he corrected her. "Remember I've got a free pass. It comes in handy too. In the summer I can go out in the country on my rest days — though that isn't much fun on my own."

They went through Trafalgar Square arm in arm, like lovers. Once they stopped outside Africa House to watch a small group of uniformed fascists standing in the shadow of Nelson's pigeon-haunted column, shouting they wanted free speech and down with the Jews. Shuddering, Elsie said, "They're horrible."

"I might not be a communist, but one thing's certain. I'd never be a fascist," Bert vowed. "Too disgusting."

"Nor me," said Elsie agreeably. "They look silly in those uniforms, don't they? Like overgrown schoolboys."

"They ought to join the Army if they want to wear uniforms. It would do them good. Come on, Elsie. Don't let's waste our time on them. They're only annoyed because they couldn't march."

They walked on. In Leicester Square, brilliant with lights of rainbow hues, a newsboy was handing out copies of a special edition of a Sunday paper as fast as his hands could move. An eye-compelling placard swinging from his waist announced:

BATON CHARGES IN EAST END STREETS

"Let's buy one," said Bert. "It's a special edition."

He gave the man twopence and walked on a little way till he stopped under the light of a streetlamp. Beneath the splashed headlines on the front page was a long account of the afternoon's disorders. They read the whole of it, breathless with interest, exclaiming now and again as they read of incidents which they themselves had witnessed. Then, turning to the back page, Elsie gasped, "look, Bert! There she is! That old woman! The one who threw the stone!"

"So it is," Bert cried, staring at the picture of an old woman in black who was being dragged along to a waiting van by two burly policemen. "Well, can you beat that —!"

"*We* might be in this," Elsie cried, pointing to another picture, one that showed a baton charge at the Aldgate crossroads. They looked closely. The scene was unfamiliar. "It must have been before we got there," she said, a little disappointed. "What a shame!"

"Never mind! We'll look in the other papers tomorrow. We might be in them. Cheer up!" He folded the paper they had bought and stuffed it into his pocket. "We'll keep this as a souvenir. Come on, Elsie. Let's go. Don't let's talk about this march any more tonight. I've just about had enough of it."

Arm in arm they walked on, talking, despite his

resolve, of the fascist march, the fighting, the old woman, Lady Stroud, and the Cable Street barricade, until they arrived at the entrance of the fun fair. It was hot inside, and the clammy, smoke-laden air made them gasp for a moment as they pushed their way through the restless people towards the centre of the building. Bert halted at a row of glittering pin tables and took a coin from his trousers pocket.

"I usually win on these," he told Elsie, slipping the coin in the machine. "It depends on my luck." He pulled back the plunger, released it after careful adjustment, and watched the bright steel ball shoot up the run and begin to bounce its way down the board.

"Well, what do you have to do to win?" Elsie asked, puzzled by the complicated game. "I've never seen any of these things before, you know."

"You have to score six hundred with five balls, see? That one's scored eighty," Bert explained, pointing at the indicator. "Not so good, though. Five eighties is only four hundred, so I'll have to do better than that!" He sent another ball up the run; it scored a hundred and fifty. "I stand a chance!" he cried, excited at the prospect of winning.

Elsie hung on to his free arm in her excitement. When the next ball left the plunger and swept up the run they watched its progress with fascinated, feverish eyes, mouths slightly open, hardly daring to breathe. Knock, knock, knock, went the ball against the bumpers, and the indicator chattered up the score: two-fifty-one, two-fifty-nine, two-sixty-four, two-seventy-five, two-eighty-eight...

"Oh, what a shame!" Elsie exclaimed as the score stopped dead at three hundred and one.

"Pretty rotten that time," Bert agreed. "Still, better luck with this one." He sent another ball up the run. "There! You see! It's scoring like blazes!"

"You can't lose now!" Elsie cried. "It's five hundred and twenty! Only eighty with this last ball. Do be careful, Bert."

"You leave that to me," said Bert with feigned calm, releasing the plunger. The ball swept up the run through the little gate at the top, and was half way across the board when it seemed to stop in its tracks, and then, with smooth, gleaming wickedness it rolled to the bottom of the board without scoring a point.

"Well, I'm damned!" Bert exploded. "Would you believe it! Of all the —!"

"It did it on purpose," Elsie said resentfully. "Just when you were winning, too."

"Never mind," he said philosophically. "Let's try again. Would you like a go?"

"No, no, Bert! It's no use me losing as well. I'll just watch and hope you win."

"Go on! You stand a chance of winning five cigarettes, or ten, if you score eight hundred."

She shook her head emphatically. "No, I'll watch you. You might win this time."

But it was no use. He scored only three hundred and twenty-one. He said damn and tried again, and said blast and tried again. Then Elsie, though she didn't want to for fear of losing, also tried, and scored less than two hundred.

"My luck's dead out," Bert said, bitterly resenting the loss of fivepence. "Come on. Let's try somewhere else."

"Maybe I've brought you bad luck," Elsie muttered superstitiously.

"Bah! That's no use, talking like that," Bert said scornfully. "I'm just off form, that's all. Come on. One more try on something else, and then if we don't win we'll pack it up and go to the pictures."

They went to a game called the Grand Hotel, around which was gathered a large crowd of speculators. This was a simple game, representing a hotel, with rooms numbered one to ten, and a bathroom, telephone, kitchen, and lift, laid out realistically beneath a glass topped table. A mechanically operated electric light circled through the rooms, lighting each one for a quivering

146

second, until the attendant turned off the power, when it came slowly to a stop, watched by the anxious eyes of the speculators. Whoever had a penny on the room thus illumined when the light stopped had a choice of twenty cigarettes or a box of chocolates for their skill.

Bert, pushing his way to the front, staked a penny on number one. Elsie pored over his shoulder. "It stopped there last time," she objected doubtfully. "I'd try number seven if I were you."

"No, let it stay," he answered. "Never change your mind at this game. That's my motto."

More pennies were extorted from reluctant pockets by the hoarse voiced attendant, until the fourteen hazards were covered, then the attendant raced the circling light until it resembled a brilliant streak of gold beneath the glass. Abruptly he cut off the power. Thirty pairs of eyes watched feverishly as the speed of the light slackened to a tantalising dawdle. Elsie's fingers dug deeper into Bert's rigid arm as the speed of the light diminished. It crawled through rooms numbered one to ten, slower still through the bathroom, kitchen, telephone, and lift, and then... three... five... six... seven.

"There!" Elsie gasped. "I told you! It's stopped at seven!"

"So you did," Bert acknowledged grudgingly, watching an elderly man pick up his winnings with envious eyes. "Never mind. It's no use crying over spilt milk. Let's try again."

"Then put it on the bath this time," Elsie implored. "I know it will win, Bert. I'm absolutely sure it will win."

"All right," he said, "but there's no need to get worked up like that. Keep calm."

"I can't keep calm," she said. "I want you to win. There! It's starting again."

Again came that period of nerve racking suspense while the light dawdled tantalisingly through the rooms; again eyes gleamed with hope that faded quickly to despair. The light seemed possessed of a malevolent

147

devil; it flickered slowly from eight to nine, to raise false hopes in the breast of an impoverished-looking youth of twenty, then it paused for a long, agonising moment at number ten. And then, as if in answer to Elsie's frantic prayers, it slipped over to the bath.

For an instant she was too overcome to move. Despite the evidence she could scarcely credit the fact that her choice had won. But when Bert reached out and took the prize with a smile of gratification on his previously scowling face, she doubted no longer. In a sudden excess of enthusiasm she flung her arms around him and hugged him in glee.

"You were right after all," Bert said, smiling happily at her upturned face. "Now what's the next choice? Hurry up, or there'll be none left."

"Bath again," she said instantly.

He put a penny on the bath. "When I bet on a number that had just won you objected."

"I know, Bert, but this time it's different. You leave it there. I know you'll win."

When it did win, Bert said, collecting his winnings, "you're a witch, Elsie! What next?"

She told him. He won again. It seemed that she couldn't lose. She gave him five winning numbers in succession, lost twice, then five more winners, whilst the crowd around them gaped, some admiringly, some enviously, as Bert's pockets became increasingly bulkier with packets of cigarettes. Then he said, "Come on, Elsie. Don't let's stay any more. We might break the run of luck."

"All right," she said happily, following him from the table. "But fancy! Ten packets!"

"Enough to last me for ages. How did you do it?"

"I dunno! I'm not usually so lucky. Perhaps it's because I met you."

"You'd better have half."

"No, no, Bert! You keep them!"

"All right then. It'll cancel out the other — what I offered you. Let's look at it that way, shall we?"

She nodded, and they walked on through the crowd that was swarming around the glittering machines until they came to a palmist's booth. Here Bert stopped, studied thoughtfully for a moment, examining the heavy black curtains stretched across the entrance.

"Look here," he suggested. "What about having our fortunes told? Just for fun! I don't believe in it, but what about it? Eh?" His eyes were as happy as a child's when they light on a bag of sweets.

"Ooo — let's!" cried Elsie. "I've never had my fortune told before. Ss-h! Who's this?"

Hearing their voices the palmist had suddenly appeared between the black curtains. Her name was Madame Dovelli. She motioned them to enter with a wave of her heavily-jewelled hand, and they cautiously followed her through the curtains into the black-draped booth beyond.

"Sit down," she said, in a rasping voice, indicating chairs.

They obeyed, intimidated, shy, nervous. Madame Dovelli seated opposite, examined them rapidly with dark, glittering eyes that seemed to pierce to their innermost souls.

"Which of you first?" she demanded. "The lady first? Yes, of course, the lady first. It's always the lady first."

She seemed to be talking to herself as she took Elsie's hand between her own and pored over it thoughtfully.

"Ah!" she cried presently, in a hissing whisper. "Ah!" she murmured again. "I see sorrow, young lady, and tragedy, despair, hopelessness. But they belong to the past. They are no more."

She waved her jewelled hand slowly in the air, as if sweeping away some floating substance with infinite patience of movement. Then she glanced rapidly at Bert, stabbing him with her bright dark eyes.

"Once a dark man entered your life and you were sad because of it," she said absently to Elsie. "But he has gone. No matter where. He has gone. Another has taken his place, a fair man, a man whom you will learn to love and cherish. You will be happy with him and he will be good and kind to you."

She sighed, bent closer over the hand, tracing the lines with a thin, sharp finger.

"Yes," she muttered. "You will not be rich, nor will you be very poor. The lines say so. You will be comfortable with this other man, this fair man, more than you can imagine at present."

Bert had watched in apparent composure. Now he coloured, and fidgeted awkwardly; for Madame Dovelli's inference was only too plain. He glanced furtively at Elsie's face, but she was watching the palmist with fixed, wide eyes, as if hypnotised. The silly little thing believed all this tripe!

"Ah!" Madame Dovelli hissed, raising her head. "Ah!" She flashed a glittering glance at Elsie, then bent again. "You will bring this fair man luck," she said. "You have already brought him luck — not a lot, but a little. You will bring him more."

She nodded, her earrings swinging to and fro like pendulums.

"Yes, and you will travel; not far, but you will travel. And you will be very, very happy together, you and this fair man."

Again the glittering eyes were raised to Elsie's face for a fleeting second, to drop again to Elsie's hand. She spoke for some while longer, prophesying children with fair hair and blue eyes and home comforts with a loving husband, and then, shrugging, announced, "That's all, my dear. Good luck."

Elsie seemed to wake from a deep sleep. She turned to Bert with a peculiar smile on her lips, but said nothing. The palmist seized Bert's hand, laid it between her own and bent over it thoughtfully, tracing the lines. Then she told him that he had travelled in far, strange places, that he had known the depths of sorrow and the heights of happiness; that he would never be very rich, but never very poor; that he would marry a dark-haired girl who would love him very much and bear him two bonnie children with hair and eyes like his own. And Elsie sat and watched as intently as she had when her own hand had lain between the palmist's thin, sharp fingers, absorbing every word, and thinking how strange it was that Bert's fresh face should show such open disbelief.

When it was over Bert paid the woman two half crowns, and she showed them out, bowing low, a triumphant sort of gleam in her glittering eyes and a thin, red smile on her lips.

"Well," said Bert, when they were out of earshot, heading for the exit. "What do you think of it?"

"I think she was marvellous!" Elsie retorted, with absolute conviction. "Don't you?"

"Oh, I dunno." He shrugged his shoulders to express his doubts. "A lot of what she said was true, but they were mainly general statements, you know."

"She said I'd had sorrow because of a dark man, and — well, I *had.*" She grew solemn for a moment — "Besides, how did she know you had travelled?"

Bert rubbed his chin thoughtfully. "Don't ask me," he said. "Still — she did seem to know you'd brought me luck tonight with these cigarettes, didn't she? That's queer."

"Yes," said Elsie. "It is queer. And she said, she said —"
"What?"

"Oh, well —" Elsie stammered. "Never mind — it's nothing — perhaps I'm just being silly —"

"I know what you mean," Bert answered, eyeing her strangely. "But come on, Elsie, my girl. Don't let's stay here all night!" he added briskly, to cover a sudden confusing thought. "Let's go somewhere else."

"All right. But don't forget I've got to see about a room, you know."

"You'll get a room, don't worry. These YWCA places are open all night. You don't want to go in yet, do you?"

"No, of course not, silly!" she cried, squeezing his arm

151

reassuringly. "I want to stay with you as long as possible."

"Fine! If we go to a YWCA place about nine o'clock, that should be early enough. In the meantime, what about going for a drink somewhere? I feel like celebrating a bit after winning all these cigarettes," he tapped his pockets, "and meeting you. You're not teetotal, are you?"

"I'll do anything you like, Bert," she said, slipping her arm through his. "Of course I'm not teetotal!"

Laughing, they walked away down the street, Elsie's eyes shining like stars.

3

PC Thurgood was let off duty later than he had anticipated, but when he reached home he still had plenty of time to have a meal, change and rest, before going to see Lady Stroud. He was feeling worn out and ill-tempered after the heat and struggles of the day, but the thought of a hot drink cheered him.

He found his mother dozing before the fire, her spectacles awry on her nose and an open Bible on her knees. The table was set for a meal and his slippers were warming in the hearth, as she had promised him that morning. She glanced up at him as if she did not immediately recognise him. Then she cried in a tone of deep relief:

"Thank heavens you're back, Harold! I thought you might have been injured in the riots!"

"Riots? What riots? Who told you about riots?" Thurgood queried.

"That young Ernie Masters —" she began.

"That young fool! No, I wasn't hurt. Just a little thing — you haven't been worrying, have you?"

"I have a bit, my boy," she admitted. "Though it was silly of me, really. I ought to know you can take care of yourself." She smiled fondly, rose, and put the spectacles and the Bible away in a drawer. "Now," she went on, "I'll get you some tea. It won't take me a minute. The kettle's boiled once and the table's ready. You can be changing into your slippers. You must be tired out. I'll soon have a meal ready and then you can sit beside the fire and rest. I'm so relieved you didn't get hurt! Young Ernie brought back a pretty bad account of the affair."

Thurgood, unbuttoning his tunic, sat down and had begun to unlace his boots when his mother returned with the kettle.

"I'll be going out this evening, after all," he said, without looking up.

"Going out?" She paused in the act of filling the teapot. "But I thought you said —?"

"I know I did, but I've remembered since that I had an appointment."

"With whom?" his mother asked suspiciously, the kettle still poised over the teapot.

"Just a friend."

"A friend?" she repeated. With pursed lips she poured the water on the tea. "Who?"

"Oh, just one of the chaps in my division," he said carelessly.

Mrs Thurgood placed the kettle in the hearth and stood next to him, staring down at his bent head. "Harold!" she said sharply. "I don't believe you."

He raised his head and met her accusing eyes with a gaze that changed to an angry flush.

"You're lying," she went on sadly. "And you needn't lie to me, Harold. I know who you are going to see. That Stroud woman."

"Oh, no, I'm not," he retorted testily; and then raising his voice, shouted, "For God's sake shut up about her!"

"I shan't shut up, Harold, so you needn't shout. I'm your mother — remember that. Now, are you or are you not going to meet that Stroud woman?"

"No, I tell you. I haven't seen her for a week, and I'm not seeing her tonight —"

"You're lying again, Harold," she returned firmly.

"Look here, Mother, I'm not going to have you pry into my affairs like this; I'm going to do what I like. Anybody would think I was a blasted kid the way you go on about my friends! Why shouldn't I see her if I want to? Answer me that! Go on, answer me that!" he snapped.

"She's far older than you are," his mother replied evenly. "You know that as well as I do. And I know her sort, running around after good-looking young men and letting them do heaven knows what to her. Yes, I know what she's after, don't think I don't. And where's it all leading to? Have you ever thought of that? Of course you haven't. Next thing you know you'll be asked to resign your job, and then where shall we be? I've never interfered with you and your friends before, and you can't say I have, but I won't stand for people like this Stroud woman. No, no!" she cried, as he tried to interrupt. "Let me have my say. I know the world far better than you. Your father and I saw most of it in our time — God rest his soul — and I know what I'm talking about. That woman wants you for only one thing, just to have you playing around with her. It's not right," she snapped indignantly. "It's immoral in the sight of God — *and* in the sight of decent folks. Nothing but evil can come of it, and when she's done with you she'll throw you aside and laugh at you, as I dare say she's done with many another before today. You've already lied to me about her once, that I know of, so it shows what she's making of you — a liar!"

His mother flushed, pained almost to tears, but she went on remorsely, "All right, all right, my boy. Call me what you will. But let me have my say —"

"I shan't listen! To hell! I'm getting out of here!"

"No, you aren't! You'll stay here and listen to me."

She thrust herself between him and the door. He would not dare remove her forcibly. Harold stood quivering with rage, towering above her, a giant in his strength but afraid to remove her.

"You listen to me," she resumed, clutching the handle

of the door and pressing her back to the panels. "It's time we had this settled. I'm only talking to you for your own good — you ought to know that without me having to tell you. Can't you see?" she asked desperately. "Can't you see this woman will get you into trouble if you carry on with her?"

"How will she?" Thurgood scoffed. "Good Lord! I can look after myself —"

"You can't stay up all night drinking and dancing and do your work properly next day, no matter how strong you are. That's one thing. For another — what does it cost you in drink? What about that? You've been taking money out of the bank for a long time now, instead of putting it in. Remember we're not worth much over five pounds a week, including my pension. Do you ever think of that?"

"I know what I'm doing, Mother. It's my money and I'll do what I like with it. Now come away from that door and let me get changed. Come on! Stop acting like a fool!"

"Yes, you want to get out to see her!" his mother retorted bitterly, tightening her grip on the doorhandle. "I don't matter. But you're going to listen to me this time, even if I don't matter."

"I'm damned if I shall! Get away from that door, Mother, or —" Thurgood's tone was menacing. He made a threatening gesture with his hand.

"Or what?" she demanded, instinctively pressing harder to the door. "What will you do?"

"I'll drag you away!" he said, between his teeth.

In a blazing fury, he seized her by the shoulders with both hands. She winced with pain, too shocked for a moment to move. Then she smacked him a stinging blow across the face. He was so surprised that he released her and fell back, holding his cheek.

"How dare you lay hands on me!" she flung at him, half-crying with fear. "Get out! Get out! Get out of my house at once!" She flung the door open with a crash. "Get out and stay out — for ever! Go to your fine woman — go to

155

your — your *whore!*" she hissed. "May God strike you dead, the two of you! You great hulking, cowardly beast! Get out!"

Without a word, pausing only to snatch up his helmet, he dashed through the door and up the stairs to his room.

He dropped on the bed burning with resentment. He touched his smarting cheek, felt again the impact of his mother's hand, and was humiliated almost to tears. He lay for a few seconds fingering his cheek, then, with sudden resolve, jumped off the bed, hurried to the bathroom and shaved, washed, and combed his hair in a rush to escape from the house. He had made up his mind. He would get out of it tonight, go to a hotel until he could find somewhere cheaper. It was impossible to stay in this house now. Utterly impossible after that scene with his mother. She must be mad, mad with jealousy, he thought, beginning to pack at a feverish pace. And she was ridiculous, absolutely ridiculous, treating him as a child when he was a grown man, able to stand on his own feet. Well, from now on he'd lead his own life, do as he pleased, have whatever woman he liked, and to hell with her interference.

It was intolerable, more than any self-respecting man could stand to be treated as a child all the time. 'My boy' this and 'My boy' that! Bah! He began to marvel as he called to mind so many little incidents from the past when she had sought to restrict his freedom, that he'd ever been able to stand her for so long. No other son would have done so, he told himself. He had been a fool. He ought to have cleared off long ago, cut the apron strings and set up on his own, as many another man had done; not be treated as a child, smacked in the face, told who to go out with, what to spend, on whom to spend it.

He packed feverishly, pressing down the things with his feet, but there was not enough room in his suitcase and trunk for all his possessions. He had to leave an old suit, a tunic, and some underclothes, but he didn't care. There was plenty of money to buy more if he wanted to, he reflected, slamming down the lid of the trunk. He had twenty-five pounds in notes in the drawer of the dressing table, and fifty or so more in the bank. He took the notes out of the drawer, counted them, and stuffed them away in his wallet. Then he changed into evening dress, slipped on his overcoat and heaved the trunk on his shoulders. It was heavy and awkward, but he could manage it as far as the front gate.

Thurgood went quietly down the stairs with the trunk. As he passed the living room door he heard the short dry sobs of his mother's sorrow. For a moment the sounds disturbed him and he had half a mind not to leave. He was being weak and sloppy, he told himself firmly. It was no use relenting now. She had started it; she had ordered him out of the house and he was going. Even if she came out and asked him to stay, he wouldn't listen.

He left his trunk just inside the front gate and returned hastily to the bedroom. He gave a final glance round the room, now disordered and forbidding after his feverish packing. There was nothing left that he wanted or had room for. He picked up his hat, jammed it on his head, and let himself out on the landing. Then he remembered that she had no money, or very little. He was tempted to leave her with nothing, but in the end he strewed five one pound notes on the bed where she would have to see them, and satisfied, made his way out to the gate and along the street searching for a taxi.

He found one cruising in the main road, hailed it, instructed the cabman, and then got in and lit a cigarette. In a few minutes they were speeding to a hotel about a mile distant which the taxi man had recommended as being reasonably cheap and comfortable.

'A fine day this has been!' Thurgood thought, smoking as the taxi rolled on its way. 'Still, I'm out of it now. I have no regrets. I'm my own boss.'

He looked at his watch. It was just after eight o'clock, and the streets were beginning to fill with courting couples heading for the glittering cinemas. He had an hour in which to book a room, get some food and get up to town. His blood quickened at the thought of Helen Stroud. It was all well worth it, this sudden disruption and the break with his mother, he thought contentedly. Come and apologise! Hell! He knew what she meant all right. No need to pretend that he didn't. Her meaning was plain enough. His mother was right about what she wanted him for — well, what the devil did she think he wanted *her* for?

The taxi slowed, jerked to a stop outside a grim looking Georgian house that had been converted a little to form a hotel where the army of unmarrieds may ply their never ending custom. The interior was drab with brown paint and worn red carpets. At the first glimpse Thurgood thought of going elsewhere, but a glance at the clock in the hall told him that he hadn't the time. He booked a room for one night, determined to make the best of it now, and followed a red-nosed, sniffing maid-of-all-work up the narrow, steeply-mounting stairs. She informed him between sniffs that she had a very bad cold and the stairs took it out of her like, but what could a body do with all this unemployment about?

"Buy a handkerchief," Thurgood said shortly, hating the girl.

"Ah, you gentlemen will 'ave your little jokes," she replied, unoffended, shaking her head at him knowingly. "'ere's your room, sir." She unlocked a door, stood back and waited patiently for a tip.

An expression of disgust crossed Thurgood's face. After his own room this was a hovel, a dirty stinking hovel. The lumpy double bed half-filling the room had probably, he thought disgustedly, known the debaucheries of hundreds of unmarried couples.

"Is there anything wrong, sir?" the maid asked anxiously.

"No, no, it will do for tonight."

"Oh, I'm so glad it's all right, sir. Will you be wanting anythin' else, sir?"

"Nothing, except my luggage."

"The porter'll bring that up, sir, when 'e gets back from a message. But," she added hopefully, "if you want it urgent, sir, I could fetch it myself."

"Here you are," retorted Thurgood, giving her sixpence, "leave the luggage to the porter."

He could stand the room no longer. He pushed past the startled maid, almost bowling her over, and ran recklessly down the stairs.

Chapter X

ALMOST dropping with fatigue, Slesser wearily examined the coins in his trousers' pocket. Eightpence. He could do without food, but he must have something to drink and another packet of Woodbines. That would leave fourpence for fares to get back home. Home! He started. Good God! Home! He hadn't thought of it for hours — and now it all came back to him in a frightening rush of memory as he stood outside a café in Shoreditch, buffeted by the people who hurried past. What would his wife be thinking?... What would she have to say when he got back?... Nag, nag, nag, and cackle, cackle, cackle... It would go on for hours; tonight, tomorrow, the next day, the day after that; she would never forgive him, never. And that shilling he had taken from her purse!... What of *that?*

He let the coins chink back in his pocket and stood, his feet hot in his shoes, his shoulders hunched in despair, his cap pulled low on his brow, moodily thinking it over. Then he jerked erect with sudden decision. Damn her! he thought. Why be afraid of her? Let her nag and cackle to her heart's content, *he* wasn't going to worry. He was a man, not a mouse, and he'd do as he liked. Ah! To hell with her!

He turned resolutely and pushed open the café door to be met with the loud, harsh blare of a radio.

The smell of cooked food made his stomach quiver as he entered the stuffy little room. Unconsciously his tongue wandered over his lips as his eyes lit on the wares stacked up on the shelves. Ham, bully beef, sausages, pickles, cheese, cold potatoes — in imagination he took a hungry mouthful of each, the saliva welling in his mouth as he passed them by. He dropped at a vacant table with his back to that tempting array, and glowered at a pile of dirty pots, his stomach retching at the sight of them.

In a moment a willowy youth with coal-black, wavy hair came and whisked the dirty pots out of sight. He returned, quickly wiped the table with a greasy cloth that hung from his waist, and asked nonchalantly, "what's yours?"

"Tea and a Woodbine," Slesser said.

"Ten?"

"No, five."

The youth gone, Slesser looked round the café. It was fairly full of girls and youths who sat drinking tea and bolting ham rolls as they jabbered away in rough coarse tones above the haunting blare of the radio. He heard one of the youths say, "Khorr! But she was a fine tart, that Judy Smith. Fixed 'er many a time afore she married Reg Tooley."

"Khorr!" said another, gulping ham roll. "Did jer?"

"Not 'arf, I didn't. 'E don't know what 'e's married, that Reg Tooley don't. Wait till 'e finds 'er out!"

Like a lot of old women, Slesser thought. Bad as that Rose, always talking scandal. Pity they had nothing else to do, pulling folks to bits behind their backs...

"Thanks," he said aloud, as the tea and Woodbines were placed in front of him.

He paid, took a mouthful of tea, and felt it slip down his throat, hot and thick and strong. That was good! He was better immediately. He drank more, slowly, to make it last, and he lit a Woodbine and smoked, resting his tired limbs.

His thoughts wandered back to the march, to those scenes of spontaneous welcome; the cheers, the songs, the saluting and that triumphantly shouted slogan; the flags at the windows of the working-class flats, the next street with its Jewish shops, and the street after that, when the column had broadened with newcomers, and then on to the Town Hall, full to over-flowing, and his own swift rush of disappointment when he found that he couldn't get in. He thought back further to the afternoon, to those dense, angry crowds of people, hundreds of thousands of them, seething and swaying and protesting hour after hour, and winning in the end. That was what being united meant, he thought approvingly. If you stood together you could win; you were invincible. There were so many of you that no power on earth could resist you, once you stood together.

He glanced up suddenly and met the eyes of a girl at the table opposite. Dark bold eyes that never blinked. Offensive eyes in a heavily rouged face. His own dropped to her lips — thick and red and sensual — and then up again to her hair — thick, dark, shiny, and waved, glinting greasily in the pale yellow light from the pendant above. What the devil was she staring at him like that for? He didn't know her, and she didn't know him — though she would if she stared much longer. He bent over his tea, sipped, and looked up again. Those offensive eyes still persisted, as steady as a watching snake's. His own glowered back from under his cap, until the circling smoke from the Woodbine wafted into them, when he had to reach for his handkerchief to wipe away the stinging tears. Through the smarting mist he saw the girl turn, a contemptuous smile on her thick, red lips, and say something to the youth at her side.

'What an insolent little bitch she is!' Slesser thought angrily. 'If she were mine I'd give her a damned good hiding. Knock all that cheap filthy colour off her face, by God I would!'

A cold draught smote suddenly on the back of his neck. Through the café door trooped half a dozen customers who flopped heavily down in the vacant chairs. Slesser's spirits rose. These were obviously people from the Town Hall meeting come in for a snack before going home. Two of the men wore crimson ties; one woman wore a crimson scarf; four of the six wore each a small red badge demanding unity. Reds, he thought, as a man and his wife came and sat at his table and began immediately to converse together about the march through the East End streets.

162

Slesser happened to glance past the pair at the black-haired girl. She was watching the newcomers with every symptom of hostility in her bold dark eyes. He saw her bend to her companion, whisper something that he guessed was 'Reds' and then stare round the café again. The youth seemed to jerk back to life; he, too, stared round the café; then he whispered to a youth nearby, who passed the whisper on to the others. Idle loafers, Slesser thought to himself, with nothing else to do but to sit in cafés and behave like trippers to the Zoo.

"Have you been on the march?" asked the man opposite, in an affable tone.

"Ah!" said Slesser proudly. "Have you?"

The man and his wife nodded. "Yes, fine turn out, wasn't it?" resumed the man.

"One of the best we've had," said Slesser confidently, thinking of Calvin's words. "Better welcome even than the hunger marchers got — and that's saying something!"

"True, true. Were you down at Royal Mint Street this afternoon?"

Slesser nodded. "They soon chased us out, didn't they?"

"Yes." The man's face hardened. Reaching in his inside pocket, he said, "Have you seen this Sunday paper? It's a special edition, just come out." He unfolded the paper, and pointed to a picture on the back page. "Look at that! That's a charge in Royal Mint Street. Look at the handsome British police bashing up the crowd."

"Good God!" Slesser ejaculated, and stared fascinated at one of the scenes of terror that the day had known. In the picture the crowd were rushing frantically away as they sought to escape a sudden baton charge. Here and there the camera had caught the full ferocity of the police — a woman being batoned by three stalwart policemen, a man on his back in the road, his arms raised despairingly to ward off a blow.

"Good God!" Slesser exclaimed again. "Why, I should be in this!" He pointed to the man in the road. "I saw that chap myself." He looked eagerly over the dense mass of people for his own capped head, but unsuccessfully. "No, I'm not there," he said, in a disappointed tone.

"We're there," said the man, pointing to a running couple. "That's us, running away!"

"He who fights and runs away, lives to fight another day," the man's wife remarked cheerfully. "If we hadn't run, God knows what would have happened. No wonder the barricades went up in Cable Street!"

"I ran away myself," said Slesser. "But not every time."

"Neither did I," the man replied. "And look what I got for my trouble." He lifted his leg above the table and exhibited a deep, blood-caked scar running down his shin. "That's what a bloody horse did —"

Suddenly a chorus of derisive cries and laughter came from the youths and girls in the café. "Ha! Ha! Ha! Serves yer right! Red rats!" they cried, and all began to chant, "The Yids! The Yids! We gotta get ridda the Yids!" and to beat with their knives and cups on the glass-topped tables.

All the newcomers turned in their chairs, eyeing the youths in amazement. The waiter stood helplessly at the counter, his mouth drooped stupidly open, he seemed too terrified to move.

"Budding fascists, looking for trouble," said the man, dropping his leg below the table. "Ignore them. They're only kids, like most of the blackshirt gang."

"Fascists!" Slesser repeated above the din. "*Are* they?"

His eyes met again the bold dark eyes of the black-haired girl. Her thick red lips were drawn back over her teeth in a sneer directed to himself. The sneer maddened him. He sprang to his feet, spluttering with rage, intending to wipe that sneer from her face. But the man at the table seized his arm and forcibly detained him.

"Leave them alone, man!" he panted. "That's just what they want — somebody to start a row. Sit down. Ignore them. They'll soon get over it. If the cops get in here it's us who'll have to suffer — not them!"

"Why-why-why! —" Slesser spluttered incoherently.

"That saucy little bitch" — he pointed at the girl who had gone suddenly pale beneath her rouge — "that bitch's been staring at me ever since I came in!"

"Never mind! Let her stare!" the man soothed, glancing round at the girl. "She's only a kid, like the others, and got no manners. Sit down."

"I'd teach her bloody manners!" Slesser growled. "I'd put her over my knee and give it her hot if she were mine."

The girl thrust out her tongue at him and added her voice to the chant, "The Yids! The Yids! We gotta get ridda the Yids!"

"You cheeky little cow!" Slesser shouted above the din, quivering with passion.

Immediately the youth at her side rose and shouted in reply, "You call my girl a cow again and I'll knock your Yiddish block off!" but not with very much conviction.

"Easy now, easy!" interrupted the man at the table, thrusting himself between Slesser and the youth. "If I were you," he said to Slesser, in lowered tone, "I'd clear off out. They think you're a Jew."

"A Jew!" Slesser gasped. "A Jew! But I'm not a Jew!"

"No, but they *think* you are. You've got a bit of a hooked nose, if you don't mind me saying so."

"Well — can't a man have a hooked nose without being a Jew?" he demanded angrily.

"Not in this district, apparently," retorted the other. "You'd better go. We'll all be mixed up in the trouble if any starts. See what I mean?"

"Ah, I see!" said Slesser, rubbing at his nose.

The chap was undoubtedly right. It wasn't fair of him to stay there just out of pride, and perhaps cause a row with those young fascists. But what silly little swine they were he thought contemptuously, eyeing them each in turn. Thinking he was a Jew just because his nose wasn't straight!

Conscious that all eyes were on him, wondering what he would do, Slesser bent to the man. "All right, chum," he said. "I'll be off. I was going soon anyway. Don't think I'm afraid of these young whelps, though. I'd soon sort the rats out if they started anything, by Christ I would!"

He glared round at them with challenging eyes, a pugnacious expression on his lined, sallow face. They flinched before his gaze and looked away, except the girl, who gave a mocking, sneering laugh, showing her strong broad teeth edged with her curved red lips.

"Have you got the time on you?" Slesser asked the man at last.

"No, chum, but it must be getting on for nine —"

"Nine! As late as that! It'll be ha' past ten by the time I get home. So long, Comrade!"

"So long," said the other.

At the café door Slesser glanced back over his shoulder. The dark-haired girl and the youth were watching him with smouldering eyes. Little fools, he thought contemptuously, and banged the door, shutting in the blaring wireless.

2

The huge, discreetly-lighted lounge of the Eagle Tavern stank of stale beer and nicotine, but it was quiet and restful after the din and glare of the funfair and the rush of traffic in the streets. They chose a dark, shadowy corner opposite the bar and flopped heavily on a leather settee, suddenly aching with tiredness. Except for themselves, the lounge was empty of customers; the waitress and the barmaid stood chattering together about some film in low, subdued voices that disturbed the restful peace of the lounge.

"Oh," Elsie whispered. "My poor feet!"

"And mine," Bert replied, rubbing his brow with a handkerchief. "We must have walked miles today. What I need is a good hot bath — and I'll have one when I get home."

The waitress broke off her chatter and came across to them, her face pleasantly inquisitive. "What'll you have?" she asked Bert.

He looked at Elsie. "A port?" he asked. "Or would you like a whisky?"

"A port, please. Whisky would kill me."

He gave the order and they lay back smoking, waiting for the drinks.

"It's nice in here," said Elsie, looking round the room with its oak beams, shaded lights, flowers, and comfortable chairs. "Have you been here before?"

"Once or twice. It's about the best place I know, but it gets a bit noisy later on, when it fills up — when the cinemas turn out."

"You don't drink much, do you?"

"No, not much. Why?" He glanced at her quickly, half surprised at her question.

"I thought you didn't," she said knowingly, as the waitress placed the drinks on the table.

When she had gone, Bert asked, "Would it matter if I did?"

Elsie laughed gently. "Of course not, silly!"

"Well, I don't, except on special occasions like this."

"Is this a special occasion?"

"A *very* special occasion. Here you are."

He gave her the port and shot soda water in his own glass with a clumsiness which told of unfamiliarity.

"Here's to you," he said, chinking her glass, "and a very special occasion."

She smiled slowly, but made no remark until she had sipped at her drink. "How is it special?" she asked, a little coyly.

"Meeting you," Bert said, embracing her. "You might not believe it, but I haven't been out with a girl for over a year, and as for spending most of the day with one —" He laughed bitterly for a moment. "It's my job. When you're working on different shifts it doesn't give you much time to make arrangements to meet anybody. The money's all right, but it doesn't make up for what you lose in other directions. Take this last month, for example. One week I had to be up at four o'clock to be at the garage at five; the next I didn't start until about ten; and next week I'm not on till five o'clock at night. So you see how it is," he ended gloomily, and drank some more of the whisky.

"But how do you go in for meals? Do you get them yourself?"

"Sometimes. It depends how I feel. But not dinners, though," he added with a laugh. "They get me down. Can you cook?"

"Why, of course I can cook! I might be a bit out of practice now, but I used to be able to."

"Then what about coming to my place next week and giving me a hand, eh?" he suggested. "What about it?"

"Well, I would, but what would your landlady think? I mean, you know what they are," said Elsie. "They talk."

"Ah, but I haven't got a landlady. I've got a flat of my own and my own furniture," he said proudly. "I can do what I like without having anybody snooping around. I've had my fill of landladies and bed-sitting-rooms — ugh! You can't call your soul your own. Well, are you going to come to my place — or daren't you?"

"Of course. Of course I dare!" Elsie protested. "I didn't really care about landladies — I was thinking of you getting into trouble, that's all."

"Splendid! I hoped you would, but I didn't know what you might think —"

He broke off hurriedly as the main door opened to admit a stocky, bald-headed man smoking a fat cigar. He glanced round the lounge, shrugged his fat shoulders, and let himself out again without a word.

"That must be the owner," Bert said. "See how the waitress pretended to be busy? Ha! Ha! Ha!" He beckoned to her to fill their glasses and then fell silent, thinking of Elsie, a thoughtful frown on his forehead as he stared with absent eyes at the table top.

Presently, nudging him, Elsie said, "You're very quiet,

Bert. What are you thinking about? The march?"

"No, not the march." He drank off the newly filled glass. "No, I was thinking of you coming round to my flat... It'll be strange having a girl there..." In a sudden burst of confidence, he added, "You know, I get so damned lonely on my own. It's no joke coming home from work and having to start washing up and so on, and then having no one to talk to."

"I know what it's like," Elsie said sympathetically, nodding. She stubbed her cigarette in the ashtray. "I've had some."

"You've been worse off than me, though, haven't you? Maybe I shouldn't grumble."

"Perhaps I have... Yes, I suppose I have. But I hate myself for this morning. I had half a mind to really jump in the river after that girl did —"

"We all get like that sometimes," Bert consoled her. "Don't you worry, Elsie. I've thought of it myself before today, when I was down to my last coppers, but I've never had the guts to carry it through. Still," he added briskly, "don't let's talk about that. Let's drink and be merry, and to hell with worry! Come on, drink up and let's have some more."

They drained their glasses and the waitress came over with her tray, her eyebrows arched enquiringly.

"Same again, only doubles this time," Bert ordered. "It'll save you a journey or two."

"Thanks," said the waitress, leaving with empty glasses.

"Lend me your comb," Elsie whispered. "My hair's awful. I know by the way that waitress looked at it."

"Your hair's lovely," Bert said, giving her the comb. "What's wrong with it?"

"Everything, but you wouldn't notice. Men never do."

Elsie tidied her hair as best she could without the aid of a mirror. Bert sat back so that her elbows were free to move, and watched her, thinking curiously of her being pulled out of the river, her hair wet and stringy, her face pale, her clothes soggy with mud, and the water pouring from her mouth. She felt him shudder when she gave him back the comb.

"What's the matter?" she asked, looking at his bare throat. "Are you cold?"

"No, I was just thinking —"

"But you shivered," she persisted. "What was it?"

He wouldn't tell her. "Here's the drinks," he said, as the waitress arrived.

"You'll have me drunk," said Elsie, picking up her port, "and then I shan't get a room at a YWCA."

"You'll be all right. Besides, what does it matter?" He drank half of the whisky in a single gulp, forgetting the soda water. It burned his throat and felt like a fire in his stomach; but soon a warm pleasant glow stole through his limbs. "Good stuff, this," he said, smacking his lips. "You ought to try some next time. It makes you feel grand."

"I feel grand now," she said softly. "I feel — oh, it's hard to explain what I feel!... Why did you speak to me on the bus, Bert?"

He shook his head and drank some more of the whisky. "You're not sorry I did, are you?" he asked in a tone of banter.

"Of course not."

She laughed, put down her glass, and drew closer to him. "You know I'm not," she said, in a whisper.

He looked at her steadily, at her firm dark eyes and moist, half-parted lips, curved in a smile. Her body was warm against his own. She touched his hand and smiled at him, gently, gratefully. The blood hammered at his temples. Setting his glass on the table, he threw a swift glance at the chattering women at the bar, and then bent and kissed her on the lips.

Laughing self-consciously, they broke apart when the door opened to admit a noisy party of men and girls who swarmed into the lounge, laughing and chattering and gesticulating together as if already drunk.

"Damn!..." Bert muttered. "They would!..."

Elsie squeezed his hand. "They didn't see us," she said happily. "Besides, what does it matter? I don't care. I'm glad you kissed me."

"So am I," he said. "So am I —" His voice trailed off, and picking up his glass he drank hurriedly. "Drink up and let's have another."

The waitress was busy serving the newcomers who were still talking noisily in raucous tones, the girls laughing hysterically when the men cracked a joke. But presently she noticed Bert's beckoning finger and came with her tray.

"Have you any cocktails?" he asked. "Good ones?"

"We make up some of our own, if you would like to try them. They're good. Two shillings each."

She flashed Elsie a rapid glance, and added, "They've got a kick in them, I can tell you."

"Then we'll have two of those; two with kicks in," Bert replied, grinning.

"Cocktails," Elsie whispered. "I've never had a cocktail. What're they like?"

"All right. They make you feel irresponsible —"

"But two shillings each —"

"What of it? This is a special occasion. And don't forget we won ten bobs' worth of fags tonight," Bert said, patting his bulging pockets. "That'll pay for the drinks indirectly. In any case it doesn't matter. Why shouldn't we have something good for a change, like those folks with all the money? They have their good times, why shouldn't we?"

His speech was blurred, his tone resentful. "That's where Ginger's right, you know," he went on unsteadily. "You know, the chap we met in that café — the Red —"

"Oh, yes," Elsie interrupted. "I know. There's something I wanted to ask him, but I daren't."

"What?" Bert demanded, suspiciously jealous and hostile.

"Maybe you know. Who's Karl Marx?"

"Ah! Karl Marx!" He was relieved. "That's the chap that

had something to do with the Russian revolution. I've heard Ginger talk about him before. He was a Jew with a big beard. I've seen his photo somewhere —"

"Here you are, sir," interrupted the waitress, returning with the cocktails in big thin glasses. "See what you think of these."

Bert sipped carefully at the dark red liquid in which the ice floated, clinking on the glass. "Lovely!" He smacked his lips.

Feeling generous, he tipped the waitress sixpence and turned to Elsie. "Here's health." They drank deeply, unaware of the liquid's potency.

"Well, what do you think of it?" Bert enquired. "Pretty good stuff, eh?"

"It's grand, lovely!"

"So are you," he whispered, suddenly drawing close to her. "You're lovely, too." His arm went round her.

"Oh, Bert!... I'm not, not really!..." she cried, but there was pleasure in her voice.

"You are. You're a grand girl," he said, boldly kissing her cheek. "You're my girl now," he added. "Aren't you?" he insisted. "Aren't you?"

"Yes, Bert," she said, her voice so low that he could barely hear. Then, "Oh, Bert, you do like me, don't you? You're not just fooling? I couldn't bear it."

"Like you?" he repeated thickly, setting his glass down. "Why should I pretend about you? I wouldn't say it if I didn't mean it. I'm not that sort."

"I know you're not," Elsie answered, impulsively kissing his cheek. "I'm sorry I said it. I didn't mean to offend you, Bert."

"I know you didn't. Forget it, Elsie." Blissfully happy, they strained together, their eyes unnaturally bright, the blood hot and surging in their veins, each oblivious to the lounge which, filling with customers, grew more noisy, more heated as the minutes passed. They talked in low, sometimes incoherent tones, about the fascist march, the luck that had brought them together, the suicide, the old

172

woman and Lady Stroud; and then followed an almost painful silence, caused by a glance at the remorselessly ticking clock and the quick realisation that soon they would have to leave.

"Oh, God!" Bert groaned suddenly. "Let's go, Elsie. It's no use putting it off."

He rose, staggered a little and clutched at the table for support. Elsie, forcing a laugh, said, "Yes, that's how I feel, too."

Bert leading, they pushed their way through the tables and down the stairs to the street. For a while they loitered undecidedly on the pavement, inhaling the cool night air, which after the heat and smoke of the lounge tasted like nectar. Their heads began to clear; they felt physically better when they moved away arm in arm.

They had gone only a few yards when he suddenly pulled her into the darkness of an alley and kissed her passionately. After a time, she said, "Bert, I don't want to leave you, but I suppose I must... it's awful..."

"I know, Elsie, I know."

He stopped, drew a deep breath to gain courage. Then he began gruffly, "Look here, Elsie. You don't have to go... you needn't..." He kissed her again, nervously. "Darling, come back with me. Will you come back with me?"

"To your flat?" she whispered.

"Yes, to my flat. Will you?"

She clung to him. "Of course, darling. Of course I will. You should have asked me before."

3

It was just on nine o'clock when Harold Thurgood reached the block of modern flats off Park Lane where Lady Stroud lived. He went up in the lift to the fifth floor, found her number and rang, wondering what she would be wearing tonight. Green, red, white, blue — perhaps black? She looked well in black. It showed off her white

173

skin, emphasised her shapely limbs — The door opened quickly. Lady Stroud herself stood smiling there.

"So you have come," she said gently, widening the door. "How nice of you."

"It is my pleasure," he said gallantly, thinking how lovely she was, how charming, how perfect. "I have come to apologise," he said mockingly.

"But you don't know what about, do you?" she suggested, arching her brows.

"No, you'll have to tell me."

"Later."

He laughed, took off his hat and coat, flung them on a stand in the hall and followed her into the drawing room. He hardly glanced at the furnishings — his eyes were only for her. She had on a gown of shimmering green which he had not seen her wearing before. It was cut so low in front that the upper part of her round, shapely breasts were open to his inspection. Her beautiful shoulders were bare, and lightly powdered, the left one lifted a trifle above the level of the other, and leaning forward seductively. Around her throat was a necklace of pearls which he mistakenly thought must be real. When she turned to pour him a drink he saw that her slender back was naked almost to the waist. His self control began to waver. The scent from her rose in his nostrils, acting like wine. His hand, when he took the proffered glass, was visibly unsteady.

Helen Stroud appeared not to notice the effect she was having on him. She motioned him to sit on a divan in the centre of the room, well out of reach of an electric fire, and remarked casually, "I had the most frightful experience on my way home today, Harold. Simply frightful!"

"Really?"

"Yes." She patted a cushion. "Do come and sit by me, Harold."

He moved up, nothing loth to be nearer, and listened attentively while she recounted the incident of the stone flung at her car by the woman in black.

"It might easily have scarred me for life," she said petulantly.

"Dreadful!" Thurgood consoled her. "I wonder I didn't see it happen. I was on duty at Leman Street all the afternoon. Of course," he added, "the trouble with these people is that they have had too much of their own way."

"Now that is really remarkable," Lady Stroud cried. "Three, or perhaps four times today someone has remarked to me that something ought to be done to stop this communist nonsense. What we need in England is a strong man at the top, someone like Hitler, to keep these people in order —" She broke off, smiled apologetically. "I'm so sorry, Harold. You must be bored stiff with politics after today. It's too bad of me, really."

"Oh, but if you want to talk politics —"

"No, no! Let me get you another drink, Harold. There are lots of more interesting things to talk about than politics."

Her smile entranced him. She rose and filled his glass, while he watched her admiringly. Never, he thought, had she looked so desirable. Every inch of her figure was a provocation. When she gave him the glass she bent low over him, her lips curved amorously, her pale grey eyes twinkling with excitement. He saw for the first time that her nipples showed plainly through the thin fabric of her gown, and was momentarily tempted to touch them. But he mustn't be too hasty, he told himself, accepting the glass.

Seating herself again, she stretched out her elegantly stockinged legs and remarked, "Shall I ring down for supper now, Harold?"

"Oh, not just yet," he said. "Hadn't you better tell me first what I'm supposed to apologise for?"

"Oh — that!" She laughed and watched him through half veiled eyes. "It is rather difficult to know how to begin, you know."

He edged a little closer until their knees touched. Her perfume stirred his senses. It was only by an effort of will that he did not embrace her immediately.

"That's better," she said, lying back on the cushions. "I hate men who keep their distance." She laughed provocatively. "Are you quite sure that you don't remember what you said last night?"

"Not very sure, you know. But I hope I didn't offend you?"

"No, no, of course not. You said some very charming things — I was thrilled. But I wonder if you meant them?" she asked dreamily, and sighed.

"You must tell me what I said before I can answer that."

"I'm not sure that I want to. After all, you were rather drunk."

"I'm not used to drink," Thurgood said in self-defence.

She reached foward and placed her glass on a table. "That's one thing you said last night, Harold."

"Well, that was true enough."

He felt more at ease with her now, more sure of himself. He was enjoying this pleasant banter. It was leading to something — but to what he was not quite certain yet.

She lay back again on the cushion, folded her hands behind her head and stared up at the ceiling." And you also said you would like to kiss me," she murmured. "Did you mean that, too?"

His heart leapt within him. There was no doubting now. He seized her in his arms, felt her own slide slowly round his neck and pull him passionately closer. For a moment he stared into her pale grey eyes; they were egging him on, sending the blood surging through his veins, hot and compelling. She gave a faint, ecstatic sigh, closed her eyes, and returned his kisses with fierce ardour.

After a time she pushed him away, gasping for breath.

"Really, Harold! You're crushing me to death," she panted happily, smoothing her hair.

He kissed her smooth, warm shoulders and felt the flesh quiver at the touch of his lips.

"Really!" she cried again. "You're adorable... but you really mustn't."

"Why not?" Thurgood asked. "Don't you want me to?"

"You haven't heard all — all you said last night, you know."

"Well — tell me."

"You might not have meant it."

"I seem to have meant the bit about wanting to kiss you," he reminded her with a short, nervous laugh.

"Yes, but this is different — very different."

She turned her head away from him and continued in a whisper. "You said you loved me."

Thurgood drew a deep breath, braced himself, slipped both arms round her and pulled her back on the cushions.

"Well," he said unsteadily. "I do."

"Oh, Harold!" She turned swiftly. "Are you serious?"

"Well, tonight I left home for your sake."

"For my sake? But how? Why?"

"My mother objected to my seeing you: she always has done. We quarrelled and she ordered me out of the house; just before I came here."

"And did you really leave?"

"Yes, I left."

"But why? Why did you quarrel? Doesn't she like me?"

"She thinks that — well, that you're —" He broke off, afraid of offending her now, wishing he hadn't said a word about the matter. He couldn't very well say: Because you're an old widow. No, that would never do. Suddenly inspired, he said, "You have a title."

"How silly!" There was relief in her laugh.

"Yes, isn't it?"

"Well, I can't do much about it, can I, darling?"

"No, of course not."

She pondered a moment, looking past him at the fire. "You're not going to let it worry you, are you?"

"No, not in the least. It was time I moved."

She laughed and dropped back into his ready arms.

"Love me," she whispered. "Love me, Harold, darling."

They lay locked in a passionate embrace, kissing constantly, their desire increasing. His free hand explored, at first cautiously, later boldly, the smooth softness of her upper limbs. She clung to him fiercely her gasping breath on his cheeks, her heart wildly pulsing beneath the gown. Presently he picked her up and carried her out of the drawing room to the room beyond.

Chapter XI

SLESSER elbowed his way through the crush that still blocked the East End streets. He had only a vague idea where he was. He had lived in London since he was born, but this was an alien world where even the trams were unfamiliar; noisy clattering giants lurching to unknown destinations with their cargo of tired humans. There were no prominent landmarks to guide him; there were no passing buses whose destination boards might give him a clue. Three times since leaving the café, he had stopped passers-by, and each time he had been given fruitless directions. He wanted very little — a bus or a tram to take him to Tower Bridge, from where he could get a tram home; but that conveyance he could not discover in this alien world.

He went past a cinema ablaze with multi-coloured lights which flickered on and off monotonously, He read the sign, in green, and red, and orange:

**ALL NEXT WEEK SALLY SELBY IN
'HER KISSES WERE REAL.'
STUPENDOUS ATTRACTION.
YOU MUST SEE HER
'HER KISSES WERE REAL'**

Why shouldn't they be real? he wondered. How can kisses be artificial? That's what I'd like to know. Silly title. He repeated it. Her kisses were real; her kisses were real. Kissing, kissing, kissing — that's all they seem to think about nowadays, the bloody fools! When I was a kid I had to work, not lounge about in cinemas, kissing and cuddling in the dark. *Or* cafés, he added to himself, remembering the insolent girl. Fancy calling me a Jew — a Yid! Me! Cheeky little bitch!...

179

Slesser halted at a crossroads where the buses sped along in the streams of winding traffic. He stood anxiously watching them roar past, examining their indicator blinds, but none was going his way apparently. Damn it! he thought. He would never get home at this rate. He was late enough in all conscience...

In gathering despair he turned about, intending to ask a passer-by again for explicit directions. And then he saw the girl who had mocked him in the café standing only a bare few feet away, a revengeful glare in her bold, dark insolent eyes. Her glance was furious, burning him; but it was not that which caused an apprehensive shiver to run down his spine. It was the two hulking men who were with her in addition to her youthful companion. They were obviously thugs, obviously trailing him, waiting to get him in a side street to have their revenge for what had happened in the café. He knew instinctively that they were all fascists — and they thought that he was a Jew.

Often he had read of the East End terror that the fascists waged nightly against the Jews, attacking them in side streets, smashing their shops, hurling bricks through the windows of their homes, and beating them up whenever they could. Now they were after him; perhaps they had bottles and knuckle dusters tucked out of sight in their pockets. It was three to one — four to one with the girl — he couldn't fight them all. For a moment he had a wild impulse to run as these thoughts speeded through his brain; then calmer reason prevailed. Let them start, that was all...

Pretending indifference, Slesser turned and walked rapidly across the road, dodging the traffic, and reached the opposite pavement, hoping to find a policeman. There was none in sight; there was not even, so far as he could see, a single supporter to whom he might have appealed for aid. He felt utterly alone in a world of enemies.

Struggling to quell his rapidly rising fears, he glanced round. The four had followed him and were watching him as a cat does a mouse before the panther-like spring that seals its doom. He quickened his pace, heading he knew not where, except that this was a main thoroughfare, liberally scattered with people whose presence afforded protection. They wouldn't dare attack him with so many people about, he thought; but doubtfully. You couldn't tell what these fascists thugs would do. They hit and ran. Oh, yes, he knew they hit and ran. One of the chaps that worked on the council had been hit on the head in the middle of Trafalgar Square by just such a gang as these. And none of them, he recollected, had ever been caught for it. They had hit and run. These at his back — he wouldn't care if they were facing him, but when they just followed, silent and grim, you never knew just when...

He glanced round again, without stopping his hasty walk, and saw they were nearer now, only half a dozen yards behind him. Damn it! he thought. Why should he run? and stopped, pretending to look into a confectioner's shop.

Glancing sideways he saw that they had stopped, too, and were looking in a shop nearby. Waiting for me to go on, he thought. They mean business. Tugging nervously at his cap, he went on, and again an apprehensive shiver assailed his spine.

A few yards ahead a bus slid gently to a halt. Slesser suddenly ran, swung aboard it, and raced up the steps to the top deck. Through the tobacco-blue haze he saw a vacant seat in the middle, and dropped into it, sighing with relief. Safe, he thought. They can't do anything now. I've dodged them. But he was wrong. Just as the bus was jerking off they came up the steps, trooped past him without a glance, and seated themselves up in front. His heart missed a beat; then it raced away again, painfully. He had half a mind to get off. He felt afraid. He half rose to do so before he realised the bus was travelling at speed. He sank back in his seat, agitatedly lit a cigarette and watched the fascists in front. Well, if they did start anything...

The conductor came up the steps for the fares; and as if

in a dream Slesser gave the man fourpence — all the coppers that he had in his pocket — without a thought as to where he was going. Only when the conductor had passed on to the people in front did it occur to him to glance at the ticket. Good God! He stared at it unbelievably. It would take him to Oxford Circus — three miles at least from where he wanted to be! Three miles! He turned the ticket over, hoping it was wrong. No, he was heading for Oxford Circus on route No. 8.

"Well, of all the —," he muttered savagely, cursing himself for his folly. Now he would have to walk from Oxford Circus to the south side of the river, for he hadn't another copper. And all because... He almost choked with rage — rage at the fascists in front, and glared at them, as if to scorch the clothes from their backs with his burning gaze. They were getting their tickets. He watched, wondering.... Yes, they were getting fourpenny tickets... then they were following him! They did intend to beat him up! He knew it! He was absolutely convinced of it now. Well, they'd have a nice long journey for nothing, he told himself grimly, for as soon as he got off the bus he would call a policeman and hand them in charge. For what he hadn't decided.

As the bus rattled on Slesser smoked furiously, watching the fascists furtively from under his cap. But they never turned; they seemed not to know he was there. They talked among themselves, sometimes laughing as if at a joke, but paid him no attention whatever. Which surprised him. Surely, if they were determined to follow him, they would keep glancing round to make sure he was still on the bus? Doubt seized him. Perhaps they weren't following him at all? Perhaps he had just imagined that they were, had suddenly got the wind up?... Indeed, why shouldn't they be journeying to Oxford Circus, the same as many of the other passengers? The more he thought of it the more he was convinced that he had acted like a fool. It was his nerves, he told himself. He was exhausted after that tiring day, after the fighting and the long march, and

182

was imagining things, thinking all who looked at him were enemies.

Blockhead! And now he would have to pay for that folly by walking three miles from Oxford Circus, when he could have ridden the whole way home from Tower Bridge. Fool that he was! He told himself bitterly. He was always doing stupid things, just like a damned old woman.

The bus reached the Bank of England, picked up some passengers, and sped on its way. Slesser, settling lower in the seat, closed his smarting eyes and reflected on the day's events. Yes, it had been an exciting day, a tiring day, too, but one of the best in his life. Easily the best. And who would have thought that, this morning, he would go to the demonstration and do all the incredible things that he had done? It just showed; you never knew what life held for you. Why, this bus might get in a smash and he might be killed, it was all so easy. Things happened on you unawares. Life was a funny business all right. Something always happened to keep you on the go, alive. Like those crowds this afternoon — something always happened just when things were getting dull. There would be a fight between a man and a policeman, and then it would grow to a battle in the twinkling of an eye, and you would find yourself in the middle of it whether you wanted to be or not, like — like? —The simile evaded him.

"Tottenham Court Road!" the conductor shouted, obviously proud of his sergeant major's lungs. "Any more for Tottenham Court Road?"

Not far now, Slesser thought, and then for that three mile walk. Oh, well. He'd be home in an hour if he stepped out. Still, it was a pretty stupid thing to do, getting the wind up like that. He glanced at the fascists; they seemed unaware of him. They had just chanced to get on the same bus as himself. Blockhead that he was!

Just past Wardour Street, Slesser rose and went stiffly below, intending to drop off the bus before it reached

Oxford Circus.

"Steady, mate!" the conductor warned, blocking his path. "There's a car behind. Wait till the bus pulls in."

"That's all right, mate," Slesser said. "I'm not getting off just yet."

"That's different." The conductor stepped aside, was silent for a moment, and then asked, "I'll bet you can't answer this one, mate: how much string will it take to go round the dome of Saint Paul's?"

"What?" Slesser asked unguardedly. "How much string? —"

"To go round the dome of Saint Paul's?"

"Dunno; how much?" he asked wonderingly, completely falling into the trap.

"Balls," said the conductor impassively.

"Ah!..." said Slesser, and laughed his sudden, barking laugh. "That's a good one, that is. Ha! Ha! Ha! Balls!"

Still chuckling, he dropped off the bus and walked on to the Circus. He would have to remember that one. How much string? — Ha! Ha! He'd catch somebody down at the dole with that all right. Ha! Ha! Ha!

"Laugh away, Yid!" said a menacing voice, just behind him.

Still with the smile on his lips, Slesser swerved round. The smile vanished; cold fear clutched at his heart. Facing him were the four fascists, their fists lifted ready to deliver blows. Without a moment's thought he lashed out, struck one in the face, turned, and ran wildly down a street on his left.

It was Argyle Street, which led through to Regent Street, cutting off Oxford Circus, and there wasn't a soul in sight between the tall blocks of offices which flanked the narrow road. Footsteps clattered behind him. He heard them rapidly gain, knew he was lost, and half turned to put up a fight when a blow knocked him flat on his stomach. Unable to check themselves, his aggressors tripped over his prostrate body and sprawled in the road in a writhing heap. He sprang up, gasping for breath, but mad now for battle. Kicking out, he heard a sharp yelp of pain, and backed swiftly into a doorway. They were on him instantly, curiously silent, their faces as mad as his own in the yellow light from the lamps. Only two at a time could get at him, and the first to come within the range of his fists went sprawling back into the road. Then blows rained on him in a fury. He struck out without thought, without precision, momentarily driving them back by his tiger-like ferocity.

Through a red haze he saw the girl rush forward, shouting, "Yid! Yid!" Without compunction he struck her hard in her red open mouth, and gloated over her thin, wild scream. Then he was down, beaten to his knees, and they were on him, kicking and pounding and tearing like wolves at a carcass. But he fought back, almost crying with pain and rage, and struggled once again to his feet, the blood salt and sticky in his gasping mouth.

He heard dimly a swift rush of feet in the road; powerful arms were thrust round his staggering body. He kicked out and butted with his capless head in a frenzy of despair. The grip relaxed; he tore himself free and ran on tottering legs down the street, somebody hard on his heels. Through that red haze before his eyes he saw a blue-clad, helmeted figure dart in his path. The police! Thank God! he thought, and stopped, to be seized again in a pair of powerful arms.

"You're under arrest!" snarled a voice, followed by a punch in the ribs from the man behind.

"Arrest!" Slesser gasped. "Arrest?"

"That's what I said. Come quietly or —"

"But I've done nothing," he protested wildly. "Those four fascists set on me —"

"Save your excuses," said another curt voice. "You're not in court — yet."

The two policemen dragged him along. They had almost to carry him, his legs were so weakened with exertion. He couldn't understand it; they had made a mistake. They must have done! The mist before his eyes cleared and he saw now that the street was filling with spectators. He saw, too, that other policemen were marching off the four fascists. The girl was still struggling, and screaming and sobbing alternately in a high-pitched, jarring tone. Her three companions were going quietly, apparently as tired as himself. He felt proud; he had given them as good as they had given him in that two minute battle. There was nothing to be afraid of now. When the police had heard his story they would have to let him go; but those others would have to be charged.

Followed by a staring crowd, Slesser and the others were hauled along to a grim red building with a blue light suspended above its open door. He went confidently up the steps, down a short, narrow passage, and then into a big cold room. Blinking in the glaring light he saw a long, deep counter, numerous files, piles of stationery, a typewriter, a wastepaper basket, two hard chairs and a telephone. Behind the counter stood a tall, helmetless policeman idly chewing a pen.

"Hullo! What's all this?" he asked, eyeing the captives and their escort in mild surprise.

"Disorderly conduct and resisting arrest," replied the policeman holding Slesser.

"I didn't resist arrest!" Slesser butted in, anxious to clear himself immediately. "It was these four fascists — they set on me as I got off the bus —"

"He's a liar," growled a fascist, glaring at Slesser.

The policeman with the pen still in his mouth raised his hands for silence. "All right, all right," he said soothingly. "You needn't get excited. Nobody's charged you with anything yet — either of you."

"It's like this," Slesser began desperately. "These four —"

"Take him inside!" snapped the policeman with the pen. "We'll deal with him later."

Still protesting, Slesser was seized by the arms and rushed hastily through to an inner room. "Wait there till you're called," said a policeman, and slammed the door.

For a moment Slesser had a wild impulse to fling himself at the panels, to beat his way through them to freedom. He wasn't guilty! He hadn't done anything, anything... Weakly, he sat down on a bench near the door and dropped his head on his hands. This was a fine thing, he thought desperately, rocking to and fro on the bench. To be accused of something you hadn't done and then be pushed in here like this!

Footsteps sounded outside the door. Slesser sat up expectantly. In came the girl fascist, sullen and resentful, followed by her three companions. They trooped past him without words and seated themselves on the bench at the far side of the room. The door closed again with a bang.

There was an utter silence in which the fascists glared across at Slesser, who glared back, his lower lip thrust out aggressively. Then one of the fascists growled through a bleeding mouth, "Just wait till we get you outside, Jew boy! Just wait! You'll pay for this!"

"Why, do you want another hiding?" Slesser challenged, half-rising to his feet.

"Just wait, that's all," said another, whose left eye was rapidly closing.

"You'd better bring some of your pals along," Slesser taunted them, "or you might have to go into hospital next time!"

"Aw! Shut up, you two!" said the girl, through her cracked lips. "It won't do any good. Leave the blasted Yid alone."

"That's right," said the youth. "Say nothing." He lowered his voice to a whisper. "Our story's this, see?" he went on cunningly. "This bloody Jew boy set about us an' we chased him to try an' arrest him."

"That's a bloody lie!" Slesser stormed, rising angrily to his feet. "You set about me —"

The door swung violently open. In came a burly policemen. "Hey! What's going on in 'ere?" he growled heavily, glaring at each in turn. "You sit down," he said, giving Slesser a push. "All of you keep quiet or it'll be the worse for you, see?"

They all obeyed instantly, but before going out, not trusting them, the policeman propped open the door so that they could all be seen from the office beyond. "Let's 'ave no more of your lip," he said, as a final warning. "Or —"

Slesser watched his thick broad shoulders vanish from his field of vision. No, no more row, he thought wearily, and settled down resignedly to wait. After a time, still sitting, with his head dropped low on his chest, he sank in exhausted sleep.

2

"These stairs are dark, aren't they?" Bert said apologetically, as Elsie panted after him to the top of the silent house. "But we're nearly there, Elsie."

After the ride home on the bus, with the cold night breeze blowing in through the open windows, he was nearly sober again. But his mouth was dry, his eyes hot and tired, and he was nervous, troubled now about Elsie. He doubted whether she really wanted to come back with him, to stay with him, or whether she had come out of a sense of indebtedness because he had bought her food, spent the day with her, and given her a 'good time.' That would be horrible. He didn't want that. He wanted her to stay of her own free will, not out of any sense of obligation, in payment for what he had done for her. As he fumbled with the key he wondered what she was thinking, standing so motionless in the half darkness of the landing, one hand holding her coat across her throat as if she were cold. Perhaps longing to go back on her word. Perhaps afraid. Perhaps just nervous like himself.

The lock turned at last. Bert switched on the light and with an effort made his voice sound cheerful when he said, "Here we are, Elsie girl!" and beckoned her into the room. She stepped past him, avoiding his eyes, and stared slowly about her.

"This is the living room," he explained. "The kitchen's through that door opposite."

He left her side and went to the window and drew the curtains, shutting out the night.

The room, Elsie noted, was just as he had described it coming here on the bus. A lino-covered floor with a black woolly rug at the hearth; a gas fire; a cushioned sofa under the window; two easy chairs with flowered print covers; three hard chairs round a polished table; a mahogany chest of drawers and a bookcase half-filled with an assortment of second-hand volumes picked up in Charing Cross Road.

"I like it very much," she said, when Bert turned from the window, his eyebrows raised inquisitively.

"It's not bad, is it?" he agreed, with a touch of pride. "It took me a long time to get it together, but it was worth it. The only snag about the flat, really, is that you have to go out on the landing to get to the bedroom and bathroom."

"Oh, have you?" she inquired disconcertingly.

"Er — yes... Well, I suppose I'd better light the fire — it's a bit cold in here."

Bert searched his pockets for matches and encountered the cigarettes they had won at the funfair. He pulled them out, packet after packet, and stacked them on the mantelpiece in a neat, high pile. "It's the first time I've ever had so many fags at once in all my life," he remarked. "Thanks to *you,* Elsie."

Elsie smiled but said nothing, watching him a little shyly as he stooped before the gas fire.

"I don't know how you managed it," Bert went on, striking a match. "Do you?"

"I don't. Unless it's because this happens to be my lucky day."

"And mine."

Bert stood up. The gas, hissing cheerfully, reddened the white radiants. "Now, Elsie, if you'll take off your coat," he suggested, "and sit here and have a rest —"

"But my dress!" she interrupted hastily. "It's not fit to be seen —"

"All right," he said. "Keep it on if you feel shy. But let's sit down by the fire, shall we?"

She sat on his knee, an arm round his neck, staring at the fire, a thoughtful little frown between her eyes. He was dismayed at her silence. He kissed her lips, but she hardly responded; she seemed suddenly cold, lifeless, perhaps afraid of him.

"Look here, Elsie girl," he said nervously. "Are you sorry you came back with me?"

"Sorry? No, of course not."

He remained unconvinced. Unsteadily he said, "You — you needn't stay here if you don't want to, you know. There's still time to get a room —"

He felt her stiffen in his arms. He held his breath, waiting anxiously for her answer, fearing it intensely. At last she said, "Why did you say that? Don't you want me to stay?"

"Want you to! Oh, God, if you knew how much!"

"If you meant what you said before," she said, kissing him lightly on the cheek, "then I want to stay more than anything else in the world."

"Yes, yes, I meant it. I mean it now," he reassured her. "I'm in love with you, really I am. I've only known you a day but — look here, will you marry me, Elsie?"

"I don't know," she said, after a thoughtful pause. "Are you sure a day's long enough? It isn't very long, you know, is it? I mean, you'd better not make a mistake."

"Long enough? Of course — for me, anyway. Why, it's twelve hours, and that's equal to four or five meetings in the usual way, and — but hell! Of course I've known you long enough," he said, hugging her.

She touched his cheek with her fingers, and he, suddenly sure and masterful, said, "You're going to marry me," and kissed her. This time she responded to his kisses with rising passion. Then, breaking away, she said, "All right, then."

"You will marry me?"

"Yes."

"Right!" His eyes shone with happiness. "Now let's have some supper, shall we?"

"I couldn't eat anything, Bert. But a cup of tea would be nice."

"That's all I want, too. I'll make you some."

"Let me help."

"No, I can manage."

"But I want to help," she pouted happily.

"No, you get a bath while I make the tea. How about that?"

"A bath? I'd love one! But oh, Bert —" She blushed. "Don't forget you'll have to lend me something to wear."

"Oh, that's all right, Elsie. You can have a pair of my pyjamas. Come, I'll show you the bathroom."

He led her into the small, somewhat over-furnished bedroom across the landing. Near the window was the large double bed, in a corner a tall wardrobe, at the opposite wall a dressing table with a small swing mirror. A faint smell of cigarette smoke clung to the room but it was scrupulously clean and tidy.

"That's the bathroom," Bert informed her, indicating an inner door. "I think you'll find everything you need — except bath salts!"

Grinning, he gave her a pair of pyjamas from a drawer in the front of the wardrobe. "These should fit you, I think. They're heaps too small for me."

"Thanks," Elsie said, measuring the pyjamas against her body. "Yes, they'll fit me all right."

She followed him into the bathroom, where he explained the simple gadgets that worked the geyser, and then, having kissed her once more, left her and lit the bedroom fire, drew the curtains, turned back the bedclothes and, having listened a moment to the sounds of running water from the bathroom, returned to the living room.

While waiting for the kettle to boil he prepared the

teapot and the cups. Now how much sugar did she take? he wondered. One? Two? Three? No, two — like himself, he recollected. *What a girl! Oh, boy, what a girl!* he thought exultantly. Elsie Lane. Elsie Forster. *Mrs* Forster. *Good lord!* What was it all about, anyway? Had he let himself in for something?...

No, she was all right. He could trust her. A good sort, Elsie. Maybe not quite the girl of his dreams, but a fine girl for all that! And she really liked him — he was certain of that. *Lord above! He'd gone and got himself a girl!* Someone to talk to at night when his work was finished. Someone to take off jaunting to the country. And so damned easy it had been! That was the funny thing... Of course, if it hadn't been for those few drinks he'd never have dared. Never! Too shy, that's what he'd been. Far too shy. Still, if he hadn't been shy he would have been married by now, and then he wouldn't have met her... *Hell, that kettle!*

He dashed into the scullery, snatched the spluttering kettle from the gas and poured the steaming water on the tea. He left the teapot brewing in the hearth while he changed his shoes. Then he had a great idea. A really great idea... He poured out the tea and carried one cupful, his face beaming with delight, through to the bedroom. Ah! That would surprise her all right. What would she say? What would she think?

He knocked timidly on the bathroom door and waited.

The splashing sounds ceased abruptly. Elsie's voice came thinly through the panels. "Is that you, Bert?"

"Yes, darling. I've brought you some tea."

"Oh, thanks..."

A short pause.

"Can I come in, Elsie?"

A long pause.

"I didn't bolt the door," she said.

He turned the knob and went in. She was sitting up in the bath, her cheeks rosy pink, but her fine dark eyes when they met his own were perfectly steady.

192

"I thought that — if you had the tea now — well, you could just, sort of — get straight into bed when you'd had your bath," Bert stammered. "You don't mind me coming in, do you?"

"No, Bert. Why should I?"

"Well, I thought you might be nervous," he replied, glancing at her firm, upstarting little breasts which showed above the soap white water.

"Perhaps I ought to be — but I'm not. I'm not so nervous as you."

"Am I nervous? Well, now you mention it, p'raps I am."

"Of course you are! But *I'm* not, not with *you*."

She took the cup in her wet fingers and began drinking. His eyes roved over her. How lovely she was! So small, slim, firm, rosy...

"I was thirsty," she said, handing him the cup. "That's just what I wanted. It was so kind of you, Bert, dear."

"Shall I get you some more? There's plenty —"

"No, thank you, darling. I say, Bert! You don't think I'm cheap — letting you come in —?"

"Good lord, Elsie, of course not. You're too precious for words! I love you!"

"Now run away and let me finish my bath. I shan't be a couple of ticks, then you can get yours, and —"

"A kiss first," Bert said, bending over her.

"No, no; I'm all soapy!" she protested. "Go on! Outside! If you don't I'll splash you!" She seized the sponge and threatened him, laughing, showing her small white teeth.

"All right, I'll have my revenge!" he vowed pleasantly.

He retreated, the cup rocking dangerously in his hand. This was great, magnificent! And she, this girl, was marvellous! Gee, what a girl! he thought, going back to the living room. One in a thousand, one in the whole wide world, the best of them all!

He drank his tea hurriedly and then sat smoking before the fire, lost in thoughts that whirled through his brain in a torrent. He wanted to marry her. He was certain.

193

They would have to marry as soon as they could. There might be a chance of doing it on Wednesday, a special licence or something, and then next Sunday — it was his day off — they could go down to the seaside, if it was fine — as it *must* be fine! — and bathe in the sea — if it was warm — and then climb up the rocks and find a large black smooth one and stay there, with their clothes off — Oh, but it was mad!

Mad! But it was real, true, lovely! No more loneliness, no more horrid washing up — unless they washed up together, and then that would be fun, not work — no more miserable, long dull days — nothing but Elsie, Elsie, Elsie! Man wasn't meant to live alone, by God he wasn't! And he wouldn't live alone any more, never again, now he had *her,* his Elsie, his Elsie girl, there in the bathroom...

He heard the gurgle of water in the wastepipe outside the window, followed soon by the sound of Elsie moving about the bathroom. How natural it was! No shyness! Everything perfect, as it should be, he thought, stubbing the end of his cigarette in the hearth. Yes, life was worth living now; and it would be for her, for poor little Elsie, too. What a hell of a time she must have had! Worse than himself, far, far worse. And now... He put out the fire, made sure that the window was securely fastened, switched off the light and joined her in the warm little bedroom.

She was sitting at the dressing table combing her soft, dark hair. The lines of her slender figure were now hidden in the folds of his pyjamas. She turned towards him a dreamy, tired face and forced a drowsy smile in response to his caress.

"I shan't be long, darling," Bert said. "Don't wait for me. Get into bed and rest. You must be tired."

"I am, Bert. Dreadfully — after that lovely bath."

"You must be."

He took his own pyjamas from under the pillow, snatched up his dressing gown, kissed her hair, and shut himself in the bathroom. As he turned on the geyser he saw his face in the mirror above the wash basin. Damn! he thought, rubbing his hand over his bristled chin. I must shave. Can't go to bed like this.

He shaved rapidly while the bath was filling, and then slipped into the water. He heard the unmistakable sound of a yawn from the bedroom, the creak of the bed, a weary sigh from Elsie. 'Tired,' he thought. 'Tired as hell after today. Don't wonder at it. I am a bit myself, though it's early for me to go to bed. Still, it's a day off tomorrow. We can lie in. *We* can lie in. Gee! It's as queer as hell!'

He soaped briskly, swilled it off and stepped out of the bath, then dried himself slowly and carefully on a rough, long towel that was still warm where she had used it before him. Then he pulled on his pyjamas, flung the green and gold dressing gown about his shoulders, released the plug in the bath and went into the bedroom. He put out the fire and advanced to the bed with an air of pleasant expectancy on his glowing face. She was lying on her side, curled up like a child, a lightly breathing form beneath the bedclothes. Only the top of her dark head, buried in the pillow, showed above the blue white sheets.

"Are you all right, Elsie?" he whispered softly.

She made no answer. He repeated the question, rather louder, and touched her shoulder gently. She didn't even stir at his touch. He drew back the covers and stared down at her face with an expression that changed swiftly from surprise to compassion.

"You must have been tired, you poor darling," he murmured, and bent and kissed her warm, soft, sleeping lips.

Then, with great care, he covered her up. He tip-toed across the room and pulled out a blanket from the drawer in the wardrobe. She was dead beat and must sleep off her exhaustion. He had to exert the strongest physical control. He mustn't wake her.

He opened the door, and after taking one more look at

her, he switched off the light and closed the door with extreme caution, and went out to sleep on the living room sofa.

3

Thurgood awoke muttering. This was ghastly! He eased himself out of bed, and pressed the switch of the bedside lamp, fearing she would waken. But she stirred only slightly, mumbled something, and began to snore. He shuddered to see her sleeping face. Lord, how awful she looked! Her hair was scattered over the pillow in extreme disorder; her mouth sagged open; the pouches were dark and heavy under her eyes. The powder and rouge was partly rubbed off, and she seemed to possess the battered face of an old, well-worn doll. Loathing filled him. So this, this haggard creature, was the beautiful, captivating Helen Stroud! Lord! he couldn't tolerate her another moment. She was too ghastly for words!

Thurgood's eyes turned from her face to the clock. It was nearly half past eleven. He found the bathroom, swilled out his mouth and dashed cold water over his head and neck. He would leave her as soon as he could. Lord, what a fool he'd been to think...! She was only an old woman, after all — a sensual old woman who must have the young crawling round her... Well, he had crawled, but it was the last time.

He was through with her now. He must have been mad to have ever thought he even liked her!

Holding his head, he returned quietly to the bedroom to dress. But despite his caution, while tying his tie at the dressing table mirror his elbow knocked over one of the many jars of cosmetics strewn on the polished top. It made a fearful clatter as it rolled and crashed among the scents and creams. He glanced round at the bed. To his horror she began to turn, muttering vaguely, and he dreaded the moment she would lift her head and see him furtively trying to escape while she slept.

Then Thurgood almost laughed with relief. Her face was turned towards him but she was still asleep. With feverish haste he arranged his tie, slipped on his shoes, and tiptoed over to the door. He was on the point of turning the knob when he heard his name.

"Harold!"

He turned slowly round. He could find no words to say, but grinned foolishly, flushing with guilt.

"What are you doing, Harold?" she cried in amazement, propping herself on her elbows.

"Well — I — you see —" Thurgood mumbled.

"Yes, I see you are going. Why did you have to creep out of bed without telling me?"

"I didn't want to waken you, of course," he said, trying not to sound irritable.

"You didn't want to waken me," she echoed. "But why, Harold?"

'Oh, to hell with her!' he thought desperately. 'If she knew what she looked like, she wouldn't ask such stupid questions.'

"Well, why should I?" he asked.

She must have sensed his hostility, for she sat up suddenly, saying sweetly, "Darling, do you mind fetching me a glass of water?"

"No, of course not."

When he got back with the water she had tidied her hair a little and had artlessly drawn down the bedclothes until she was bare to the waist. She sat up unashamed. The thought passed through his mind that it would relieve his feelings and do her good if he dashed the water over her body.

"How do you feel, darling?" she asked pleasantly, taking the glass from his hand.

"So-so."

"Only so-so?"

She gave a low, irritating sort of laugh. "You make love marvellously, Harold, you know," she said, and drank

197

slowly, her eyes on his face over the rim of the glass.

She took her time over the water. Brooding, he watched her, wondering all the more why he had ever thought her beautiful. With each second that she loitered, sipping the water as if it were a rare, old wine, his annoyance increased, his face grew redder and harder under the possessive stare in her pale grey eyes.

"Thank you," she said at last.

Thurgood snatched the glass rudely.

"Harold!" she cried. "What is it? What have I done? Tell me what's wrong."

He said nothing, but banged the glass on the dressing table, and then made hurriedly for the door.

"Harold!" she cried in alarm. "Darling! You've changed so suddenly. Please tell me what's wrong."

Consumed with overwhelming rage, he turned to her. The old fool! All he wanted was to get away from her!

With amazed eyes she sprang out of bed, rushed naked across the room and flung herself in front of the door. Thurgood immediately thought of his mother.

"Harold! Whatever is the matter? Why do you treat me like this?"

"Please don't make a scene."

"What has happened to you?" she asked piteously, and tried to kiss him.

He pushed her away, was about to answer, then closed his mouth in a thin hard line. She could see his jawbones working in suppressed anger. His terrifying silence brought a swift change to her pleading face. It blazed red like his own. She stepped back, her eyes seemed to sparkle with sudden venom, and he flinched beneath her scorn.

"Oh, so now you're tired of me!" she hissed at him. "Now you've had all you want you think you can treat me like this! But I'll tell you what you are before you go. You're nothing but a silly, cheap little policeman, you — you —"

"Shut up, and get out of my way!" he shouted back. "You ugly society wh..."

"Take that — and that!" she screamed, hitting him in

the mouth twice. "Now get out! Get out of my flat! Never come near me again. Go on, get out! Oh! how I hate you!"

He momentarily drew himself up to his full height.

That was the second time a woman had hit him in the face... by God! Then his hands shot out and seized her throat in an iron grip, choking off a strangled scream. She struggled wildly, kicked with her bare feet at his crutch, beat his flaming face with her fists and clawed at his eyes. But he felt nothing. There was a strange, roaring sound in his ears, like maddened surf, and a strange joy in his heart as his grip tightened, the muscles of his shoulders and arms bulging with the effort. Madly he pressed her head back against the door. Her lips turned blue black, her eyes, almost starting from her head, rolled wildly. Then suddenly she went limp in his grasp. He released his grip slowly and watched her slump to the carpet, where she lay with twitching limbs. He watched, fascinated with horror, till she lay still.

Thurgood stared wildly down at her body. Suddenly panic seized him. He turned and rushed from the room in terror. The lights and the fire were still on in the drawing room; he hardly noticed them in his headlong dash to the hall. In his fumbling, haste to get into his coat he ripped the lining of a sleeve. Cursing at the delay, he tore it from its stitchings, stuffed it in his pocket, jammed on his hat, and let himself out of the flat on the verge of hysteria.

There was no one in sight, thank God! Afraid of the lift, he staggered weakly down the stairs, his knees beginning to give way at every step. He must pull himself together. He began to fasten his coat, and hurry on down, obsessed with only one thing — to get safely away. He hadn't a doubt but that he had killed her, and left her dead on the bedroom floor. But he wouldn't hang. Oh, no. He wouldn't hang. They'd have a hell of a job to catch him, once he got out of this building. The whore! He thought viciously, stopping on the bottom landing to straighten his hat. She deserved what she got. Hit him, would she! The whore!

The porter and the liftman were talking together

beside the lift when Thurgood reached the bottom of the stairs. He saw them look up, stare queerly at his face as he walked quickly towards them. Now why the devil? — — A cold shiver ran through him as he remembered his bleeding mouth. They would detain him, ask awkward questions, find the body upstairs...

"Excuse me, sir," said the porter, stepping forward.

"Leave me alone," he shouted, and thrust the man aside. He ran recklessly into the street.

Chapter XII

WAKING slowly from exhausted sleep, through rapidly blinking eyes, Slesser saw that a blue-clad figure stood beside him, shaking his shoulder with a large, red hand.

"Hi!" said an affable voice. "Do you want to stay here all night? Come on! Show a leg! It's your turn now."

"Wha'?" asked Slesser drowsily. "Wha's tha'?"

"Come on! No more snoring," the voice went on. "You can't stay here, you know. This is a police station — not a sanatorium!"

It all came back to him in a rush — the fight with the fascists, the arrest, and then being bundled in here and told to wait. But now the room was empty except for himself; the fascists must have gone while he slept.

"I must ha' been asleep," Slesser muttered. He made to rise. "Christ! My back!" he gasped painfully, clutching at his spine.

Groaning he sank on the bench. Every muscle in his body was stiff and sore. From his feet to the top of his bare head there seemed to be nothing but pain, the deep, dull pain of over-taxed limbs that have stiffened in sleep. "Christ!" he said again. "I can't move!"

"Well, you can't stay here, old chap. You'll have to be charged. Come on. I'll give you a hand," said the policeman kindly, and lifted him up by the arms.

Wincing, Slesser stood up slowly and straightened his aching back. "They must ha' kicked me," he said. "The dirty curs! Where are they now?"

"What? Those other guys? They've gone. They were charged while you were asleep. Come on, or we'll be here all night at this rate."

Slesser suffered himself to be led through the door to the room beyond. Standing officiously behind the charge table was a police sergeant, and also the younger policeman with the teeth-bitten pen between his lips. They both eyed Slesser keenly as he stopped, grabbing for support at the table.

"Your name and address?" asked the sergeant brusquely, raising his bushy brows interrogatively.

Slesser told him in weary tones, as yet hardly able to think. The policeman with the pen nonchalantly scratched the information on a form that lay before him. Then they asked him his age, was he married or single, what was his trade, was he working or unemployed, had he any previous convictions — and all his answers were duly entered on the form with the scratching pen.

"Now," said the sergeant. "Have you got any proof of this information? Any old letters, club cards or anything like that? If you haven't," he added, "you'll have to stay here till we make enquiries, and that," he glanced round at a clock hanging on the wall at his back, "might take till after midnight."

Slesser, also glancing at the clock, saw with a shock that the time was after 11pm.

"That's not the right time, is it?" he asked, in an anguished tone. "It can't be!"

"Whether it can't be or not, it is," the sergeant retorted.

"But it wasn't ten o'clock when I came in here!" Slesser protested wildly. "What's it going to be when I get home?"

"You went to sleep, didn't you? Well then, you can't grumble if we left you till last. Have you got any letters on you? If so, hand 'em over — or you'll be here another hour or more."

Obediently Slesser felt in his pockets and drew out a collection of old papers, which he laid in a pile on the counter.

"Is this any good?" he asked, producing a tattered unemployment card.

The sergeant took the card, noted the name. "This hasn't any address on it. Have you got a letter or anything?"

"No," said Slesser, with gathering impatience. "The

only letters I get are bloody bills, and I don't carry them about with me. But is this any good?" he asked, offering his Health Insurance card for their inspection. "It's got my address on it."

"That'll do," said the sergeant, handing back the card.

Slesser put the card and papers away again, and waited patiently for something to happen. The sergeant examined a form, raised his head and shouted, "Harris! Harris! Where the devil have you got to?"

Immediately from an inner room came a policeman, furtively wiping his lips on the back of his hand. Slesser recognised him instantly as the one who had arrested him after the fight. He watched the man slip round the back of the charge table and take his stand beside the sergeant. Now what? he wondered. How much longer would they keep him there asking all those bloody silly questions, when they knew he wanted to get home?

"You arrested this man, Harris?" the sergeant asked, pointing at Slesser.

"Yes, sergeant."

"And this is your report?" picking up a form.

"Yes, sergeant."

"That's all, Harris. You can go. Now," said the sergeant, turning to Slesser, "you're charged with disorderly conduct in Argyle Street at 9.52pm on October fourth nineteen-hundred and thirty-six, resisting arrest and assault of PO Harris in execution of his duty. Report to — court tomorrow morning at ten, sharp!"

"But I never resisted arrest!" Slesser expostulated.

"Tell that to the court," the sergeant cut in brusquely. "Don't forget. Ten o'clock tomorrow, sharp! That's all."

"But look here," Slesser began.

A policeman seized his arms and marched him into the corridor. "Arguing won't do you any good, mate," he said, releasing his grip. "Better get off home right away."

"It's a lie!" Slesser cried." I didn't assault no cop! I didn't —"

His voice trailed off, ending in a startled gasp. He knew

now that he had assaulted a cop, he had resisted arrest —
but not intentionally. Those strong arms that had seized
him when he struggled to his feet to run from the fascists
had been those of Harris. He had butted Harris hard
under the chin, and broken away!

"Christ!" he said weakly, and staggered down the steps
to the road, appalled at his discovery. Now it would be
impossible to defend himself in court. They might even
send him to prison. In gathering despair he trudged on,
forgetting his aching limbs, and brooding over his misfor-
tunes. Over and over again he thought: 'It's true, I did
assault the cop, but I didn't do it on purpose. I didn't
know it was a cop. That's what I'll tell 'em in court.
They'll have to believe it and let me off. They can't punish
me for what I did in mistake. How the hell was I to know
who it was?'

The cold night breeze fanned lightly on his grey brown
hair as he turned a corner into Oxford Street. His hand
strayed to his head. 'Blasted cap's lost as well,' he
thought. He shrugged his shoulders indifferently. 'Ah,
what the hell's it matter! To hell with worry. I've had
enough of it for one fine day. There'll be plenty to worry
about when I get back home and *she* gets to know what's
happened.'

He gazed down the broad stretch of Oxford Street that
led to Marble Arch, wondering which way to take.
Perhaps it would be better to go straight on down to the
Arch, and along by the park, instead of cutting down
Regent Street. If it hadn't been for those fascists, those
blasted fascists, he wouldn't have had this three mile
walk! The black rats! Ah, well... He shrugged his shoulders again, pushed back a wisp of hair from his eyes, and
set off for the Arch, shoulders hunched, hands pushed
down in his empty pockets, indifferent to his troubles.

Except for the passing buses and an occasional car, at
that hour the street was almost deserted. But here and
there in the dark doorways between the brilliantly
lighted shops he saw the ever-watching policemen flash

him a glance of suspicion as he trudged past. Three times this happened before he wondered why; and then he caught a glimpse of himself in a plateglass window. Good God! he thought, stopping and staring at the tramp-like reflection. He could hardly believe his eyes. His face was a mass of bruises and blood-caked cuts; his hair and clothes thick with dust from his fall in the road; his collar was fixed to his neck only by the knot in his rumpled tie. He looked like an American criminal after undergoing the third degree. No wonder the police had stared! It was a miracle they hadn't arrested him!

Snatching out his handkerchief, he wetted a corner and furtively rubbed at his face to remove that repulsive mask. The caked blood came away in scales, exposing the cuts beneath, which exuded fresh blood in thin, tiny streams that trickled warmly down to his chin. He dabbed frantically knowing that he looked worse now than he had done before, but the blood welled down as hard as ever. Damn it! he thought, walking on, dabbing at his face. If anyone should meet him now they'd think he had been in an accident, perhaps stop him, ask awkward questions, perhaps even send for the police.

High up on a building on his left he saw the sign: NORTH AUDLEY STREET. The name seemed familiar. Surely he had worked here at one time, on a building job, labouring for an Irish bricklayer? Yes, there was the very building, he recognised it down the street. If he turned down here, he recollected, he would cut off Marble Arch and come eventually to Hyde Park Corner, saving a few hundred yards of his three mile walk.

'If only this bloody bleeding would stop,' he thought as he turned into the street, dabbing away at his face. 'Anybody would think I'd done a murder! A fine to-do, this is. There'll be a hell of a row when I get home, after this lot. She won't let me get a bloody word in edgeways. Nag, nag, nag, and cackle, cackle, cackle, like — like I dunno what. What a day! Nothing but rows — rows this morning, rows this afternoon, rows tonight, and more rows to come. Still, I sorted them fascists out right good and proper. Didn't know I had it in me. Why, it must be nigh on fifteen years since I had a scrap! Easy fifteen years; nigh on sixteen to be exact — about the time when I started courting *her*. Just wait till she sees my face! She'll have a blue fit. Wish it would stop bleeding. This handkerchief's about soaked through. Wish to Christ I didn't have to walk. As if I hadn't done enough walking today, as it is. Must be over ten miles; maybe twelve — God knows. Wonder what Claire's doing now? And Calvin? Nice couple that. Clever. Wonder what they'd say if they could see me now? Eh? Fine sight I look, messed up like this! I'll tell them about what happened to me if I ever see them again...'

Thus, alternately gloomy and rejoicing, Slesser walked on, dabbing at his face with the blood-soaked handkerchief. The street was strangely deserted. Hardly a light showed from the windows, hardly a sound came from the surrounding streets to distract his racing thoughts. Only from afar, subdued by the intervening buildings, came the steady drone of the traffic as it whirled round Marble Arch. It was like walking in a dead city, from which the inhabitants had fled, suddenly, hastily, forgetting to turn out the street lamps as they rushed from an oncoming doom.

That flow of uncanny silence was suddenly, harshly interrupted by the piercing scream of brakes, followed immediately by a metallic crash. Jerked rudely from his thoughts, Slesser halted, the handkerchief still at his face, and listened holding his breath, crouched half forward as if to spring at an onrushing foe.

Shouts and excited cries issued from a street nearby. Gathering his wits, he ran swiftly towards the sounds, his heart pounding heavily inside him. There'd been a smash. He had heard that sort of metallic crash before, the crash of car wings buckling under sudden impact.

Turning into a narrow road that was darkened by towering buildings he came on the scene of the accident. A taxi stood shattered, its blunt nose buried deep in some area railings, and beside the taxi, tended by a man in a chocolate-coloured uniform, the driver lay groaning. Twenty feet away lay the still figure of a man in evening dress.

"What's up?" Slesser panted to the uniformed man. "Is he dead?"

"This one isn't," was the answer, in a significant tone. "Just had a shock, that's all."

"Shall I fetch the ambulance or something?" Slesser asked hurriedly, throwing an apprehensive glance at the silent body.

"No, my mate's phoning now. You might help me sit this guy on the running-board. He'll be all right in a minute. Shock, you know." He added, to explain himself, "I used to be in St. John's, see?" He added again, "I'm porter in the flats there."

"Ah!..." said Slesser, feverishly lifting the taxi-driver, and propping him up against the shattered taxi. "How'd it happen?" he whispered.

"How'd it happen? That's easy," replied the porter. "I saw everything. That chap there" — he indicated the body in the road — "that chap came running down the steps from the flats like a madman and ran right in front of this taxi. Hadn't an earthly! Not a bleedin' earthly! Smack! an' he was fini'. Just as if a shell had hit him. Broke his neck. Never even moved after it. Say," he said, glancing up, "what's the matter with your face, mate? You weren't in this, were you?"

"*My* face?" Slesser's hands stole to his cheeks and came away wet. "Oh, that! That's nothing. Been in a scrap, that's all."

"Looks pretty bad to me. What you get fighting for, mate?"

"Four bloody fascists set on me," said Slesser. "I sorted 'em out, though," he added hastily.

"You a Red?"

"Ah!" proudly answered Slesser.

The porter fell silent, slapping the taxi driver's cheeks in an effort to bring him to consciousness. In a moment the groaning ceased; the man opened his eyes, his mouth working with pain. He was a stumpy old man with greying hair and round, weather-beaten features. "It weren't my fault," he moaned. "It weren't my fault."

"No, that's right, chum," said the porter soothingly. "Got any pain anywhere?"

"Dunno. It weren't my fault, were it? Chap came running out — couldn't stop — he ain't? —"

"No, he's all right, chum. Don't worry. Sit quiet and the ambulance will be here in a minute."

He placed himself between the body in the road and the taxi driver.

"You'll soon be all right," the porter said. "Shock, you know."

Another man in uniform came running down the steps from the flats and joined the group at the taxi. "Is he all right, Alf?" he asked quickly, addressing the porter.

"Shock, that's all. Did you get through?"

"Yeah. Ambulance is on its way now. And a police car. What about the other chap?"

"Go and see," said the porter, in a low tone, in case the driver should hear.

Stemming his dread, Slesser followed the newcomer the few paces to the silent body. The two bent over curiously.

"Dead, all right."

"Ah, dead, poor devil. Looks like a gent, too," Slesser whispered, eyeing interestedly the unfamiliar dress clothes.

"Yeah. Been visiting somebody in the flats and came running downstairs, his face all blood — like yours — and ran like hell in front of that taxi. Must have been drunk, I fancy, and fell on the stairs and then just ran out like a fool — listen! That's the ambulance. About time, too."

They stood up as the ambulance tore into view and stopped close to the scene of the crash. Right at its heels came a small black police car, containing a policeman in uniform and two others in plain clothes. Ambulance men and police hurriedly examined the victims and held a whispered consultation. As a result, the taxi driver was carried inside the flats to get a rest, since he was not a hospital case, while the plain clothes police bent over the body in the road and began to search through the dead man's pockets.

Slesser, the liftman and the porter stood aside, watching. The searchers drew out a wallet stuffed with various papers and a few pound notes.

"Seems like he was a policeman himself," said the plain clothes man with the wallet, holding up a sports club card for the other's inspection. "Look, he was in your old division. Know him? Name's Thurgood — Harold Thurgood."

"Thurgood, Thurgood," repeated the other, taking the card. "No, never heard of him. He must have been after my time."

"Probably. Well, the poor devil's done for now. We'd better measure up and take some statements."

Turning to Slesser and the others, he raised his voice, "Did any of you see this happen?"

"I did," replied the porter instantly. "It's like this —"

"Just a minute." The policeman drew out his notebook and licked a stubby pencil. "Go on."

"It's like this. I was on duty in the flats there — I'm night porter, see? — when I saw this chap come running down the stairs with his face all blood —"

"His face all blood?"

"Yes, something like this chap here," the porter said, indicating Slesser.

Slesser started. "I had nothing to do with it," he cut in hastily. "I just heard the smash and came along."

"Oh! How did you get like that, then?"

"Well —" Slesser shuffled uneasily, wishing he had gone before the police arrived. "You see," he blurted out, "I've been in a scrap up at Oxford Circus — four fascists — set on me — I know nothing about this here —"

209

"All right, all right. You needn't get excited. I was only asking," said the policeman, and licked his pencil again. "Now you go on," he said to the porter. "You say this chap" — jerking his foot at the body — "came running down the stairs and you saw his face bleeding. What happened next?"

"Well," said the porter. "I was talking to my mate — he's inside now — near the lift, when this chap came running down, as I said, and o' course, seeing his face like that we thought he'd fallen down the stairs or something, and tried to stop him to ask if he wanted any help or anything. He shouted, 'Leave me alone,' and rushed past us like a mad bull — drunk, I think he was — and we followed, my mate and me, and he ran right in front of that taxi — wallop!"

"Yes, and what then?"

"Well, I shouted to my mate to phone for an ambulance and you chaps, and saw that this chap was dead, then did what I could for the driver. I used to be in St. John's, see?"

"Had you seen this man before?" asked the policeman, meaning the body of Thurgood.

"No, never set eyes on him. Nor has my mate. He don't live in the flats."

"No, I should imagine he doesn't! But do you know who he might have been visiting?"

"Couldn't say. My pal took him up to the fifth floor about nine o'clock — he told me that before you arrived — but he didn't see which flat he went in."

"Uhm!" said the policeman thoughtfully, tapping with his pencil on his notebook. "Well, that'll be all for now. You'd better give me your name and address, and then I'll have a word with that pal of yours."

The group moved off towards the flats, and Slesser was momentarily left alone with the body in the road. He looked down again at the dead man, noticing the handsome features, daubed a little with blood from the twisted mouth, and thick, dark, curly hair, ruffled and untidy. Poor devil! he thought compassionately. I bet you wish

210

you hadn't been drinking now. He shrugged his shoulders, turned and walked, on his way, heading for Hyde Park Corner.

Moaning every now and again, Helen Stroud crawled slowly to her feet and clutched at the bedroom door. For a time she stood there dazed, swaying like one drunk, her hair falling down into her horrified eyes. Every little bit of her flesh quivered uncontrollably, and her throat burned as if scorched with a flame.

This was terrible, terrible! He had nearly killed her! The beast! The brute! He must have been mad! She shuddered all over; hatred and fear intermingled as she recalled that frightening scene. His eyes glaring into her own while his fingers sank in her throat, and then the deep, red-seared, light shot darkness.

"Oh, my God!" she cried, in a whisper, and crawled over to the bed on her hands and knees like an animal.

Painfully she pulled a dressing gown over her shoulders and slumped on the end of the bed, living the whole scene over again, while her throat burned and her head throbbed and her flesh convulsively quivered. Dimly she heard through her torrents of thoughts the sound of excited voices in the street five storeys below. But she paid no heed to them; they could find no place to repose in her whirling brain.

"The beast!" she muttered incoherently. "The beast, he almost killed me..."

She hated him. And she was terribly hurt; but less because he had savaged her with his hands than because he had shown her his loathing. Loathing had oozed from him, from his eyes, from the set of his jaw, from his every action. And that was what hurt her most. *He loathed her.* Once he had had his fill of her she meant nothing to him; she would never mean anything again. Nothing at all. Which meant — Oh, it could only mean one thing — one dreadful thing!

None of the others had ever looked at her like that. None of the others had ever exhibited such haste to leave her. Rather had they been reluctant, had gone unwillingly, had asked to be allowed to come again. But this one, this Thurgood — *he* hadn't wanted to stay. He hadn't even wanted to kiss her. He had loathed her so much that he couldn't even *make* himself kiss her. He had struck her, nearly killed her, rather than kiss her. And that was what hurt.

It wasn't that men were different. Oh, no! She knew them too well to make mistakes about that. They weren't different. It was she, herself, who was different. *She was getting old.* She *was* old. She could hide the fact no longer. And now nobody would want her ever again, none of the nice men, anyway, none of the young ones, the ones who pulsed with virile life. Those hours before the mirror, at the hairdresser's, at the beauty specialist's — these pounds and pounds spent on preserving an appearance of youth — would now be unavailing. Through the mask her age would show, inexorably — and that was what hurt.

Very wearily she dragged herself to her mirror and sat there examining the haggard face, thinking bitter thoughts in her anguish. He had called her a whore — a society whore, she remembered, stroking her discoloured throat. The young fool! She wasn't a whore. Oh, no, to be one of those you had to be young; you had to have looks that would stand the wear and tear; she had neither now. And she wasn't even 'society.' He was even wrong about that. She was merely the widow of a beer baron who had managed to buy himself a title and then had ingloriously died. Worse, the demand for beer had declined; the value of the shares had declined; the dividends had declined; she herself had declined. And now — here she was, a one-time beer baron's widow — impoverished, lonely, haggard — and old. Old. That was what hurt.

She rose at last from the mirror and the voices from the street below found a place in her weary mind. 'Why must they brawl at this time of night?' she thought tiredly. 'Why can't they leave me in peace. I'm an old woman, a lonely old woman — why can't they leave me in peace?'

She entered the beautiful bathroom, suddenly thirsting for water, and drank glass after glass of it without quenching her thirst. She bathed her eyes, and examined curiously her discoloured throat in the mirror. There were two large, horribly inconvenient bruises where his thumbs had sunk, and two little wounds where his nails had bitten into the flesh. For a fraction of time she was consumed with rage. She wanted revenge; she would phone for the police; she would hound him to hell!... But no, that was no use, no use at all. She must keep this thing quiet. The certain ensuing scandal would be far too terrible to bear. She and a policeman — oh, no, that would never do! It must never get out, never!

Thirst consumed her again. She went hunting in the drawing room for whisky. Two glasses and an empty bottle lay on the carpet beside the divan, just as they had left them two hours before. The lights were on, the fire was burning, and the room was hot, stuffy, redolent of cigarette smoke mingled with perfume. She switched out the fire and thought, with a bitter smile on her lips, of his ardent caresses, there, on that very divan. What incredible stupidity! she thought. A policeman! — I should have known, oh, I should have known... She picked up the empty bottle, shook it, frowned, turned it upside down and watched a trickle of golden liquid dribble to the carpet.

"But I must have a drink!" she exclaimed suddenly, pitching the bottle on the floor where it thudded softly and rolled glinting in the light, until it stopped against the leg of a chair.

Pulling her dressing gown closer, in her bare feet she went into the hall and phoned the porter to bring her another bottle.

The porter came in a very few minutes, hugging a bottle. She had waited for him in the hall, brooding, completely forgetting her undressed appearance, and the comment that it might provoke. But the porter did not seem to notice it. He gave her the bottle still wrapped as it had come from the restaurant cellar, and promptly blurted out, "Did you know there had been an accident, madam? Down in the street? —"

"Oh," said Lady Stroud, remembering the voices, "is that what all the noise is about?" She took the bottle and clutched it under her right arm; with her left she held her dressing gown close against her throat, hiding the telltale marks.

"Yes, madam," the porter continued breathlessly. "A gentleman got killed — taxi ran over him —"

"Really?"

She wished he would go. Couldn't he see that she wanted to be left in peace, that she wasn't interested in the accident?

"Yes, madam, and the funny thing is — he came running out of these flats — face bleeding — I saw him myself —"

"Out of these flats — face bleeding?" she repeated. "Did he really?"

"Yes, madam. And as a matter of fact, my mate — I mean the liftman, madam — he said he brought him up to this very floor about nine o'clock —"

"Nine o'clock," she repeated in a hollow voice. A horrible thought was beginning to take shape in her mind. But it couldn't be! "Are you sure?" she asked.

"Well, he's the only gent that's called since nine o'clock, so there can't be much mistake about it. And the police," the porter gabbled on, "the police want to know whose flat he was in — his face being bloody like it was when he came running down, he might have been up to something, you see, madam."

"Yes," Lady Stroud said faintly, staring past the porter with absent eyes.

For the first time noticing her strange demeanour, the porter thought she was drunk and began to back to the lift, saying, "Well, madam, I just thought I'd better let you know in case the police come up to make inquiries. They — they want to know which flat he was in, and —"

Starting, she made a great effort to compose herself, and asked, still not really believing, "Do you happen to know — who he was? Was he a tenant?"

"No, madam, he wasn't a tenant. The police know though."

And she knew. Oh, yes, she knew — beyond a shadow of doubt.

Fearfully she clutched at her mouth with the hand that held the dressing gown. The folds of the wrap parted and for a fraction of a second the porter saw her nakedness. He was still staring goggle-eyed and horrified at her when she slammed the door in his face.

"Drunk," he said aloud. "But, Jesus! —"

She walked unsteadily back to the drawing room, and there opened the bottle with feverish fingers and drank down two glasses of the neat whisky. The liquid tore at her throat, already painfully inflamed, but she felt nothing. 'Dead,' she thought incessantly. 'Dead,' and stared dumbly at the nearby divan, imagining him there caressing her. But the picture became too horrible. Taking the bottle, she lurched to her bedroom and flung herself down on the bed. But that was worse still, far worse. She got up and paced up and down, repeatedly drinking from the bottleneck, trying to shut out the voices in the street below. They rang up insistently on the still night air, demanding her attention. At last, fearfully, she went to the window, released the catch, and peered down to where a little group of figures were bent over an indistinct form in the road. Nearby was a shattered taxi, its nose buried deep in the area railings, and near that, white, grim, silent, an ambulance. The figures straightened up, laboriously carrying the body, and moved slowly over to the ambulance. She withdrew hurriedly, closed the window and tilted the bottle. She drank deeply, in great gulps, until she could hardly remain on her feet.

"Oh Lord," she muttered, the tears rolling down her haggard cheeks. "I can't stay here after this — I can't — I must get right away — to the country — where it's

215

quiet, peaceful. I'll leave firs' thing in morning, go quiet lil' village, buy cottage, four rooms an' gard, garden an' never come Lunnon 'gain 's long's I — live!"

With this vow and the bottle to comfort her, she was unsteadily getting into bed when the bell shrilled in the hall. After a moment's hesitation she went drunkenly, still clutching the bottle, to answer it, muttering vaguely, punctuating her words with waves of the bottle which she held by the neck, "Wha' they wanna come — ring my bell for — when they know I wanna go to sleep — that's wha' I wanna know..."

She flung open the door, staggered, and nearly fell. "Wha's marrer now?" she demanded aggressively, brandishing the bottle at an indistinct face.

"I'm a police officer," said a voice from the face. "A man's been killed outside and we wondered whether he might have been up to something in the flats. Sorry to trouble you, Lady Stroud — isn't it? — but do you happen to have had any visitors tonight? —"

"Vishtors?" she demanded thickly. "Vishtors? Why should 'ave vishtors, eh? Tha's wha' I' like know." Suddenly her voice rose to a scream." Go 'way! Go 'way! Can't you see I'm lonely ol' woman! Go 'way leave me in peace!"

She dropped the bottle and began to beat on her breasts and to tear at her hair in a drunken, demoniacal frenzy. "Go 'way will you!" she screamed hoarsely. "Damn you, go 'way! Can't you see I'm lonely old woman want left in peace! Go 'way!"

The policeman suddenly pushed her inside, disgustedly slammed the door and walked off, her voice still ringing in his ears.

Chapter XIII

IN distant Westminster, Big Ben chimed out the midnight hour. Slesser paused, counting the strokes. Twelve o'clock! Ah, well! He'd soon be home. It wasn't far now to the bridge, and then over it and down by the park — and home. He lit his last cigarette, gently fingered his tender face, found that the bleeding had ceased, and walked on again.

'Life's a funny business,' he began to muse. 'You never know really what the day's going to bring. But then, if you did, life wouldn't be worth living, would it? Though there hasn't been much fun in my life since I've been on the bloody dole; nag, nag, nag, and cackle, cackle, cackle, day after day, week after week, month after month — ever since I lost the job on the council... Still, there's some changes and maybe I was wrong about that. Maybe I should have joined the union, then they wouldn't have laid me off when the work got scarce, me being married and with four kids *(and* another on the way!). But I don't like having to join anything, union or not. And why should I? If they'd come up quietly and said, "Look here, Slesser, wouldn't you like to join our union?" I might have done so. But when a little whipper-snapper only half my age comes round and says, "Hey, you — if you haven't a card I'm not going to work with you, I'm going on strike," that's beyond a bloody joke. Think I was a mouse, not a man! Still, I've half a mind to go up to the council tomorrow afternoon, as Rose says, and see about getting a job again. Can't go on like this, nagging and cackling week after week. It gets a body down. Christ! Some poor folks stay on the dole for years and years — so what sort of a life do they have? Must be worse than mine — and mine's bad enough. Still, I'm as much to blame as her, I suppose. She wasn't always like it. When I was working she was all right, one o' the best, and we hardly ever had a row. It's this being on the dole, her having to worry about the food and the rent and the kids, that does it. And now she's five weeks overdue and another kid on the way! That's Rose's bloody fault! If she'd never said about those tablets we'd never have tried them and then we wouldn't be in this bloody fix. Wish to Christ she'd keep her nose out of my affairs. Her and that nancy husband of hers! What would *he* have done if four bloody fascists had set about him. Run like hell, I suppose, the spineless little whelp. Can't even make a bloody baby!'

Slesser came to the bridge that spanned the Thames and walked slowly over it towards the park, which spread dark and mysterious from the opposite bank of the river to the sleeping homes in the distance. The night before, he recollected, a girl had leapt from this very bridge to her death in the water below. It was a thrilling, morbid, fascinating thought. He tried to imagine the exact spot from which she had jumped, but there were no traces of disaster, no blood, no tattered clothing, no water splashes, on the grey stone parapet to guide him. Such people came, he thought, hung around, fearful of doing it when faced with it, and then they suddenly jumped — splash! — and it was all over, fini', as the porter said.

'But *I'm* not finished,' he decided resolutely, leaving the bridge and heading down the road past the park. 'Not by a bloody long chalk.'

Old Tom Whiteley's acetylene lamp glared steadily into the night from his kiosk at the closed park gates. Hearing footsteps approaching from the bridge, he looked out hopefully, thinking of a possible customer. At first he failed to recognise the hatless, badly battered man who walked with dragging feet towards him as Slesser. Then he let out a gasp, "Joe!"

"Hullo, Tom!" Slesser cried cheerfully, grinning with his cracked lips. "How's trade?"

"What — what?" Tom Whiteley stuttered. "What's up with your face, man?"

"Been in a scrap," Slesser answered, pulling himself erect, proud as a peacock. "Bit of a mess, aren't I?"

"Bit of a mess! You're like a side of bloody beef!"

"Ah!.. Four fascists set on me — up at Oxford Circus."

"Fascists?"

"Ah, followed me from the East End and set about me."

"Look here," Tom said. "You have a cup o' tea and tell me all about it —"

"Don't think I've time, Tom. I ought to be getting back home — the missus, you know. Besides," as Tom started to pour, "I'm broke to the wide."

"This is on me," Tom retorted. "Lord! Last night I see a tart dead and now you come along like I dunno what! Good job I ain't superstitious. Here, drink that; it's newly made. Would you like a ham roll to go with it?"

"No, thanks, Tom. I haven't much time. And besides, I'm not feeling like eating with this lot," Slesser retorted, fingering his swollen lips.

"Anyway, let's have the story, Joe. You say these fascists followed you from the East End? —"

"Ah!" Slesser mumbled, sipping the hot thick tea.

Hurriedly he recounted the story of the day's events, while Tom Whiteley emitted appropriate gasps, now commiserating, now approving, now condemning. "But what troubles me," Slesser ended, "is this court business. Do you think I'll get time?"

Tom Whiteley shook his head, his lips pursed. "Hardly likely, Joe. Maybe you'll get fined a couple o' quid, but they won't put you inside."

"A couple o' quid! But I couldn't pay that! —"

"Still, it's better than doing time. Maybe you could borrow it?"

"Ah, maybe," Slesser muttered, thinking of Rose. "Well, Tom, thanks for the tea. I'll have to be going or the missus'll be having a fit, me being out at this time o' night."

"All right, Joe. But have a fag to smoke on the way," Whiteley suggested. "And say, Joe," he added suggestively, "I heard there'll be some work for such as you on the council shortly. They're building some new flats."

"I heard about that, too," Slesser said cautiously, taking the proffered Woodbine and striking a match. "As a matter of fact, I was thinking of going up there tomorrow, if I don't get time at the court."

"It means joining a union this time —"

"Ah, I know. But —" Slesser paused, not yet prepared to commit himself. "Well, so long, Tom. And thanks for the tea," he said finally.

At a brisk pace Slesser headed for home, first through the street of clean little houses with their neat front gardens and gravelled paths, then into the contrasting, over-crowded squalor of South Park Road. Here his pace slowed almost to a shuffle, for in a little while now, he remembered in despair, he would have to face the row with his wife that he knew not how to avoid. It seemed so inevitable that even to think of excuses was a waste of energy. And it appalled him. He hated to row with her, to see her face grow distorted with passion — absolutely hated it. For a frantic moment he was tempted not to go home tonight, to stay away and put it off... But that was silly, and it was cowardly. He thrust the thought immediately aside. Useless to think like that, he told himself gloomily. She had to be faced. She would nag and she would cackle, and the Lord only knew she would have enough to nag and cackle about. Of course, she might be in bed and asleep. She might. But it wasn't very likely. She wasn't that sort. More likely she'd be up, sitting under the gas light, waiting to pounce as soon as he opened the kitchen door. And then she would start, 'Where have you been all this time, might I ask? Eh? Who do you think *you* are, coming home at this time of night? Eh? And what do you mean by stealing the food money out of my purse? Eh? What have you done with it? Eh? Why did you sneak out this afternoon as if I was a leper? Eh? You lazy, good for nothing brute! You ought to be ashamed of yourself! But you're not! Oh, no! You never are! You don't know what shame is. You just loaf about and steal the only bit of money we've got when you know quite well that those poor kids have hardly a rag to their backs! *And* another on the way! What? What's that you say? What? You've been *arrested!* You've got to go to the court! You'll be *fined,* perhaps sent *to prison!* Well!... If that isn't the limit! If that just isn't the very limit! Here I slave to keep home and children tidy and you — you — you! — You lazy, good for nothing scoundrel! I must have been mad when I married you — mad as a hatter. Madder. It's just as Rose says: *you don't want work.* No, all you want to do is to loaf about the house all day, smoking those filthy Woodbines of yours, while I work like a slave. But I've had enough this time. This is the end, Joe Slesser, the very end. I'm going. I'm going now. Rose'll keep me, *and* the kiddies. I won't stay here and be treated like this any more. You idle, good-for-nothing loafer! You scoundrel! You thief!'

Quietly he let himself indoors and along the dark, mildew-smelling passage to the kitchen. A narrow streak of light shone under the kitchen door, signifying her presence in the room beyond. He turned the knob slowly, putting off meeting her as long as he possibly could, and then went sheepishly inside, and stood blinking in the gaslight. He almost slunk in, his head sunk low on his chest to avoid her eyes, and closed the door very softly.

"Joe!" came a startled gasp. "Joe! Oh Joe! —"

"What?" he asked sheepishly, and grinned, and blinked, still unaccustomed to the light.

"Joe!" she cried again. "Oh, Joe, your face!"

"My face," he repeated, stroking his chin with a wondering hand. "Ah... that, that's — some chaps set on me. Four of 'em —"

"Four men set on you! Oh, you poor thing! And here I've been thinking — Joe, you're not hurt bad, are you?"

She came right up to him, peering at his battered face with anxious, questioning eyes.

He hadn't expected this welcome. It bewildered him; he hardly knew how to cope with it. "Well," he stammered at last. "It does hurt a bit — like —"

"Then sit down, Joe," she urged. "Sit down beside the fire while I get you some hot water to bathe it. Why, your left eye's nearly closed right up! You poor thing. Joe, who did it?" she asked ominously.

"Four fascists," Slesser said, allowing her to seat him in the chair. "But don't think I didn't put up a fight," he said hastily, "because I did. I gave 'em as good as they gave me."

"I should think so, the brutes! The cowards! And I've been sitting here all night thinking — It just shows."

She ended mysteriously, and declaiming, "Cowards! brutes!" hurried into the scullery to put on the kettle.

Slesser still couldn't grasp that all this attention was meant for him. More, he felt strongly that he didn't deserve it. And, of course, she didn't know the whole story yet. When she did...

"But where did it happen, Joe?" his wife asked, returning from the scullery. "At the march?"

"What march?" he queried, for a moment not thinking.

"The fascist march. I've seen the special paper about it; Mrs upstairs sent it down. I expected that's where you were."

"Oh, no! No. As a matter of fact, they set about me at Oxford Circus, in a back street —"

"Oh, but what were you doing up there?"

Her tone had altered, almost imperceptibly, but Slesser noticed it. Now for it, he thought. He should have known it was too good to last.

"Well," he said, and cleared his throat noisily. "I *was* at the march, but these chaps followed me to Oxford Circus —"

"But why did you go to Oxford Circus? The march was in the East End, wasn't it? And what made you so late getting back?"

Trapped, Slesser looked at her helplessly. He couldn't tell her the truth — because he had got afraid and had tried to run away from the fascists? No, no! That would never do!

"Well, I — I — you see, I got on the wrong bus and —"

"Just a minute," she interrupted. "The kettle —" and darted to the scullery.

Slesser breathed a sigh of relief. He had a minute's respite in which to gather his scattered wits. He mustn't rile her now. He must go very carefully, keep her in this wonderful humour, keep her anxious — Yes, that was it! Keep her anxious. He groaned aloud three times, and lay back and closed his eyes as if on the point of collapse.

"Joe! Joe!" she cried instantly, hastening in with a steaming bowl. "Are you all right, Joe? Shall I fetch a doctor?"

"No, no," he muttered weakly. "Just a bit of dizziness. Soon pass off."

"Look! Have an aspirin!" she cried. "Now where did I put them? Oh, dearie me! Whenever I want things they're sure to be missing —"

She banged the bowl on the table, and hunted feverishly through the chest of drawers, recklessly upsetting the folded clothes in her desperate haste. They were not there. She stood on the fender and searched through the assorted ornaments stacked on the mantelpiece, even looking under the clock, but they were not there. And Slesser, watching her through narrowed eyes, marvelled constantly at her obvious concern. It seemed that he had never really known her before. Never, never had he thought she could get so genuinely concerned about him. He had misjudged her utterly. He had been a fool, an ungrateful, pig headed fool, he told himself, with something like a lump beginning to form in his throat. And it wasn't fair to pretend like this, to groan, to wilfully deceive her, to make her upset, flustered, anxious, when he didn't really feel ill at all. Damn it! 'I'll tell her and risk it,' he thought, and half rose from the chair.

"No, no! You sit there!" she cried instantly, waving him back. "I'll find them in a minute — somewhere." She picked up the clock again, searching for the aspirins.

"Still, perhaps I'd better bathe your face while the water's warm," she amended, abandoning the search and bringing the bowl of water and a lump of cottonwool to his side. "Oh, dearie me! I might have expected something like this had happened! I might have known all along when you didn't come home."

"Look here —" Slesser began; but she silenced him quickly by dabbing the wet cottonwool on his swollen lips.

"You lie quiet," she said firmly. "You rest, and don't get excited. I wish I had some raw beef to put on this eye. It's supposed to be better than any of the stuff you can buy at the chemist's. I dunno! I've never seen a face like this before! Never! Wait till the kiddies see you!"

Slesser lay quietly while she swabbed his swollen flesh with a gentleness that stirred him profoundly. Again and again that lumpy feeling welled in his throat and the moisture started to his eyes. Her thick broad fingers were as soft, somehow, as a newborn child's — and equally as disconcerting. They almost reduced him to abject tears of repentance.

Suddenly she said, "Joe!"

"What?" he muttered, surprised at her tone, for it was humble.

"I was wrong about you," she said, swabbing fiercely.

"But what do you mean, wrong?"

"About where you were. I didn't really think you were at the march — I only said that to cover myself. But now I know you were — and it's all right, Joe. I was wrong."

Flabbergasted at her tone and her words, Slesser made to sit up, to confront her. But she pushed him back, quickly soaked some more cottonwool, and dabbed it near his eyes. He had to shut them.

"You see, Joe," she resumed in that curiously humble apologetic tone. "I thought you were out with another woman."

To think she had thought he was out with another woman!... He wanted to tell her everything, to blurt it all out, about the arrest and everything, but she gave him no time. She pushed him back and swabbed away at his battered face, though that was no longer necessary.

"No, you hear *me* out first," she said. "I've been wrong about you, Joe. All night I've sat here — thinking — thinking you were out with another woman. But that's not all. There's something else, Joe. I've been thinking about that job on the council that Rose was on about, and now I know you're right. You didn't ought to join a union if you don't want to — even if it means being on the dole for ever. You're right about that —"

"No, no!" Slesser cried wildly. "I'm wrong!" He started up at last and faced her. "I've been wrong all the time! I've been a bloody fool! I ought to have joined the union years ago. Everybody ought to join a union. Don't you see?" he asked passionately. "We must all stand together. All us working folks must be organised. That's the only way we'll ever fight the bosses, that's the only way we'll ever get the rich off our backs. That's —"

"But, Joe!" she cried anxiously, alarmed at his wild demeanour. "Joe! You're not well —"

"No, no. I'm all right," he insisted heatedly. "You stay and listen to me. I've been wrong. You've been wrong. Rose's been wrong. The whole blasted lot of us's been wrong! Don't you see? We all ought to be organised, stand together —"

"Joe! Joe! Please —" she cried again.

"All right. All right. I'm just a bit excited." He drew a deep breath, forcing himself to be calm. "I've learned something today," he resumed in a steadier tone. "Yes. I've learned a hell of a lot. You listen to me. I've learned a hell of a lot —"

"And who from, may I ask?" she inquired pointedly.

"Now stop getting jealous and listen. Here — you sit on my knee — there, like you used to before I got on the dole. Remember?"

"But, Joe!" she protested, half angry, half confused, but sitting on his knee nevertheless.

"You listen to me, Waffles," Slesser urged, grinning

225

triumphantly, and reviving a term of endearment that had long ago ceased to be uttered. "Say what you like when I've finished, but just keep quiet for now. It's like this. You needn't be jealous! Old Tom Whiteley spoke of going to the fascist march, and I did. I took a shilling to pay for the fare, got in the fighting in Royal Mint Street and met a girl there. It's all right," Slesser said airily as his wife opened her mouth to object, "her bloke was with her so I've nothing to hide. Besides, an old man like me —" he added humorously.

"You're not old, Joe! You're not forty yet!" she protested.

"No, maybe not. But another year on the dole and I'd be fifty!"

"Don't be silly, Joe! Get on with what you were saying."

"All right. Well, us three stuck together all afternoon and then I went on a march with them — an anti-fascist march — you should have seen the crowds! And after that I went in a café for a cup of tea, and these four fascists got nasty. Said I was a Jew!"

"*A Jew?*"

"Yes, because my nose is a bit bent, see?" Slesser explained, fingering his nose. "Not that I've anything against the Jews."

"And they set on you?"

"Not there. No. As a matter of fact they followed me out and — well, I got the wind up for a minute and — well, I jumped on the first bus that came along —"

"To Oxford Circus?"

"Ah!... They set on me there and —" He stopped now. This was the test. He looked away from her at the dying fire, at the hissing gas, at the bowl of lukewarm, reddish water and transparent, floating swabs of cottonwool.

"Well," he said at last, looking back to her, "the cops came and we all got —"

"Arrested?"

He nodded. "And I had to walk back, too."

"Oh, poor Joe! And here's me been thinking —"

Slesser grinned sheepishly and shrugged his shoulders, round which she placed a sympathetic arm.

"That's how it is," he said. "I'm up at the court tomorrow — I mean today — and the worst of it is, I wanted to go to the council to see about getting taken on —"

"Joe, are you really going?"

"Ah! Why not? If I don't get time. Shouldn't do that, though," he added, his thoughts flashing momentarily to old Tom Whiteley and his lonely vigil by the park gates.

"Well," said his wife, after a thoughtful pause, "hadn't we better be getting off to bed? It's nearly two o'clock. But there! You must be hungry —"

"No, I'm not. I don't know why, but I'm not. Too much excitement, maybe. Let's go to bed."

They rose. Slesser vaselined his face while she cleared away the bowl and bolted the door on the yard; and then they put out the gas and went quietly to their bedroom at the front of the house, fearing to disturb the children.

"How much will the fine be, Joe?" she asked, when they had got into bed.

"About a couple o' quid, I should think. Why?"

"Rose'll lend it us. You can always rely on her. She's been good to us."

"In some ways. But if it wasn't for her and those tablets you wouldn't be as you are, would you?"

"Oh, Joe! I am silly! I forget to tell you — I'm all right now — this afternoon."

"Are you? Thank God!"

"Yes, I think that's why I was jealous. I shouldn't be, really. You've been a good husband to me, Joe."

"Have I? Well, you've been a good wife, Waffles."

They were silent, lying back to back, sinking into sleep. And in the room, in the street outside, in all the other streets in London, the night was pressing gently on to another October day.

"Joe," she said drowsily. "You meant what you said about going after that job, didn't you?"

"A-a-ah!" Slesser muttered from the edge of sleep.

More Five Leaves' books on the Battle of Cable Street

Battle for the East End: Jewish responses to fascism in the 1930s
David Rosenberg

Everything Happens in Cable Street
Oral history from Roger Mills

The Battle of Cable Street
by The Cable Street Group

Street of Tall People
a children's book by Alan Gibbons

<u>www.fiveleaves.co.uk</u>

New London Editions

King Dido
Alexander Baron
Introduction by Ken Worpole
New London Editions 1

Rosie Hogarth
Alexander Baron
Introduction by Andrew Whitehead
New London Editions 2

Scamp
Roland Camberton
Introduction by Iain Sinclair
New London Editions 3

Rain on the Pavements
Roland Camberton
New London Editions 4

Forthcoming

Adrift in Soho
Colin Wilson

The Furnished Room
Laura Del-Rivo

This Bed Thy Centre
Pamela Hansford Johnson
Introduction by Zoë Fairbairns

Neighbours of Ours: slum stories of London
Henry Nevinson
Introduction by Andrew Whitehead

Baron's Court, All Change
Terry Taylor

www.fiveleaves.co.uk